THE SIAMESE TWIN MYSTERY

"*God!*" whispered the Inspector. He had stopped short in his tracks and gripped Ellery's arm with convulsive fingers. He was staring with sagging jaw, naked terror in his eyes, grey little face greyer than Ellery had ever seen it, past his son's shoulder at something down the hall.

His nerves already frayed by the harrowing experiences of the evening, Ellery whirled about. The skin of his arms was prickling, and the flesh was crawling at the base of his scalp.

But he saw nothing unusual; the corridor was dim and empty, as before. Then he heard a faint *click*! as of a door closing.

"What in God's name is the matter?" he whispered nervously, searching his father's horror-struck face.

The Inspector's taut body relaxed. He sighed and passed a trembling hand over his mouth. "El, I—I—— Did you see what I——"

They both jumped at a light footstep behind them. Something large and shapeless was stalking them from the rear, where the corridor was blackest. Two burning eyes . . .

THE SIAMESE TWIN MYSTERY

A Problem in Deduction

Ellery Queen

A Hamlyn *Whodunnit*

Hamlyn Paperbacks

THE SIAMESE TWIN MYSTERY

ISBN 0 600 20075 2

First published in Great Britain 1933
by Victor Gollancz Ltd
Hamlyn Paperbacks edition 1980
Copyright © 1933 by Ellery Queen

Hamlyn Paperbacks are published by
The Hamlyn Publishing Group Ltd,
Astronaut House,
Feltham,
Middlesex, England

Made and printed in Great Britain by
William Collins Sons & Co Ltd, Glasgow

CONTENTS

PART I

PART II

PART III

PART IV

CHARACTERS

MEMBERS OF THE HOUSEHOLD

DR. JOHN S. XAVIER . . . whose god is Science
SARAH ISÈRE XAVIER . . . . . his lady
MARK XAVIER . . . . . . his brother
MRS. WHEARY . . . . . his housekeeper
DR. PERCIVAL HOLMES . . . . his assistant
" BONES " . . . . . . his vassal

VISITORS TO THE HOUSEHOLD

MRS. MARIE CARREAU . . . *une grande dame*
FRANCIS . . . . her son
JULIAN . . . . her son
ANN FORREST . . . . . her secretary
MR. SMITH . . . . . . a stranger

FOREWORD

As the keeper of Ellery Queen's conscience, as it were, I have long felt it my duty so to annoy and shame him as to make him get down in type, between the usual pasteboard covers, the story of his fascinating investigation many years ago on that isolated peak of iniquity known as Arrow Mountain—not, I hasten to explain, in Darien, but in those more indigenous mountains to the north, the Tepees, in the heart of the ancient Indian country.

In many ways it is a remarkable story ; not only because of its strange locale, the peculiarity of at least two of its characters, and the melodic theme of fire which ran through it like a Wagnerian *leit-motif* ; but also because it represents, for the first time among Mr. Queen's published adventures, an investigation conducted wholly without benefit of official interference. For with the exception of his father, Inspector Richard Queen, the scene was utterly unencumbered by the customary impedimenta of murder cases—detectives, police, medical examiners, fingerprint men, ballistics experts, *et al.*

How this came about in a country like ours, wherein mere suspicion is sufficient to bring a brigade of heavy-footed sleuths tramping over the scene of a crime, is one of the most interesting elements of a story crammed with surprises. I wish you joy of it.

J. J. McC.

Claremont, N. H.
July 1933

PART I

" The human element is the only factor that keeps this world from being overrun by untouchable murderers. The complexity of the criminal mind is also its greatest weakness. Show me a so-called ' clever ' murderer and I will show you a man already condemned to death."—Crime and the Criminal by LUIGI PERSANO (1928).

CHAPTER I

THE BURNING ARROW

THE ROAD looked as if it had been baked out of rubbly dough in a giant's oven, removed in all its snaky length, unwound and laid in coils around the flank of the mountain, and then cheerfully stamped upon. Its crust, broiled by the sun, had risen quite as if one of its ingredients were yeast; it erupted like brown cornbread for fifty yards at a stretch and then, for no sane reason, sucked itself in to form tyre-killing ruts for fifty more. To make life exciting for the unfortunate motorist who chanced upon that unhappy highway it had been so moulded as to slew and curve and dip and wind and swoop and climb and broaden and narrow in a manner truly wonderful to behold. And it raised swarms of dust, each grain a locust ferociously bent upon biting into such damp crawling human flesh as it happened to alight upon.

Mr. Ellery Queen, totally unrecognisable by virtue of specked sun-glasses over his aching eyes, linen cap pulled low, the wrinkles of his linen jacket filled with the grit of three counties, his skin, where it showed, a great raw wet irritation, humped his shoulders over the wheel of the battered Duesenberg, wrestling with it with a sort of desperate determination. He had cursed every curve in the alleged road from Tuckesas forty miles down the Valley, where it officially began, to the present point; and he had quite run out of words.

"Your own damn' fault," said his father peevishly. "Cripes, you'd think it would be cool in the mountains!

I feel as if somebody's scraped me all over with sand-paper."

The Inspector, grey little Arab swathed to his eyes against the dust in a grey silk scarf, had been nursing a grudge which, like the road itself, bucked skyward and erupted at every fifty yards. He twisted, groaning, in his seat beside Ellery and peered sourly over the pile of luggage strapped behind at the lumpy stretch of paving in their wake. Then he slumped back.

"Told you to stick to the Valley pike, didn't I ? " He brandished his forefinger at the rush of hot sticky air.

" ' El,' I said, ' take my word for it—in these blasted mountains you never know what kind of squirty road you run into,' I said. But no ; you had to go and start explorin' with night coming on, like—like some damn' Columbus ! " The Inspector paused to grumble at the deepening sky. "Stubborn. Just like your mother—rest her soul ! " he added hastily, for he was after all a God-fearing old gentleman. " Well, I hope you're satisfied."

Ellery sighed and stole a glance from the zigzag expanse before him to the sky. The whole arc of heaven was purpling very softly and swiftly—a sight to rouse the poet in any man, he thought, except a tired, hot, and hungry one with a querulous sire at his side who not only grumbled but grumbled with unanswerable logic. The road along the foothills bordering the Valley *had* looked inviting ; there was something cool—by anticipation only, he thought sadly—in a vista of green trees.

The Duesenberg bucked on in the gathering gloom.

" And not only that," continued Inspector Queen, cocking an irritated eye upon the road ahead above a fold of the dusty scarf, " but it's one hell of a way to top off a vacation. Trouble, just trouble ! Gets me all hot and—and bothered. Damn it all, El, I *worry* about these things. They spoil my appetite ! "

" Not mine," said Ellery with another sigh. " I could eat a Goodyear-tyre steak with French-fried gaskets and gasoline sauce right now, I'm so famished. Where the devil are we, anyway ? "

" Tepees. Somewhere in the United States. That's all *I* know."

" Lovely. Tepees. There's poetic justice for you ! Makes me think of venison broiling over a woodfire. . . . Whoa, Duesey ! That *was* a daisy, wasn't it ? " The Inspector, who at the peak of the bump had almost had his head torn off, glared ; it was quite evident that to his way of thinking " daisy " was scarcely the appropriate word. " Now, now, dad. Don't mind a little thing like that. One of the normal hazards of motoring. What you miss is the Montreal Scotch, you renegade Irishman ! . . . Now look at that, will you ? "

They had reached a rise in the road around one of the myriad unexpected bends ; and for sheer wonder Ellery stopped the car. Hundreds of feet below and to the left lay Tomahawk Valley, already cloaked in the purple mantle which had dropped so swiftly from the green battlements jutting against the sky. The mantle billowed as if something huge and warm and softly animal stirred beneath it. A faint grey tapeworm of road slithered along far down, already half-smothered by the purple mantle. There were no lights, no signs of human beings or habitations. The whole sky overhead was suffused now, and the last cantaloupe sliver of sun was sinking behind the distant range across the Valley. The edge of the road was ten feet away ; there it dipped sharply and cascaded in green sheets toward the Valley floor.

Ellery turned and looked up. Arrow Mountain swelled above them, a dark emerald tapestry closely woven out of pine and scrub-oak and matted underbrush. The bristly fabric of foliage towered, it seemed, for miles above their heads.

He started the Duesenberg again. " Almost worth the torture," he chuckled. " Feel better already. Come out of it, Inspector ! This is the real thing—Nature in the raw."

" Too damn' raw to suit me."

The night suddenly overpowered them and Ellery switched his headlights on. They bounced along in silence. Both stared ahead, Ellery dreamily and the old gentleman with irritation. A peculiar haze had begun to dance in the shafts of lights stabbing the road before them ; it drifted and curled and eddied like lazy fog.

" Seems to me we ought to be getting there," growled the Inspector, blinking in the darkness. " Road's going down now, isn't it ? Or is it my imagination ? "

" It's been dipping for some time," murmured Ellery. " Getting warmer, isn't it ? How far did that hulking countryman with the lisp—that garageman in Tuckesas —say it was to Osquewa ? "

" Fifty miles. Tuckesas ! Osquewa ! Cripes, this country's enough to make a man throw up."

" No romance," grinned Ellery. " Don't you recognise the beauty of old Indian etymology ? At that, it's ironic. Our compatriots visiting abroad complain bitterly about the ' foreign ' names—Lwów, Prague (now why *Pra-ha*, in the name of merciful heaven ?), Brescia, Valdepeñaz, and even good old British Harwich and Leicestershire. Yet those are words of one syllable——"

" Hmm," said the Inspector in an odd tone ; he blinked again.

"—compared with our own native Arkansas and Winnebago and Schoharie and Otsego and Sioux City and Susquehanna and goodness knows what else. Talk about heritage ! Yes, sir, painted redskins roamed them thar hills across the Valley and this here mount-ing falling on our heads. Redskins in moccasins and tanned deerskin, braided hair and turkey-feathers. The smoke of their signal-fires——"

"Hmm," said the Inspector again, suddenly bolting upright. "Looks damned near as if they were still setting 'em!"

"Eh?"

"Smoke, smoke, you son! See it?" The Inspector rose, pointing ahead. "There!" he cried. "Right in front of us!"

"Nonsense," said Ellery in a sharp voice. "What would smoke be doing up here, of all places? That's probably some manifestation of evening mist. These hills play peculiar pranks sometimes."

"This one's acting up," said Inspector Queen grimly. The dusty scarf fell into his lap, unheeded. His sharp little eyes were no longer dull and bored. He craned backward and stared for a long time. Ellery frowned, snatching a glimpse into his windshield mirror, and then looked quickly ahead again. The road was definitely dipping toward the Valley now, and the peculiar haze thickened with every downward foot.

"What's the matter, dad?" he said in a small voice. His nostrils quivered. There was an odd and faintly disagreeable pungency in the air.

"I think," said the Inspector, sinking back, "I think, El, you'd better step on it."

"Is it——?" began Ellery feebly, and swallowed hard.

"Looks mighty like it."

"Forest fire?"

"Forest fire. Smell it now?"

Ellery's right foot squeezed the accelerator. The Duesenberg leaped forward. The Inspector, his grumpiness gone, reached over the edge of the car on his side and switched on a powerful sidelamp which swept the slope of the mountain like a broom of light.

Ellery's lips tightened; neither spoke.

Despite their altitude and the mountain chill of evening, a queer heat suffused the air. The swirling mist through which the Duesenberg ploughed was yellowish now, and thick as cotton. It was smoke, the smoke of desiccated wood and dusty foliage burning. Its acrid molecules suddenly invaded their nostrils, burned their lungs, made them cough, brought smarting tears to their eyes.

To the left, where the Valley lay, there was nothing to be seen but a dark smother, like the sea at night.

The Inspector stirred. " Better stop, son."

" Yes," muttered Ellery. " I was just thinking that myself."

The Duesenberg halted, panting. Ahead of them the smoke was whipping in furious dark waves. And beyond—not far, a hundred feet or so—little orange teeth began to show, biting into the smoke. Down toward the Valley, too, were more little orange teeth, thousands of them ; and tongues, long flicking orange tongues.

" It's directly in our path," said Ellery in the same queer tone. " We'd better turn round and go back."

" Can you turn here ? " sighed the Inspector.

" I'll try."

It was nervous, delicate work in the boiling darkness. The Duesenberg, an old racing relic Ellery had picked up out of perverted sentiment years before and had had reconditioned for private use, had never seemed so long-legged and cantankerous. He sweated and swore beneath his breath as he swung it back, forward, back, forward—inching his way around by imperceptible degrees while the Inspector's little grey hand clutched the windshield and the ends of his moustache fluttered in the hot wind.

" Better make it snappy, son," said the Inspector quietly. His eyes darted upward to the silent dark slope of Arrow Mountain. " I think——"

" Yes ? " panted Ellery, negotiating the last turn.

" I think the fire's climbed up to the road—behind us."

" Lord, no, dad ! "

The Duesenberg shuddered as Ellery stared fiercely into the murk. He felt the impulse to laugh. It was all too silly. A fire-trap ! . . . The Inspector sat forward, alert and quiet as a mouse. Then Ellery shouted and brought his heel down, hard, upon the accelerator. They surged forward.

The whole mountainside below them was burning. The mantle was ripped in thousands of places and the little orange teeth and the long orange tongues were greedily nibbling and licking away at the slope, hostile and palpable in their own light. An entire landscape, miles long, seen in miniature from their elevation, had suddenly burst into flames. In that numbing moment as they rushed back along the crazy road they both realised what must have happened. It was late July, and the month had been one of the hottest and driest in years. This was almost virgin timberland—a tangled mat of tree and bush long since sapped by the sun of its water. It was crumbly tinder inviting flame. A camper's carelessly trodden fire, or a forgotten cigarette, even the friction of two dead limbs rubbed against each other by a breeze, might have started it. Then it would slither swiftly along beneath the trees, eating its way along the sole of an entire mountain foot, and suddenly the slope would burst into flame spontaneously as the fire burned through to the dry upper air. . . .

The Duesenberg slowed down, hesitated, lunged forward, stopped with a screeching of brakes.

" We're hemmed in ! " cried Ellery, half-rising behind the wheel. " Back and front ! " Then, calming suddenly, he sank back and fumbled for a cigarette. His chuckle was ghostly. " It's ridiculous, isn't it ? Trial by fire ! What sins have *you* committed ? "

"Don't be a fool," said the Inspector harshly. He stood up and looked quickly from right to left. Below the lip of the road flames were gnawing.

"The odd part of it is," muttered Ellery, drawing a lungful of smoke and expelling it without sound, "that I got you into this. It's beginning to look like my last stupidity. . . . No, it's no use looking, dad. There's no solution except to dash right through the thick of it. This is a narrow road and the fire's already nibbling at the timber and brush beyond." He chuckled again, but his eyes were hot behind his goggles and his face was damp chalk. "We shan't last a hundred yards. Can't see—the road twists and spins. . . . The chances are, if the fire doesn't get us, that we'll go rocketing off the road."

The Inspector, nostrils flaring, stared without speaking.

"It's so damned melodramatic," said Ellery with an effort, frowning over the Valley. "Not my notion at all of how to pass out. It smacks of—of charlatanry." He coughed and flung his cigarette away with a grimace. "Well, what's the decision? Shall we stay here and fry, or take our chances with the road, or try scrambling up the slope overhead? Quickly—our host is impatient."

The Inspector flung himself down. "Get a grip on yourself. We can always take to the woods up there. Get going!"

"Right, sir," murmured Ellery, his eyes full of a pain that was not caused by the smoke. The Duesenberg stirred. "It's really no use looking, you know," he said, pity suddenly invading his voice. "There's no way out. This is a straight road—no side-roads at all. . . . Dad! Don't get up again. Wrap your handkerchief around your mouth and nose!"

"I tell you to get going!" shouted the old man with exasperation. His eyes were red and watery; they glared like damped coals.

The Duesenberg staggered drunkenly ahead. The combined brilliance of the three lamps served only to bring out more starkly the yellow-white snakes of smoke wrapping their coils about the car. Ellery drove more by instinct than sense. He was trying desperately, beneath a rigid exterior, to recall the exact vagaries of the insane road ahead. There had been a curve. . . . They were coughing constantly now ; Ellery's eyes, protected by the goggles as they were, nevertheless began to stream. A new odour came to their tortured nostrils, the smell of scorched rubber. The tyres. . . .

Cinders speckled their clothes, dropping softly.

From somewhere far below and far away, even above the snapping and crackling about them, came the faint persistent scream of a country fire-siren. A warning, thought Ellery grimly, from Osquewa. They had seen the fire and were gathering the clans. Soon there would be hordes of little human ants with buckets and flails and hand-made besoms swarming into the burning woods. These people were accustomed to fighting fires. No doubt they would master this one, or it would master itself, or providentially rain would come and smother it. But one thing seemed certain, thought Ellery as he strained into the smoke and coughed in hacking spasms : two gentlemen named Queen were destined to meet their fate on a blazing road along a lonely mountain miles from Centre Street and upper Broadway, and there would be no one to watch their exit from a world which had suddenly become impossibly sweet and precious. . . .

" *There !* " shrieked the Inspector, jumping up. " There—El ! I knew it, I knew it ! " and he danced up and down in his seat, pointing to the left, his voice a wild blur of tears, relief, and satisfaction. " I thought I remembered one side-road. Stop the car ! "

With a wildly beating heart Ellery jammed on his

brakes. Through a rift in the smoke appeared a black cavernous gap. It was apparently a road leading up through the steep and almost impassable tangle of forest which matted the chest of Arrow Mountain like a giant's hair.

Ellery wrestled powerfully with the wheel. The Duesenberg darted back, screamed, surged forward with a roar. In second gear it bit into a hard-packed dirt road set at an alarming angle to the main highway. The motor whined and keened and sang—and the car clawed its way up. It gathered speed, creeping up. It hurtled on, flashing up. Now the road began to wind ; a curve, a swift wind inexpressibly sweet, scented with pine-needles, a delicious chill in the air. . . .

Incredibly, within twenty seconds, they had left fire, smoke, their fate and their death behind.

.   .   .   .

It was utterly black now—the sky, the trees, the road. The air was like liquor ; it bathed their tortured lungs and throats with coolness that was half warmth, and they both became silently intoxicated upon it. They gulped it down, sniffing mightily until they felt their lungs must burst. Then they both began to laugh.

" Oh, God," gasped Ellery, stopping the car. " It's all—all too fantastic ! "

The Inspector giggled : " Just like that ! Whew." He took out his handkerchief, trembling, and passed it over his mouth.

They both removed their hats and exulted in the cold feel of the wind. Once they looked at each other, trying to pierce the darkness. Both fell silent soon, the mood passing ; and finally Ellery released his hand-brake and set the Duesenberg in motion.

If the road below had been difficult, this ahead was impossible. It was little more than a cowpath, rocky and overgrown. But neither man could find it in his heart to curse it. It was a boon sent from heaven. It kept winding and climbing, and they wound and climbed with it. Of human beings not a trace. The headlights groped ahead of them like the antennæ of an insect. The air grew steadily sharper, and the sweet sharp arboreal smell was like wine. Winged things hummed and dashed themselves against the lights.

Suddenly Ellery stopped the car again.

The Inspector, who had been dozing, jerked awake. " What's the matter now ? " he mumbled sleepily.

Ellery was listening intently. " I thought I heard something ahead."

The Inspector cocked his grey head. " People up here, maybe ? "

" It seems unlikely," said Ellery dryly. There was a faint crashing from somewhere before them, not unlike the sound of a large animal in undergrowth far away.

" Mountain lion, d'ye think ? " growled Inspector Queen, feeling a little nervously for his service revolver

" Don't think so. If it is, I daresay he's in for more of a scare than we. *Are* there catamounts in these parts ? Might be a—a bear or a deer or something."

He urged the car forward again. Both were very wide awake, and both felt distinctly uncomfortable. The crashing grew louder.

" Lord, it sounds like an elephant ! " muttered the old man. He had his revolver out now.

Suddenly Ellery began to laugh. There was a comparatively long stretch of straight road here, and around the far curve came two fingers of light, as if fumbling in the darkness. In a moment they straightened out and glared into the Duesenberg's own brilliant eyes.

" A car," chuckled Ellery. " Put that cannon away, you old lady. Mountain lion ! "

" Didn't I hear you say something about a deer ? "

retorted the Inspector. Nevertheless he did not return the revolver to his hip-pocket.

Ellery stopped the car once more ; the headlights of the approaching automobile were very close now. "Good to have company in a place like this," he said cheerfully, jumping out and stepping before his own lights. "Hi !" he shouted, waving his arms.

It was a crouching old Buick sedan that had seen better days. It came to rest, its battered nose snuffling the dirt of the road. It seemed occupied by only one passenger : a man's head and shoulders were dimly visible behind the dusty windshield, illuminated by the mingling lights of the cars.

The head popped out of the side window. Away from the disfiguring glass, its every feature was sharply limned. A tattered felt hat was jammed over the man's ears, which stood away from the enormous head like a troglodyte's. It was a monstrous face : gross, huge, wattled, and damp. Frog's eyes were imbedded in lumps of flesh. The nose was broad and flared. The lips were tight lines. A big unhealthy face, but somehow hard and quieting. The owner of that face, Ellery felt instinctively, was not to be trifled with.

The eyes, luminous slits, fastened on Ellery's lanky figure with batrachian steadiness. Then they shifted to the Duesenberg behind, surveyed the indistinct torso of the Inspector, and clicked back.

"Out of the way, you." It was a rumbling voice, harshly vibrant in its bass tones. "Get out of the way !"

Ellery blinked in the strong light. The gargoyle head had retreated behind the translucent shelter of the windshield again. He could see a suggestion of vast humped shoulders. And no neck, he thought irritably. Indecent of the fellow. Ought to have a neck.

"I say," he began, pleasantly enough. "That's not nice——"

The Buick snorted and began to snuffle forward. Ellery's eyes flashed.

" Stop ! " he cried. " You can't go down that way, you—you surly fool ! There's a fire down there ! "

The Buick halted two feet from Ellery and ten feet from the Duesenberg. The head popped out again.

" What's that ? " said the bass voice heavily.

" Thought that would get you," replied Ellery with satisfaction. " For heaven's sake, isn't there anything remotely resembling courtesy in this part of the domain ? I said there's a very neat and thorough conflagration raging down below—must be past the road by now, so you'd better turn round and go back."

The froggy eyes stared for an instant without expression.

Then : " Out of the way," the man said again, and touched his gears.

Ellery stared incredulously. The fellow was either stupid or insane.

" Well, if you want to be smoked up like a side of pork," snapped Ellery, " that's your affair. Where's this road lead to ? "

There was no reply. The Buick kept impatiently edging up inch by inch. Ellery shrugged and trudged back to the Duesenberg. He got in, slammed his door, muttered something impolite, and began backing off. The road was much too narrow to permit lateral passage of two machines. He was forced to back into the underbrush, crashing through until he smacked against a tree. There was barely enough room for the Buick to pass. It roared forward, kissing Ellery's right fender none too gently, and disappeared in the darkness.

" Funny bird," said the Inspector thoughtfully, putting away his revolver as Ellery steered the Duesenberg on to the road again. " If his mug was any fatter it would just naturally float away. The hell with him."

Ellery uttered a savage chuckle. " He'll come back soon enough," he said ; " damn his infernal cheek ! " and thenceforward devoted his whole attention to the road.

.   .   .   .

They climbed, it seemed, for hours—a steady upgrade which taxed the powerful resources of the Duesenberg. Nowhere the faintest sign of a habitation. The forest, if it were possible, grew thicker and wilder than before. The road, instead of improving, grew worse—narrower, rockier, more overgrown. Once the headlights picked out directly in the road ahead the glowing eyes of a coiled copperhead.

The Inspector, perhaps as a reaction from the emotional disturbances of the past hour, frankly slept. His low snore throbbed in Ellery's ears. Ellery gritted his teeth and pushed on.

The branches overhead dipped lower. They kept up an incessant rustle, like the gossip of old foreign women in the distance.

Not once through the interminable minutes of that remorseless ascent did Ellery catch sight of the stars.

" We escaped dropping into Hell," he muttered to himself, " and now, by George, we seem headed straight for Valhalla ! " How high was the mountain, anyway ?

He felt his lids droop and shook his head angrily to keep himself awake. It was unwise to doze on this journey ; the dirt-road twisted and pirouetted like a Siamese dancer. He set his jaw and began concentrating upon the turmoil in his empty belly. A cup of steaming consommé, now, he thought ; then a smoking rare cut of thick sirloin, with gravy and browned potatoes ; two cups of hot coffee. . . .

He peered ahead, alert. It seemed to him that the road was widening. And the trees—they seemed to be receding. Lord, it was time ! There was something doing ahead ; probably they had reached the crest of this confounded mountain and would soon be slipping down the road on the other side, bound for the next valley, a town, a hot supper, and bed. Then to-morrow a swift trip south, refreshed, and the day following New York and home. He laughed aloud in his relief.

Then he stopped laughing. The road had widened for excellent reason. The Duesenberg had pushed into a clearing of some sort. The trees receded left and right into the darkness. Overhead there was hot thick sky speckled with millions of brilliants. A wilder wind fluttered the loose crown of his cap. To the sides of the expanded road lay tumbled rocks, from shards to boulders, out of the crevices and interstices of which sprouted an ugly, dried-up vegetation. And directly ahead . . .

He swore softly and got out of the car, wincing at the ache in his cold joints. Fifteen feet in front of the Duesenberg, boldly revealed in the headlights' glare, stood two tall iron gates. To both sides ran a low fence built out of stones unquestionably indigenous to this forbidding soil. The fence stretched away divergently into the darkness. Beyond the gates for the short distance illuminated by the headlights ran the road. What lay still farther ahead was cloaked in the same palpable blackness that covered everything.

This was the end of the road !

He cursed himself for a fool. He might have known. The winding of the road below had not *circled* the mountain. It had merely seesawed erratically from side to side, following, now that he thought of it, the line of least resistance. This being the case, there must be a reason for the failure of the path to spiral completely about Arrow Mountain in its ascent to the summit. The reason could only be that the other side of the mountain was impassable. Probably a precipice.

In other words, there was only one way down the mountain—and that was by the road they had just climbed. They had run headlong into a blind alley.

Angry with the world, the night, the wind, the trees, the fire, himself and all living things, he strode forward to the gates. A bronze plaque was attached to the iron grille of one of them. It said simply : *Arrow Head*.

" What's the matter now ? " croaked the Inspector sleepily from the depths of the Duesenberg. " Where are we ? "

Ellery's voice was gloomy. " At an impasse. We've reached the end of our journey, dad. Pleasant prospect, isn't it ? "

" For cripes' sake ! " exploded the Inspector, crawling down into the road. " Mean to say this God-forsaken road doesn't lead anywhere ? "

" Apparently not." Then Ellery slapped his thigh. " Oh, God," he groaned, " flay me for an idiot ! What are we standing here for ? Help me with these gates." He began to tug at the heavy grilles. The Inspector lent a shoulder, and the gates gave balkily, squealing in protest.

" Damned rusty," growled the Inspector, examining his palms.

" Come on," cried Ellery, running back to the car. The Inspector trotted wearily after. " What's the matter with me ? Gates and a fence mean human beings and a house. Of course ! Why this road at all ? Someone lives up here. That means food, a bath, shelter——"

" Maybe," said the Inspector disagreeably as they began to move and swung in between the gates, " maybe there's nobody living here."

" Nonsense. That would be an intolerable trick of fate. And besides," said Ellery, quite gay now, " our fat-faced friend in the Buick came from somewhere, didn't he ? And yes—there are the tracks of tyres. . . . Where the deuce are these people's lights ? "

The house was so near it partook of the nature of the darkness about it. A wide gloomy pile which blotted out the stars in an irregular pattern. The Duesenberg's headlights focused upon a flight of stone steps leading to a wooden porch. The sidelamp under the Inspector's guidance swept to right and left and disclosed a long terrace running the entire length of the house, occupied only by empty rockers and chairs. Beyond the sides lay the rocky brush-covered terrain ; only a few yards separated the house from the woods.

" That's not polite," muttered the Inspector, switching the lamp off. " That is, *if* anyone lives here. I have my doubts. Those French windows off the terrace are all closed and it looks as if they've got blinds drawn right to the floor. See any lights in the upper story ? "

There were two stories and an attic floor beneath the slate shingles covering the gabled roof. But all the windows were black. Dry bedraggled vines half-covered the wooden walls.

" No," said Ellery, a note of misgiving creeping into his voice, " but then it's—it's *impossible* that the house is untenanted. That would be a blow from which I should never recover ; not after our fantastic adventure to-night."

" Yes," grunted the Inspector, " but if anybody lives here why the devil hasn't someone heard us ? Lord knows this rattletrap of yours made enough racket coming up here. Lean on that horn."

Ellery leaned. The klaxon on the Duesenberg possessed a singularly disagreeable voice ; a voice, one would have said, capable of rousing the dead. The voice ceased and with pathetic eagerness both men bent forward and strained their ears. There was no response from the lifeless pile before them.

" I think," said Ellery doubtfully, and stopped. " Didn't you hear some——"

"I heard a blasted cricket calling to his mate," growled the old gentleman, "that's what I heard. Well, what the devil are we going to do now? You're the brains of this family. Let's see how good you are getting us *out* of this mess."

"Don't rub it in," groaned Ellery. "I'll admit I haven't displayed precisely genius to-day. God, I'm so hungry I could eat a whole family of *Gryllidæ*, let alone one!"

"Hey?"

"Saltatorial orthopters," explained Ellery stiffly. "Crickets to you. It's the only scientific term I remember from my Entomology. Not that it does me any good at the moment. I always said higher education was perfectly useless against the ordinary emergencies of life."

The Inspector snorted and wrapped his coat more closely about him, shivering. There was an eerie quality about their surroundings which made his usually impervious scalp prickle. He strove to drive away the unaccustomed phantoms of his roused imagination by thoughts of food and sleep. He closed his eyes and sighed.

Ellery rummaged in a car-pocket, found an electric torch, and scrunched across the gravel to the house. He mounted the stone steps, tramped across the wooden flooring of the porch, and searched the front door in the light of his torch. It was a very solid and uninviting door. Even the knocker, a chunk of chipped stone fashioned in the shape of an Indian arrowhead, was darkly forbidding. Nevertheless Ellery lifted it and began to pound the oak panels. He pounded with vigour.

"This," he said grimly between assaults on the door, "is beginning to resemble a nightmare. It is utterly unreasonable that we should go"—rap! rap!—

" through the ordeal by fire"— *rap! rap!*—" and emerge without the customary rewards of penitence. Besides "— RAP ! RAP !—" I would welcome even a Dracula after what we've gone through. Lord, this *does* remind me of that vampire's roost in the mountains of Hungary ! "

And he pounded until his arm ached without evoking the faintest response from the house.

" Oh, come on," groaned the Inspector. " What's the use of knocking your arm off like a fool ? Let's get out of here."

Ellery's arm dropped wearily. He flicked the torch's beam over the porch. " *Bleak House*. . . . Get out ? And where shall we go ? "

" Hell, I don't know. Back to get our hides scorched, I guess. At least it's *warm* down there."

" Not me," snapped Ellery. " I'm going to get that laprug out of the luggage and camp right here. And if you're sensible, dad, you'll join me."

His voice carried far through the mountain air. For an instant only the hindlegs of the amorous cricket answered him. Then without warning the door of the house opened and a parallelogram of light leaped out on to the porch.

Black against the light, framed by the rectangle of the door, stood the figure of a man.

CHAPTER II

THE "THING"

So suddenly had the apparition appeared that Ellery instinctively retreated a step, tightening his grip on the electric torch. From below he could hear the Inspector groaning with a sort of pleasant pain at the miraculous appearance of a Good Samaritan at the time when the last hope had fled. The old man's heavy step crunched on the gravel.

The man stood in the foreground of a dazzlingly illuminated entrance-hall which, from Ellery's position, disclosed only an overhead lamp, a rug, a large etching, the corner of a refectory table and an open doorway at the right.

" Good evening," said Ellery, clearing his throat.

" What d'ye want ? "

The apparition's voice was startling—an old man's voice, querulously crackling in its upper tones and heavily hostile in its undertones. Ellery blinked. With the strong light shining in his eyes all he could see of the man was a silhouette, revealed by a steady glow of golden light pouring on him from behind. The outline, which made the man look like a shape created by the luminous tubes of a Neon sign, was that of a shambling, loose-jointed figure, long arms dangling, sparse hair sticking up at the top like singed feathers.

" Evening," came the Inspector's voice from behind Ellery. " Sorry to be bothering you at this time of night, but we've sort of "—his eyes yearned hungrily at the furniture in the entrance-hall—" we've sort of got ourselves into a jam, you see, and——"

" Well, well ? " snarled the man.

The Queens regarded each other with dismay. Not an auspicious reception !

" Fact of the matter is," said Ellery, smiling feebly, " that we've been forced up here—I suppose this is your road—by circumstances beyond our control. We thought we might get——"

They began to make out details. The man was even older than they had thought. His face was marble-grey parchment, multitudinously wrinkled, and hard as stone. His eyes were small, black, and burning. He was dressed in coarse homespun that hung from his emaciated figure in ugly vertical folds.

" This isn't a hotel," he said savagely and, stepping back, began to close the door.

Ellery gritted his teeth ; he heard his father begin to snarl. " But good lord, man ! " he cried. " You don't understand. We're stuck. There's no place for us to go ! "

The rectangle had squeezed together, and at its foot there was a thin wedge of light now ; it made Ellery, licking his chops, think of a slab of mince pie.

" You're only about ten-fifteen miles from Osquewa," said the man in the doorway in a surly voice. " Can't go wrong. Only one road down the Arrow. You hit a wider road several miles below, turn right and keep on it until you get to Osquewa. There's an inn there."

" Thanks," barked the Inspector. " Come on, El ; this is one hell of a country. God, what swine ! "

" Now, now," said Ellery with desperate rapidity. " You still don't understand, sir. We can't take that road. It's on fire ! "

There was a little silence ; the door opened wider again. " On fire, d'ye say ? " said the man suspiciously.

" Miles of it ! " cried Ellery, waving his arms. He warmed to his subject. " The whole shooting-match ! Foothills one mass of flame ! A—a monstrous conflagration! The burning of Rome was simply a piddling little campfire compared with it ! Why, man, it's as much as your life is worth just to get within a half-mile of it ! Burn you crisper than a cinder before you could say antidisestablishmentarianism ! " He drew a deep breath, surveying the man anxiously ; made a face, swallowed his pride, smiled with child-like faith (thinking of succulent food and already hearing the blessed sound of running water), and said : " Now can we come in ? " plaintively.

" Well . . . " The man scratched his chin. The Queens held their breaths. The issue hung quivering in the balance. Ellery began, as the seconds flew by, to feel that perhaps he had not stated the case strongly enough. He should have spun a veritable saga of tragedy to soften the granite lump occupying this creature's breast.

Then the man said sullenly : " Wait a minute," slammed the door in their faces—thus vanishing as miraculously as he had appeared—and left them once more in darkness.

" Why, the gosh-blamed son of a so-and-so ! " exploded the Inspector wrathfully. " Did you ever *hear* of such a thing ! All this confounded bunk about the hospitality of——"

" Sssh ! " whispered Ellery fiercely. " You'll break the spell. Try to screw that writhing face of yours into a smile ! Look pretty, now ! I think I hear our friend returning."

But when the door swept open it was another man who confronted them—a man, one would have said, from a different world. He was impressively tall and generously shouldered, and his smile was slow and warming. " Come in," he said in a deep pleasant voice. " I'm afraid I must apologise abjectly for the rotten bad manners of my man Bones. Up here we're a little cautious about night-visitors. Really, I'm sorry. What's all this about a fire down on the mountain road ? . . . Come in, come in ! "

Overwhelmed by this excess of hospitality after the tempestuous reception of the surly man, the Queens blinked and gaped and rather dazedly obeyed. The tall pleasant man in tweeds closed the door softly behind them, still smiling.

They stood in a foyer, warm and comforting and delightful. Ellery, with his habitual and irrelevant restlessness, noted that the etching on the wall which he had glimpsed from the terrace was remarkably fine, etched after the grisly Rembrandt painting, *The Anatomy Lesson.* He had time, as their host closed the door, to wonder at the nature of a man who compelled his guests to be greeted with a realistic revelation of a Dutch cadaver's viscera. For an instant he felt a chill, looked sidewise at the distinguished features and pleasant expression of the tall man, and ascribed the chill to his depressed physical condition. The Queen imagination, he ruminated, was overwrought ; if the man were surgically inclined. . . . Surgically inclined ! Of course. He suppressed a grin. No doubt this gentleman was of the scalpel-wielding profession. Ellery felt better at once. He glanced at his father, but the subtleties of wall ornamentation had apparently escaped the old gentleman. The Inspector was licking his lips and sniffing furtively. Yes, there was the unmistakable odour of roast pork in the air.

As for the old ogre who had first greeted them, he had disappeared ; probably, Ellery thought with a chuckle, to slink back in his lair and sullenly lick the wounds of his fear of night-visitors.

.   .   .   .

As they passed through the foyer, holding their hats expectantly in their hands, they both caught a glimpse through the half-open door at the right, of a large room unilluminated by any light save that of the stars coming through the French windows off the terrace. Apparently then someone had raised the blinds of the windows in that room while their host was ushering them into the foyer. The remarkable creature to whom their host inexplicably referred as " Bones " ? Probably not ; for to their ears from the room on the right came the sibilant sounds of several whispering voices ; and among them Ellery detected at least one of unmistakably feminine pitch.

But why were they sitting in darkness ? Ellery experienced a recurrence of the chill, and shook it off impatiently. There were several things uncommonly mysterious about this house. Well, it was quite clearly none of his business. Let well enough alone ! The important thing was that food lurked in the offing.

The tall man ignored the door on the right. Still smiling, he motioned them to follow him and led them through the foyer a few steps along a corridor which bisected the house, running from front to back to terminate in a closed door vaguely seen at the end of the long passageway. He paused at an open door on the left.

" This way," he murmured, and motioned them into a large room which, they instantly saw, fronted the entire half of the terrace between the foyer and the left side of the house.

It was a living-room, dim with tall hangings over the French windows, sparsely starred with lamps, dotted with armchairs and small scatter-rugs and a white bearskin and small round tables bearing books and magazines and humidors and ash-trays. A fireplace occupied a good section of the far wall ; oil paintings and etchings hung about, all of a faintly dismal character, and elaborate tall candelabra threw swaying shadows which flowed and mingled with the shadows caused by the flames in the fireplace. The whole room for all its warmth and inviting chairs and books and cosy lights struck the Queens as unaccountably depressing. It was —*empty*.

"Please sit down," said the big man, "and take off your things. We'll get you comfortable and then we can chat." He pulled a bell-rope near the door, still smiling ; and Ellery began to feel a tiny irritation. Damn it all, there was nothing to smile about !

The Inspector, however, was made of less critical stuff. He sank into an overstuffed chair with a loud sigh of satisfaction, stretched his short legs, and murmured : "Ah, this *is* good. Makes up for a lot of grief, sir."

"I daresay, after the chill of your ascent," smiled the big man. Ellery, standing, was slightly puzzled. In the light of the fire and lamps the man was vaguely familiar-looking. He was a powerful fellow of perhaps forty-five, big in every way, and despite his predominating blondness, Ellery thought, a Gallic type. He wore his rough clothes with the unconscious carelessness of a man indifferent to convention ; a brute of a chap with distinct charm and physical attractiveness. His eyes were rather remarkable—deep-set and glowing, a student's eyes. His hands were strangely alive ; big broad and long-fingered, and given to authoritative gesture.

"It was warm enough to start with," said the Inspector with a grin ; he looked quite comfortable now. "Barely escaped with our lives."

The big man frowned. "As bad as that ? I'm horribly sorry. Fire, did you say ? . . . Ah, Mrs. Wheary ! "

A stout woman in black, white-aproned, appeared in the corridor doorway. She was rather pale, Ellery thought, and distinctly nervous about something.

" D-did you ring, Doctor ? " She stammered like a schoolgirl.

" Yes. Take these gentlemen's duds, please, and see if you can't scrape together something in the way of food." The woman nodded silently, took their hats and the Inspector's duster, and vanished. " I've no doubt you're famished," went on the big man. " We've already had our dinner or I should invite you to something perhaps a little more elaborate."

" To tell the truth," groaned Ellery, sitting down and feeling very good all at once, " we're both reduced almost to the point of cannibalism."

The man laughed heartily. " I suppose we should introduce ourselves after the unfortunate manner of our meeting. I'm John Xavier."

" Ah ! " cried Ellery. " I thought you looked familiar. Dr. Xavier ? I've seen your picture in the papers numberless times. As a matter of fact, I'd rather deduced a medico as the master of this house when I saw that etching after Rembrandt on your foyer wall. No one but a medical man would have displayed such—ah—original taste in decoration." He grinned. " Remember the doctor's face, don't you, dad ? " The Inspector nodded with vague enthusiasm ; in his mood at the moment he would have remembered anything. " We're the Queens, father and son, Dr. Xavier."

Dr. Xavier murmured something gracious. " Mr. Queen," he said to the Inspector. The Queens exchanged glances. Their host, then, was ignorant of the police connection of the Inspector. Ellery's eyes warned his father. And the Inspector nodded imperceptibly ; it did seem pointless to bring up his official title. People as a rule stiffened up on such creatures as detectives and policemen.

Dr. Xavier sat down in a leather chair and produced cigarettes. " And now, while we're waiting for my excellent housekeeper's no doubt frenzied preparations to bear fruit, suppose you tell me something about this . . . fire."

His mild and slightly absent expression did not change ; but something queer had crept into his voice.

The Inspector went into lurid detail, their host nodding at every sentence and maintaining a perfect air of polite perturbation. Ellery, whose eyes were paining him, took his spectacle-case out of his pocket, polished the lenses of his *pince-nez* wearily, and perched them on the bridge of his nose. He was in a mood to feel hypercritical about everything, he told himself glumly ; why shouldn't Dr. Xavier show polite perturbation ? The man's house was perched on top of a hill whose base was burning. Perhaps, he thought, closing his eyes, Dr. Xavier wasn't showing *enough* perturbation. . . .

The Inspector was saying sententiously : " We really ought to be making inquiries, Doctor. Have you a 'phone ? "

" At your elbow, Mr. Queen. There's a branch line running up the Arrow from the Valley."

The Inspector took the instrument and put in a call to Osquewa. He had considerable difficulty getting a connection. When he finally succeeded it was to discover that the entire town had been impressed into service for the purpose of fighting the flames, including the Sheriff, the Mayor, and the Town Board. The lone telephone operator supplied the information.

The old man put down the telephone with a grave look. " I guess this is a little more serious than usual. The fire's ringing the whole base of the mountain, Doctor, and every able-bodied man and woman for miles around is fighting it."

" Good lord," muttered Dr. Xavier. Perturbation had increased, but politeness had vanished. He rose and began to stride about.

" So," said the Inspector comfortably, " I guess we're stuck here, Doctor, at least for the night."

" Oh, that." The big man waved his muscular right hand. " Naturally. Wouldn't think of letting you push on, even under normal circumstances." He was frowning deeply and biting his lip. " This thing," he went on, " begins to look . . ."

Ellery's head was spinning. Despite the thickening atmosphere of mystery—his intuition told him that something very odd indeed was taking place in this lonely house perched on the shoulder of a mountain— he yearned most of all for bed and sleep. Even hunger had crept off, and the fire seemed far away. He could not keep his lids up, where conventionally they belonged. Dr. Xavier in his grave voice, now touched with the faintest mixture of excitement and dissimulation, was saying something about " the drought . . . probably spontaneous combustion . . ." and then Ellery heard no more.

. . . .

He awoke with a guilty start. A woman's unsteady voice was saying in his ear : " If you don't mind, sir . . ." and he leaped to his feet to find the stout squat figure of Mrs. Wheary standing by his chair with a tray in her broad hands.

" Oh, I say ! " he exclaimed, reddening. " Execrable manners. Please excuse it, Doctor. The fact is—the long drive, the fire——"

" Nonsense," said Dr. Xavier with an abstracted laugh. " Your father and I were just commenting upon the inadequate capacity of the younger generation for standing up under physical punishment. It's quite all right, Mr. Queen. Would you care to wash up before——? "

" If we may." Ellery eyed the tray hungrily. The

pangs had returned, catching him unaware, and he could have devoured the cold food before him on the spot, tray and all.

Dr. Xavier conducted them to the corridor, turned left, and led the way to a staircase overlooking another corridor which crossed the one leading out of the foyer. They ascended a flight of carpeted stairs and found themselves on the landing of what was apparently the sleeping-quarters floor. Except for a dim night-light above the landing the single hall was dark. All doors were tightly closed. The rooms behind the doors were silent as niches in a tomb.

" Brr ! " muttered Ellery in his father's ear as they followed the stately figure of their host down the hall. " Nice place for a murder. Even the wind is performing in character ! Listen to that silly howling, will you ? The banshees are out in full force to-night."

" You listen to it," growled the Inspector contentedly, " or even them. Not even an army of banshees could ruffle my hair to-night, old son. Why, this place looks like the Marble Palace to me ! Murder ? You're off your nut. This is the nicest damned house I've ever set foot in."

" I've seen nicer," said Ellery gloomily. " Besides, you've always been primarily a creature of the senses. . . . Ah, Doctor ! This is perfectly angelic of you."

Dr. Xavier had flung open a door. The room was a vast bedroom—all the rooms in this gargantuan establishment were enormous—and neatly grouped on the floor at the foot of the wide double bed were the heterogeneous components of the Queens' luggage.

" Not another word," said Dr. Xavier. And yet he said it absently, without the proper heartiness one might expect from an otherwise impeccable host. " Where on earth could you go with the fire burning below ? This is the only house for miles around, Mr. Queen. . . .

I've taken the liberty, while you were—resting down-stairs, of having my man Bones carry your luggage up here. Bones—odd name, eh? He's an unfortunate old derelict I picked up years ago; quite devoted to me, I assure you, despite a certain gruffness of manner, ha-ha! Bones will take care of your car. We've a garage here; cars get frightfully damp outdoors at this elevation, you know."

" Bully for Bones," murmured Ellery.

" Yes, yes. . . . And now, there's the lavatory. The general bathroom is behind the landing. I'll leave you to your ablutions."

He smiled and left the room, closing the door gently. The Queens, left alone in the centre of that colossal bedchamber, stared wordlessly at each other. Then the Inspector shrugged, stripped off his coat, and made for the indicated lavatory door.

Ellery followed, muttering : " Ablutions ! That's the first time I've heard that word in twenty years. Re-member the fussy old Greek who taught me at the Crosley School ? Did a Mrs. Malaprop with the word, misusing it for ' absolution.' Ablutions ! I tell you, dad, the more I see of this ominous establishment the less I like it."

" The more fool you," burbled the Inspector to the accompaniment of snorts and running water. " Good, by God ! I needed this. Come on, son ; get going. That grub downstairs won't last for ever."

When they had washed and combed and brushed the dust from their clothes, they went out into the dark corridor.

Ellery shivered. " What do we do now—just hurl ourselves downstairs ? Being the perfect guest, and considering the generally mysterious air of this house-hold, I'd rather not blunder in on anyth——"

" *God !* " whispered the Inspector. He had stopped

short in his tracks and gripped Ellery's arm with convulsive fingers. He was staring with sagging jaw, naked terror in his eyes, grey little face greyer than Ellery had ever seen it, past his son's shoulder at something down the hall.

His nerves already frayed by the harrowing experiences of the evening, Ellery whirled about. The skin of his arms was prickling, and the flesh was crawling at the base of his scalp.

But he saw nothing unusual ; the corridor was dim and empty, as before. Then he heard a faint *click* ! as of a door closing.

" What in God's name is the matter ? " he whispered nervously, searching his father's horror-struck face.

The Inspector's taut body relaxed. He sighed and passed a trembling hand over his mouth. " El, I—I—— Did you see what I——"

They both jumped at a light footstep behind them. Something large and shapeless was stalking them from the rear, where the corridor was blackest. Two burning eyes. . . . But it was only Dr. Xavier detaching himself from the region of intensest shadows.

" Quite ready, eh ? " he said in his deep charming voice, as if he had noticed nothing amiss, although he must have heard the Queens' tense whispers and— Ellery saw in a flash—must have seen both the Inspector's horror and the cause of it. The surgeon's voice was as pure, as rich, as mildly unruffled as it had been a few moments before. He linked their arms in his. " Then let's go downstairs ; shall we ? I daresay you're both ready to do justice to Mrs. Wheary's little snack."

And he urged them gently but firmly toward the landing.

* * * * * * * *

As they descended, three abreast on the side staircase, Ellery stole a glance at his father. Except for a certain slackness about the lips the old man betrayed no sign of his agitation of a moment before. But there was a deep furrow between his grey brows and he was holding himself stiffly erect, as if by a great effort of will.

Ellery shook his head in the half-light. All desire for sleep had fled before the excitement boiling in his brain. What mess of wriggling human relationships had they innocently blundered into ?

He frowned, treading the steps quietly. There were three major problems which required immediate solution if his restless brain was to relax and succumb to sleep : the cause of the Inspector's unaccountable and unprecedented horror, the reason their host had lurked near their door in the darkness of the upper corridor, and a rational explanation for the extraordinary fact that Dr. Xavier's big arm, where it touched Ellery's, was as rigid and hard as if the man had died and his body were in the grip of *rigor mortis*.

CHAPTER III

THE QUEER PEOPLE

In later years Ellery Queen was to remember every brilliant detail of that remarkable night in the Tepee Mountains, with an animate wind whistling about the summit of a peak on which stood a veritable house of mystery. It would not have been so bad, he would point out, had not the palpable blackness of the mountain night provided a dark breeding-ground for the phantoms of their imagination. And then, too, the fire miles below worked in and out of their minds, like a plaited thread of phosphorescent wool. Beneath everything they both realised that there was no escaping from the house, that they must eventually confront whatever of evil it concealed—unless they were willing to throw themselves upon the doubtful mercies of the wilderness and the conflagration below.

To make it worse, neither father nor son was offered the opportunity to discuss their common fears in private. Their host did not leave them alone for even a moment. Engulfing the cold pork sandwiches and blackberry tarts on the trays, and the steaming coffee Mrs. Wheary silently provided when they returned to the living-room on the main floor, the Queens would gladly have dispensed with the presence of Dr. Xavier. But the big man remained with them, ringing for Mrs. Wheary and ordering more sandwiches and coffee, pressing cigars upon them—in every way except the important one acting the perfect host.

Ellery, watching the man as he ate, was puzzled. Dr.

Xavier was not a charlatan nor a sinister figure out of bloody fiction. There was nothing of the Cagliari nor of the Cagliostro about him. He was a cultured, handsome, genial man approaching comfortable middle age, with an air of expertness in his profession—Ellery recalled that he was sometimes referred to as " the Mayo of New England "—and a quiet charm which was even more captivating on closer acquaintance. The ideal dinner guest, for example ; unquestionably, from his physique, a man of athletic tendencies ; a scientist and student and gentleman. But there was something else, something he was concealing. . . . Ellery racked his brains as his jaws rose and fell, but he could think of no explanation except the Thing that had raised the Inspector's hackles upstairs. Good lord, he thought to himself, it can't be one of these—these scientific monstrosities ! That would be too much, he conceded. The man was a famous surgeon, had performed pioneer work in unexplored surgical fields ; but to visualise him as a sort of Wellsian Dr. Moreau. . . . Nonsense !

He eyed his father. The Inspector was eating quietly. Terror had gone. But in its place lurked a sharpness, a sleepless vigilance which he strove to mask under the necessary movements of mastication.

And suddenly Ellery realised something else. The light coming in from the corridor was stronger. There were voices, too—almost normal voices—from that direction where there had been only whispering before. It was as if a veil had been lifted, as if by telepathic command the doctor had influenced the owners of those voices, who had whispered before, to make a pretence of normality.

.   .   .   .

" And now, if you've quite finished," said Dr. Xavier, surveying the ruins in the two trays with a smile, " suppose we join the others ? "

" The others ? " echoed the Inspector innocently, as if he had not even suspected the existence of others in the household.

" Why, yes. My brother, my wife, my medical assistant—I do some research up here, you know ; quite a laboratory at the rear of the house—and a . . ." Dr. Xavier hesitated ". . . a guest. I suspect it's a little too early to retire—— ? "

He stopped on an ascending note, as if mutely hoping that the Queens might be willing to forgo the pleasure of meeting " the others " for the more immediate delights of sleep.

But Ellery said quickly : " Oh, we've quite recovered ; haven't we, dad ? " The Inspector, accustomed to accepting cues, nodded. There was even a certain eagerness in his nod. " I don't feel a bit sleepy now. And then, after all the excitement," Ellery added, laughing, " it will be good to plunge into congenial human society again."

" Yes, yes, naturally," said Dr. Xavier. There was the faintest note of disappointment in his voice. " This way, gentlemen."

He conducted them out of the living-room across the corridor to a door almost directly opposite. " I suppose," he said hesitantly, his hand on the knob, " I should explain——"

" Not at all," said the Inspector heartily.

" But I feel . . . You see, I don't doubt it's all a little —odd to you, our behaviour to-night," he hesitated again, " but it's most uncommonly lonely up here, you know, and the ladies were slightly—ah—alarmed at the sounds of your pounding on the front door. We thought it best to send Bones——"

" Not another word," said Ellery handsomely, and Dr. Xavier hung his head and turned back to the door. It was as if he realised very well how lame the explanation must sound to intelligent ears. Ellery began to feel compassion for the big man. He abruptly dismissed from his mind, for once and all, the possibility of the scientific monstrosity his fertile imagination had conjured up a few moments before. This big chap was as gentle as a girl. Whatever it was that agitated him, it was something that concerned others, not himself. And it was a rational thing, not a fantastic horror.

.   .   .   .

The room they entered was a combined music-and-game room. A concert grand occupied one whole corner, and armchairs and lamps were artfully arranged about the instrument. The greater part of the room, however, was occupied with tables of varied sizes : for bridge, chess, checkers, backgammon, ping-pong and even billiards. The room had three other doors : one on the wall to their left ; another door leading from the foyer on the corridor wall—through which they had heard the whispering people—and a door on the opposite wall apparently opening, from the glimpse Ellery had of the room beyond, into a library. The entire front wall was composed of French windows which looked out upon the terrace.

All this he grasped in the first circumambient glance ; and more, for on two of the tables were scattered cards and this, it seemed to Ellery, was the most provocative fact of all ; and then, following the doctor and his father, he devoted his whole attention to the four people in the room.

Of one thing he was instantly certain : all four, like Dr. Xavier, were labouring under some intense excitement. The men showed it more than the women. Both men had risen, and neither glanced directly at the Queens. One of them, a big blond with broad shoulders and sharp eyes—unquestionably Dr. Xavier's brother—

covered his nervousness by masking it under action : he crushed his cigarette, barely smoked, in an ash-tray on the bridge-table before him, quickly, holding his head low. The other for no outward reason flushed : a young man of delicate features but keen blue eyes and squared-off jaw, with brown hair and chemical-stained fingers. He shuffled his feet twice as the Queens approached, his fair skin reddening more deeply at their every step, and his eyes fluttered from side to side.

"The assistant," thought Ellery. "Nice-looking youngster. Whatever it is this crowd is holding back, he's holding it back with them—but he doesn't like the feeling, that's evident ! "

The women, with the usual feminine capacity for rising to emergencies, scarcely betrayed their nervousness. One was young and the other—ageless. The young woman was big and competent, Ellery felt at once ; twenty-five, he judged, and quite capable of taking care of herself ; a quiet composed creature with alert brown eyes, pleasant features indefinably charming, and a certain controlled immobility that bespoke a capacity for decisive action should the necessity arise. She sat perfectly still, hands in her lap, even smiling a little. Only her eyes betrayed her : they were swimming with tension, snapping, brilliant.

Her companions was the dominating figure of the tableau. Tall even in her chair, deep-bosomed, with proud black eyes and jet hair touched with grey, with a clear olive complexion barely cosmetised, she was a woman to dominate any group. She might have been thirty-five or fifty ; and there was something strikingly French about her which Ellery could not analyse. A woman of passionate temperament, he felt instinctively ; dangerous woman, dangerous in hate and deadly in love. Her type should be given to quick little gestures, an overflow of movement reflecting the volatile personality.

Instead, she sat so still that she might have been mesmerised ; the liquid black of her eyes was fixed in space midway between Ellery and the Inspector. . . . Ellery dropped his eyes, composed himself, and smiled.

The amenities were preserved. It was an awkward meeting. " My dear," said Dr. Xavier to the extraordinary woman with the black eyes, " these are the gentlemen whom we mistook for marauders," and he laughed lightly. " Mrs. Xavier, Mr. Queen. Mr. Queen's son, my dear." Even then she did not look at them fixedly ; one flashing side-glance from her remarkable eyes, a polite smile. . . . " Miss Forrest, Mr. Queen ; Mr. Queen. . . . Miss Forrest is the guest I spoke of."

" Charmed," said the young woman instantly. Did a glance of warning pass from the doctor's deep-set eyes ? She smiled. " You'll have to forgive our bad manners. It's a—a ghastly night and we were taken rather by surprise." She shivered ; a genuine shiver.

" Can't say I blame you, Miss Forrest," said the Inspector genially. " I guess we didn't realise what sane people would think at having somebody pound at their front door at night in a place like this. But that's my son—impulsive scoundrel."

" There's an introduction for you," smiled Ellery.

They all laughed, and then silence again.

" Ah—my brother, Mark Xavier," said the surgeon hastily, indicating the tall blond man with the sharp eyes. " And my colleague, Dr. Holmes." The young man smiled in a strained fashion. " There ! Now that we've all met, won't you sit down ? " They found chairs. " Mr. Queen and his son," Dr. Xavier murmured casually, " were brought here more by circumstances than inclination."

" Lost your way ? " said Mrs. Xavier slowly, looking at Ellery directly for the first time. He felt a physical shock ; it was like peering into a furnace. And she had a throbbing husky voice as passionate and baffling as her eyes.

"Not that, my dear," said Dr. Xavier. "Don't be alarmed, but the fact is there's something of a forest fire down below and these gentlemen, returning from a holiday in Canada, were forced on to the Arrow road in self-protection."

"Fire !" they all exclaimed ; and Ellery saw that their surprise was genuine. This was undoubtedly the first intelligence they had had of the conflagration.

And so the gap was bridged, and for some time the Queens were occupied answering excited questions and repeating the story of their narrow escape from the flames. Dr. Xavier sat quietly by, listening and smiling courteously, as if this were the first time he, too, had heard the story. Then the conversation petered out and Mark Xavier went abruptly to one of the French windows to stare out at the darkness. The ugly Thing that lurked in the recesses reared its head again. Mrs. Xavier was biting her lip and Miss Forrest was studying her rosy fingers.

"Now, now," said the surgeon suddenly, "don't let's pull such long faces." Then he had seen it, too. "It's probably not very serious. Communication's cut off temporarily, that's all. Osquewa and the neighbouring villages are well equipped for fighting forest fires. There's one almost every year. Remember the blaze last year, Sarah ?"

"Indeed I do." The glance Mrs. Xavier flung at her husband was enigmatic.

"I suggest," said Ellery, lighting a cigarette, "that we discuss pleasanter things. Dr. Xavier, for example."

"Now, now," said the surgeon, flushing.

"There's an idea !" cried Miss Forrest, jumping from her chair suddenly. "Let's talk about you, Doctor, and how famous and kind and miraculous you are ! I've been dying to for days, but I haven't dared for fear Mrs. Xavier would tear my hair out, or something."

" Now, Miss Forrest," said Mrs. Xavier grimly.

" Oh, I *am* sorry ! " cried the young woman, swinging about the room. Her self-control seemed to have deserted her ; her eyes were extraordinarily bright. " I guess I'm just all nerves. With two doctors in the house, perhaps a sedative. . . . Oh, come *on*, Sherlock ! " and she pulled at Dr. Holmes's arm. The young man was startled. " Don't stand there like a stick. Let's do something."

" I say," he said quickly, almost stammering. " You know——"

" Sherlock ? " said the Inspector, smiling. " That's an odd name, Dr. Holmes. . . . Oh, I see ! "

" Of course," said Miss Forrest, dimpling. She clung to the young physician's arm to his evident embarrassment. " Sherlock Holmes. That's what *I* call him. Real name is Percival, or some such dismal thing. . . . He's a Sherlock at that ; aren't you, darling ? Always messing about with microscopes and nasty liquids and things."

" Now, Miss Forrest," began Dr. Holmes, scarlet.

" And he's English, too," said Dr. Xavier with a fond glance at the young man, " which makes the name astonishingly appropriate, Miss Forrest. But you're an impertinent baggage. Percival's very sensitive, like most Britons, you know ; you're really embarrassing him. "

" No, no," said Dr. Holmes, whose conversational capacity seemed limited. He said it very quickly, however.

" Oh, lord ! " wailed Miss Forrest, throwing her arms about as she flung the young man's aside. " Nobody loves me," and she went to join silent Mark Xavier at the window.

" Very pretty," thought Ellery grimly. " This crowd

ought to go on the stage, *en masse*." Aloud he said with a smile : " You'd rather not be named after Holmes of Baker Street, Dr. Holmes ? In some circles it would be considered rather an accolade."

" Can't abide shockers," said Dr. Holmes briefly, and sat down.

" There," chuckled Dr. Xavier, " Percival and I part. I'm fatuously fond of them."

" Trouble is," said Dr. Holmes unexpectedly, with a furtive glance at the smooth back of Miss Forrest, " their atrocious medical stuff. Sheer bilge, you know. You'd think the blighters would take the trouble to get accurate medical information. And then when they put English characters into their stories—the American ones, I mean, do you see—they make 'em talk like. . . . like . . ."

" You're a living paradox, Doctor," said Ellery with a twinkle. " *I* thought no Englishman breathes who uses the word ' blighter.' "

Even Mrs. Xavier permitted herself to smile at that.

" You're too captious, my boy," went on Dr. Xavier. " Read a story once in which murder was committed by injecting the victim with air from an empty hypodermic. Coronary-explosion sort of thing. Well, the fact is, as you know, death won't occur from that cause once in a hundred times. Didn't bother me, though."

Dr. Holmes grunted ; Miss Forrest was deep in conversation with Mark Xavier.

" Refreshing to meet a tolerant medico," grinned Ellery, recalling some vitriolic letters he had had from physicians because of alleged errors of fact in his own novels. " You read for entertainment purely ? I should deduce, seeing this wealth of games, Doctor, that you're the puzzle type of fan. Like to figure them out, eh ? "

" It's my one abiding passion—much, I fear, to the disgust of Mrs. Xavier, whose own taste runs to French novels. Cigar, Mr. Queen ? " Mrs. Xavier half-smiled again—a dreadful smile ; and Dr. Xavier surveyed his game-tables imperturbably. " As a matter of fact, I've an abnormally developed game-sense, as you've noted. All sorts of games. I find I need that sort of thing as sheer diversion from the physical strain of surgery. . . . I *did* find, I mean to say," he added with an odd change of tone. A shade passed over his pleasant face. " It's been some time since I've presided in an operating theatre. Retired, you know. . . . Now it's a habit, and it's excellent relaxation. I'm still fussing about with my laboratory." He flicked ashes from his cigar, bending forward to do so ; and as he bent forward his eyes searched his wife's face for an instant. Mrs. Xavier was sitting with the same vague smile on her extraordinary face, nodding at every word. But she was frigid and remote as Arcturus. A frigid woman who was volcanic beneath ! Ellery studied her without seeming to do so.

" By the way," said the Inspector suddenly, crossing his legs, " we met a guest of yours on our way up."

" Guest of ours ? " Dr. Xavier seemed puzzled ; the fair skin of his forehead wrinkled inquiringly. Mrs. Xavier's body stirred ; the movement reminded Ellery of the squirming of an octopus. Then she became as still as before. The low voices of Mark Xavier and Ann Forrest at the window ceased abruptly. Dr. Holmes alone seemed unaffected ; he was staring rebelliously at the cuff of his linen trousers, his thoughts apparently eons away.

" Why, yes," murmured Ellery, alert. " Bumped into the chap during our flight from that private Hades of ours below. He was driving a rather ancient Buick sedan."

" But we haven't——" began Dr. Xavier slowly, and stopped. His sunken eyes narrowed. " That's rather odd, do you know ? "

The Queens looked at each other. What now?

" Odd ? " said the Inspector mildly. He refused his host's mechanical offer of a cigar and, taking a worn brown box from his pocket, sniffed a pinch of its contents. " Snuff," he said apologetically. " Dirty habit. . . . Odd, Doctor ? "

" Quite. What sort of man was he ? "

" Very stout, from what I saw of him," said Ellery quickly. " Froggy eyes. Voice like a bassoon. Tremendous breadth of shoulder. About fifty-five, at a rough guess."

Mrs. Xavier stirred again.

" But we've had no visitor at all, you know," said the surgeon quietly.

The Queens were astonished. " Then he didn't come from here ? " muttered Ellery. " But I thought no one else lives on this mountain ! "

" We're quite sequestered up here, I assure you. Sarah, my dear, you don't know of anyone—— ? "

Mrs. Xavier licked her full lips. A struggle seemed to be raging within her. There was speculation, bafflement, and subtle cruelty in her black eyes. Then she said in a surprised voice : " No."

" That's funny," murmured the Inspector. " He was headed lickety-cut down the mountain, and if there's only one road and this is at the end of it and nobody else lives up here . . ."

There was a crash from behind. They turned quickly. But it was only Miss Forrest, who had dropped her compact. She straightened up, her cheeks fiery, eyes so strangely bright, and said gaily : " Oh, shoot ! The next thing we know we'll all be babbling of bogies. If you people insist on introducing unpleasant subjects, you know, I'll be *just* as unpleasant. What with men prowling about and all, somebody will have to tuck me into bed to-night. You see——"

" What do you mean, Miss Forrest ? " said Dr. Xavier slowly. " Is there anything——? "

The Queens crossed glances again. These people were not only concealing a common secret, but they possessed little private secrets as well.

The girl tossed her head. " I wasn't going to mention it," she said, shrugging, " because it was really nothing and—and . . ." It was evident that she already regretted having begun. " Oh, let's forget all about it and play ducks and drakes, or something."

Mark Xavier came forward with short quick steps. There was a brutal gleam in his sharp eyes and his mouth was hard. " Come on, Miss Forrest," he said gruffly. " Something's bothering you and we might as well know what. If there's a man skulking about the place . . ."

" Of course," said the girl quietly, " that's what it is. Very well, if you insist ; but I apologise in advance. No doubt that's the explanation. . . . Last week I—I lost something."

It seemed to Ellery that Dr. Xavier, more than any of them, was startled. Then Dr. Holmes rose and went to a small round table, groping for a cigarette.

" Lost something ? " asked Dr. Xavier in a thick voice.

The room was incredibly quiet ; so quiet that Ellery could hear the suddenly laboured breathing of their host. " I missed it one morning," said Miss Forrest in a low voice ; " I think it was Friday of last week. I thought I might have mislaid it. I looked and looked all over but I couldn't find it, you see. Perhaps I *did* lose it. Yes, I'm sure I lost it." She stopped in confusion.

No one spoke for a long time. Then Mrs. Xavier said harshly : " Come, come, child. You know that's non-sense. You mean some one *stole* it from you, don't you ? "

" Oh, dear ! " cried Miss Forrest, flinging her head back. " Now you've made me talk about it. I wasn't going to. I'm sure I either lost it or that—that man Mr. Queen was telling about stole into my room somehow and—and took it. You see, it *couldn't* have been anybody h . . ."

" I suggest," stammered Dr. Holmes, " th-that we put off this charming conversation to another time ; eh ? "

" What was it ? " asked Dr. Xavier in a quiet voice. He had himself perfectly under control again.

" Was it valuable ? " snapped Mark Xavier.

" No ; oh, no," said the girl eagerly. " Absolutely worthless. You couldn't get a wooden nickel on it from a pawnbroker or—or anybody. It was just an old heirloom, a silver ring."

" A silver ring," said the surgeon. He rose. Ellery noticed for the first time that there was something gaunt about his appearance ; drawn and bleak. " Sarah, I'm sure your remark was needlessly unkind. There isn't anyone here who would stoop to theft, my dear ; you know that. Is there ? "

Their eyes met briefly ; it was his that fell. " You never can tell, *mon cher*," she said softly.

The Queens sat still. This talk of thievery was, under the circumstances, acutely embarrassing. Ellery slowly removed his *pince-nez* and began to scrub them. Unpleasant female, that woman !

" No." The surgeon gripped himself visibly. " And then Miss Forrest says the ring was valueless. I see no point in suspecting a theft. You probably dropped it somewhere, my dear, or else, as you suggest, this mysterious skulker is in some way responsible for its disappearance."

" Yes, of course that's it, Doctor," said the girl thankfully.

" If you will pardon an unpardonable interruption,"
murmured Ellery. They turned to stare, freezing in
their attitudes. Even the Inspector frowned. But Ellery
replaced his *pince-nez* with a smile. " You see, if this man
we met really is an unknown quantity and unconnected
with the household, then you are faced with a peculiar
situation."

" Yes, Mr. Queen ? " said Dr. Xavier stiffly.

" Of course," said Ellery with a wave of his hand,
" there are minor considerations. If Miss Forrest lost her
ring last Friday, where has this prowler been ? Not
necessarily an insurmountable point, however ; he may
have his headquarters in Osquewa, say. . . ."

" Yes, Mr. Queen ? " said Dr. Xavier again.

" But, as I said, you are faced with a peculiar situation.
Because, since the fat-faced gentleman is neither a
phœnix nor a devil out of Hell," continued Ellery, " the
fire will stop him to-night as effectually as it stopped
my father and me. Consequently he will find himself—
has already found himself, no doubt—unable to leave
the mountain." He shrugged. " A nasty situation.
With no other house in the vicinity, and the fire possibly
a stubborn one . . ."

" Oh ! " gasped Miss Forrest. " He—he'll be back ! "

" I should say that is a mathematical certainty," said
Ellery dryly.

There was silence again. About the house Ellery's
postulated banshees, as if this were a signal, redoubled
their howling. Mrs. Xavier shivered suddenly, and even
the men glanced uneasily at the black night beyond the
French windows.

" If he's a thief," muttered Dr. Holmes, crushing out
his cigarette, and stopped. His eyes met Dr. Xavier's and
his jaw tightened. " I was about to say," he went on
quietly, " that Miss Forrest's explanation is undoubtedly
correct. Oh, undoubtedly. For you see, I myself missed

a signet ring last Wednesday. Worthless old scrap, to be sure ; don't wear it much and it means nothing to me, but—there you are. Gone, you see."

The silence resumed where it had left off. Ellery, studying those faces, wondered again with weary tenacity what cesspool lay beneath the polite surface of this household.

The silence was shattered by Mark Xavier, whose big body moved so suddenly as to cause Miss Forrest to utter a little scream. " I think, John," he snapped, addressing Dr. Xavier, " that you'd better see that all the doors and windows are locked tight to-night. . . . Good night, all ! "

He stalked out of the room.

.   .   .   .

Ann Forrest—whose aplomb seemed irremediably shaken for the evening—and Dr. Holmes excused themselves soon after ; Ellery heard them whispering to each other as they strode down the corridor toward the staircase. Mrs. Xavier still sat with the Mona Lisa half-smile that was as stiff and inexplicable as the expression on the painted face of Leonardo's *Gioconda*.

The Queens rose awkwardly. " I guess," said the Inspector, " we'll be trotting off to bed, too, Doctor, if you don't mind. I can't tell you how all-fired grateful we are——"

" Please," said Dr. Xavier roughly. " We're rather short-staffed here, Mr. Queen—Mrs. Wheary and Bones are our only servants—so I'll show you to your room myself."

" Not at all necessary," Ellery hastened to reply. " We know the way, Doctor. Thank you all the same. Good night, Mrs. Xav——"

" I'm going to bed myself," announced the doctor's wife suddenly, rising. She was taller even than Ellery had supposed ; she drew herself up to her full height, breathing deeply. " If there's anything you'd like before retiring . . ."

" Nothing at all, Mrs. Xavier, thank you," said the Inspector.

" But, Sarah, I thought——" began Dr. Xavier. He stopped and shrugged, his shoulders set at an oddly hopeless slope.

" Aren't you coming to bed, John ? " she said sharply.

" I think not, my dear," he replied in a heavy voice, avoiding her eyes. " I believe I'll do a bit of work in the lab before I turn in. There's a chemical reaction I've been meaning to make on that ' soup ' I prepared. . . ."

" I see," she said, and smiled that dreadful smile again. She turned to the Queens. " This way, please," and swept out of the room.

The Queens muttered subdued " good nights " to their host and followed. The last glimpse they had of the surgeon was as they turned into the corridor. He was standing where they had left him, in an attitude of the most profound dejection, sucking his lower lip and fingering a rather gaudy bar-pin securing his necktie to his rough woven shirt. He looked older than before and mentally exhausted. Then they heard him cross the room in the direction of the library.

.   .   .   .

The instant the door of their bedroom closed upon them and Ellery had switched on the overhead light, he whirled on his father and whispered fiercely : " Dad ! What in the name of God was that awful thing you saw in the corridor outside just before Xavier sneaked up on us from behind ? "

The Inspector sank into a Morris-chair very slowly, loosening the knot of his cravat. He avoided Ellery's eyes. "Well," he mumbled, "I don't rightly know. I guess I must have been a little—well, jumpy."

"You jumpy?" said Ellery scornfully. "You've always had the nerves of a cuttlefish. Come on, out with it. I've been bursting to ask you all evening. Blast that big chap! He didn't leave us alone for an instant."

"Well," muttered the old gentleman, pulling his cravat off and unbuttoning his collar, "I'll tell you. It was—weird."

"Well, well, what was it, dad, for heaven's sake?"

"To tell the truth, I don't know." The Inspector looked sheepish. "If you or anybody else in this world described that—that thing to me I swear I'd call for the nut-wagon. Cripes!" he burst out, "it didn't look like anything human, I'd bet my life!"

Ellery stared at him. This from his own father! The prosaic little Inspector, who had handled more corpses and wallowed in more illicitly spilled human blood than any other man in the New York Police Department!

"It—it looked," went on the Inspector with a feeble grin that held no mirth whatever, "it looked just like—a crab."

"*A crab!*"

Ellery gaped at his father. Then his flat cheeks ballooned out and he put his hand over his mouth, doubled over in a spasm of the heartiest laughter. He rocked to and fro, eyes streaming.

"A crab!" he gasped. "Ho, ho, ho! A *crab*!" and he went off into another gale.

"Oh, stop it!" said the old gentleman irritably. "You sound like Lawrence Tibbett singing that flea-song. Stop it!"

"A crab," gasped Ellery again, wiping his eyes.

The old man shrugged. "Mind you, I'm not saying it *was* a—a crab. Might have been a couple of crazy acrobats or wrestlers or something doing a little home-work on the hall-floor. But it *looked* like a crab—a giant crab. Big as a man—bigger than a man, El." He rose nervously and grasped Ellery's arm. " Come on, be nice. I look all right, don't I ? I haven't got de—delusions, or something, have I ? "

" Blessed if I know what you have," chuckled Ellery, flinging himself on the bed. " Seeing crabs ! If I didn't know you so well I'd lump the crab with a particularly violent purple elephant and say you'd had a wee drappie too much. Crab ! " He shook his head. " Now look here ; let's examine this thing like rational human beings, not kids in a haunted house. I was talking to you, facing you. You were looking straight ahead, down the corridor. Exactly where did you see this—this fantastic beast of yours, Inspector dear ? "

The Inspector took snuff with shaking fingers. " Second door down the hall from ours," he muttered, and sneezed. " Of course, it was just my imagination, El. . . . It was on our side of the hall. It was pretty dark at that spot——"

" Pity," drawled Ellery. " With a little more light I'm sure you'd have seen at least a tyrannosaurus. Just what was your friend the crab doing when you spotted him and got the shivers ? "

" Don't rub it in," said the Inspector miserably. " I just got a glimpse of—of the thing. Scuttled——"

" Scuttled ! "

" That's the only word for it," said the old gentleman in a dogged voice. " Scuttled through the doorway, and then you heard the click yourself. Must have."

" This," said Ellery, " calls for investigation." He jumped from the bed and strode to the door.

" El ! For God's sake be careful ! " wailed the Inspector. " You simply can't go snooping about a man's house at night——"

" I can go to the bathroom, can't I ? " said Ellery with dignity ; and he pulled open the door and vanished.

.   .   .   .

Inspector Queen sat still, gnawing at his fingers and shaking his head. Then he rose, pulled off his coat and shirt, his suspenders sagging below his seat, and stretching his arms yawned prodigiously. He was very tired. Tired and sleepy and—afraid. Yes, he admitted to himself in the privacy of that doorless chamber of the mind to which no outsider can gain admittance, old Queen of Centre Street was afraid. It was a queer thing. He had felt fear often before ; it was silly to set oneself up as a Jack Dalton ; but this was a new kind of fear. A fear of the unknown. It did queer things to his skin and made him want to whirl about at purely imaginary sounds behind him.

Consequently he yawned and stretched and busied himself with the score of slow little unimportant things a man does when he is undressing for bed. And all the while, despite the very genuine laughter of Ellery echoing in his brain, fear lurked there and would not be banished. He even began—sneering bitterly to himself in the same instant—to whistle.

He slipped out of his trousers and folded his clothes neatly on the Morris-chair. Then he bent over one of the suitcases at the foot of the bed. As he did so something rattled at one of the windows and he looked up, prickling and alert. But it was only a half-drawn window-shade.

Moved by an unconquerable impulse he trotted quickly across the room—a grey mouse of a man in his underwear—and pulled the blind. He caught a glimpse of the outdoors as the blind came down : a vast black abyss, it seemed to him ; and indeed it was, for he was to find later that the house was perched on the edge of a precipice, with a sheer drop of hundreds of feet into the next valley. His small sharp eyes flicked sidewise. In the same instant he sprang back from the window, releasing the shade so that it flew up with a crash, and darting across the room flicked the light-switch, plunging the room in darkness.

.   .   .   .

Ellery opened the door of their bedroom, stopped short in astonishment, and then slipped into the room like a wraith, shutting the door quickly and softly behind him.

" Dad ! " he whispered. " Are you in bed ? Why's the light off ? "

" Shut up ! " he heard his father say fiercely. " Don't make any more noise than you have to. There's something damned fishy going on around here, and I think I know now what it is."

Ellery was silent for a moment. As his pupils contracted under influence of the dark, he began to make out shadowy details. A faint starlight shone through the rear windows. His father, bare-legged and in shorts, was crouched almost on his knees across the room. There was a third window on the right-hand wall ; and it was at this window that the Inspector crouched.

Ellery ran to his father's side and looked out. The side window overlooked a court formed by the recession of the rear wall of the house in the middle. The court was narrow. Propped against the outside of the rear wall in the court at the first-floor level there was a balcony which led, apparently, from the bedroom adjoining the Queens'. Ellery reached the window just in time to see a flowing shadowy figure slip from the balcony through a French door and vanish. A white feminine hand shone in the starlight as it reached out of the room and drew the double-door shut.

The Inspector rose with a groan, pulled all the blinds, pattered back to the door, and turned on the light-switch. He was perspiring profusely.

"Well?" murmured Ellery, standing still at the foot of the bed.

The Inspector dropped on to the bed, hunched over like a little half-naked kobold, and tugged fretfully at one end of his grey moustache. "I went over there to pull the blind," he muttered, "and just then I saw a woman through the side-window. She was standing on the balcony staring off into space, seemed like. I ran back and turned off the light and then watched her. She didn't move. Just stared up at the stars. Moony, sort of. I heard her sniffle. Cried like a baby. All by herself. Then you came in and she went back to that room next door."

"Indeed?" said Ellery. He slipped over to the wall on the right and pressed his ear against it. "Can't hear a thing through these walls, damn the luck! Well, and what's fishy about that? Who was it—Mrs. Xavier, or that very frightened young woman, Miss Forrest?"

"That," said the Inspector grimly, "is what makes it so fishy."

Ellery stared at his father. "Riddles, eh?" He began to strip off his jacket. "Come on, out with it. Somebody we haven't seen to-night, I'll wager. And *not* the crab."

"You've guessed it," said the old gentleman glumly. "It wasn't either of 'em. It was . . . Marie Carreau!" He uttered the name as if it were an incantation.

Ellery stopped struggling with his shirt. "Marie Carreau? Come again. Who the devil's she? Never heard of her."

"Oh, my God," moaned the Inspector. "Never heard of Marie Carreau, he says! That's what comes of raising an ignoramus. Don't you read the papers, you idiot? She's society, son, society!"

" Hear, hear."

" Bluest of the blue. Pots of money. Runs official Washington. Her father's Ambassador to France. Of French stock, dating from the Revolution. Her great-great-what-is-it and Lafayette were just like that." The old gentleman twined his middle finger about his forefinger. " Whole damn' family—uncles and cousins and nephews—all in the diplomatic service. She married her own cousin—same name—about twenty years ago. He's dead now. No children. Never remarried, though she's still young. She's only about thirty-seven." He paused for sheer lack of breath and glared at his son.

" Bravo," chuckled Ellery, flexing his arms. " There's the complete woman for you ! That old photographic memory of yours operating again. Well, what of it ? To tell the truth, I'm immensely relieved. We're beginning to dig into some tangible mysteries. This crowd had some reason, obviously, to conceal the fact that your precious Mrs. Carreau is among those present. *Ergo*, when they heard an automobile roaring up tonight they bundled your precious social *ranee* into her bedroom. All that stuff about being afraid of visitors this time of night was pure hogwash. What gave mine host and the rest the jitters was trying to keep us from suspecting she's here. I wonder why."

" I can tell you that," said the Inspector quietly. " I saw it in the newspapers before we started out on our trip three weeks ago, and you would have seen it, too, if you paid the least attention to what's going on in the world ! Mrs. Carreau is supposed to be in Europe ! "

" Oho," said Ellery softly. He took a cigarette out of his case and went over to the night-table to hunt for a match. " Interesting. But not necessarily inexplicable. We've a famous surgeon here—perhaps the little lady has something wrong with her blue blood, or her gold-plated innards, and doesn't want to have the world know. . . . No, that doesn't seem to wash. It's more than that. . . . Very pretty problem. Crying, eh? Perhaps she's been kidnapped," he said hopefully. " By our excellent host. . . . Where in hell's a match? "

The Inspector disdained to reply, tugging at his moustache and scowling at the floor.

Ellery opened the drawer of the night-table, found a packet of matches, and whistled. " By George," he drawled, " what a thoughtful gentleman our precious doctor is. Just look at the junk in this drawer."

The Inspector snorted.

" There's a man," said Ellery admiringly, " with admirable singleness of purpose. Apparently gaming of the innocuous sort is a phobia with him, so that he can't forbear inflicting his phobia on his guests. Here's the complete solution to a dull week-end. A crisp new pack of cards, never opened, a book of crossword puzzles —actually virgin, by Vesta!—a checker-board, one of those questions-and-answers books, and heaven knows what else. Even the pencil is sharpened. Well!" He sighed, closed the drawer, and lit his cigarette.

" Beautiful," muttered the Inspector.

" Eh? "

The old gentleman started. " I was thinking out loud. The lady on the balcony, I mean. Really a gorgeous creature, El. And crying——" He shook his head. " Well, I suppose it's all really none of our business. We're a pair of the world's nosiest louts." Then he jerked his head up and some of the old wariness leapt into his grey eyes. " I forgot. Anything doing outside? Find out anything? "

Ellery deliberately lay down on the other side of the bed and crossed his feet on the footboard. He puffed smoke toward the ceiling. " Oh, you mean about the— ah—giant crab? " he said with a twinkle.

" You know damn' well what I mean ! " snarled the Inspector, blushing to his ears.

" Well," drawled Ellery, " it's problematical. Corridor was empty and all the doors closed. No sounds. I crossed the landing noisily and went into the bathroom. Then I came out—without noise. Didn't remain there long. . . . By the way, do you happen to know anything about the gastronomical predilections of crustaceans ? "

" Well, well ? " growled the Inspector. " What's on your mind now ? You always have to say it with trimmings ! "

" The point is," murmured Ellery, " that I heard footsteps on the stairs and had to dodge back into the darkness of the corridor near our door. Couldn't cross the landing to get into the bathroom again, or whoever it was that was coming up would have spotted me. So I watched that patch of light at the landing. It was our buxom Demeter, our nervous provider of provender, Mrs. Wheary."

" The housekeeper ? What of it ? Probably going to bed. I suppose she and that lout of a scoundrel, Bones —cripes, what a name !—sleep on the attic floor upstairs."

" Oh, no doubt. But Mrs. Wheary was not bound for blessed dreamland, I'll tell you that. She was carrying a tray."

" Ah ! "

" A tray, I might add, heaped with comestibles."

" Bound for Mrs. Carreau's room, I'll bet," muttered the Inspector. " After all, even society women have to eat."

" Not at all," said Ellery dreamily. " That's why I asked you if you knew anything about the gustatory tastes of crustaceans. I've never heard of a crab drinking a pitcher of cow's milk and eating meat sandwiches of whole-wheat bread, and gulping fruit. . . . You see, she barged right into the room next to Mrs. Carreau's with not the faintest sign of fear. The room," he said slyly, " into which you saw your giant crab—ah " —the Inspector threw up his hands and dug into the suitcase for his pyjamas—" scuttle ! "

CHAPTER IV

BLOOD ON THE SUN

ELLERY opened his eyes and saw brilliant sunlight splashing the counterpane of the unfamiliar bed on which he lay. For a moment he did not remember where he was. There was a singed soreness in his throat and his head felt like a pumpkin. He sighed and stirred and heard his father say : " So you're up," in a mild voice ; and he twisted his head to find the Inspector, fully dressed in clean linen, fastidious little hands clasped behind his back, staring out of one of the rear windows with quiet abstraction.

Ellery groaned, stretched, and crawled out of bed. He began to peel off his pyjamas, yawning.

" Take a look at this," said the Inspector, without turning.

Ellery shuffled to his father's side. The wall with two windows between which stood their bed was at the rear of the Xavier house. What had seemed a profound black abyss the night before turned out to be a sheer drop of contorted stone ; so deep and disturbing that for a moment Ellery closed his eyes against a surge of vertigo. Then he opened them again. The sun was well over the distant range ; it painted microscopic details of valley and cliffside with remarkable clarity. They were so high that the still, deserted world in the cup of the mighty well was the merest miniature ; fluffy clouds drifted a little below them, striving to cling to the mountain's top.

" See it ? " murmured the Inspector.

" See what ? "

" 'Way down there, where the cliff begins to slope into the valley. At the sides of the mountain, El."

Then Ellery saw. Curling around the edges of Arrow Mountain, far down at the knife-edge sides where the tight green mat of vegetation abruptly ended, were little fluttering pennants of smoke.

" The fire ! " exclaimed Ellery. " I'd almost got myself to the point of thinking the whole blessed thing was a nightmare."

" Drifting around at the back, where the cliffside is," said the Inspector thoughtfully. " All stone at the back here and the fire can't get a grip. Nothing to feed on. Not that it does *us* any good."

Ellery halted on his way to the lavatory. " And what does that mean, my good sire ? "

" Nothing much. Only I was just thinking," said the old gentleman reflectively, " that if the fire really got bad . . . "

" Well ? "

" We'd be stuck good and proper, my son. A bug could hardly crawl down that cliff."

For a moment Ellery stared ; then he chuckled. " There you go spoiling a perfectly lovely morning. Always the pessimist. Forget it. Be with you in a moment ; I want to splash some of that monstrous cold mountain water over me."

But the Inspector did not forget. He watched the little streamers of smoke without blinking all the while Ellery showered, combed, and dressed.

.   .   .   .

As the Queens descended the stairs they heard subdued voices below. The lower corridor was deserted, but the front door off the foyer was open and the dark hall of the night before was almost cheerful in the strong morning light. They went out upon the terrace and found Dr. Holmes and Miss Forrest engaged in an earnest conversation which ceased abruptly at the Queens' appearance.

" 'Morning," said Ellery briskly. " Lovely, isn't it ? " He stepped to the edge of the porch and breathed deeply, eyeing the hot blue sky with appreciation. The Inspector sat down in a rocker and fumbled with his snuff-box.

" Yes, isn't it ? " murmured Miss Forrest in an odd voice. Ellery turned sharply to search her face. She was rather pale. She was dressed in something pastel and clinging and looked very charming. But the charm was half tension. . . .

" Going to turn hot," said Dr. Holmes nervously, swinging his long legs. " Ah—did you sleep well, Mr. Queen ? "

" Like Lazarus," said Ellery cheerfully. " Must be the mountain air. Curious place Dr. Xavier has built here. More like an eagle's eyrie than a roost for human beings."

" Yes, isn't it," said Miss Forrest in smothered tones, and there was silence.

Ellery examined the terrain in the bright daylight. The summit of Arrow Mountain was level for only a few hundred feet. With the wide sprawling house backed against the lip of the precipice, very little ground remained to front and flank it, and that had apparently been cleared only with the greatest difficulty. Some effort had been made to level the terrain and remove the tumbled clusters of rock ; but the effort had obviously been abandoned in short order, for except for the automobile drive leading from the grilled gates the ground was a petrified morass of jutting stones and rubble sparsely covered with tangled dusty vegetation. The woods began abruptly in a three-quarter circle about the summit, dipping down the mountainside. The whole effect was stark, lonely, and grotesque.

" Nobody else up ? " inquired the Inspector pleasantly, after a while. " It's kind of late and I thought we'd be the last."

Miss Forrest started. " Why—I really don't know. I haven't seen anyone but Dr. Holmes and that awful creature Bones. He's rooting around at the side of the house somewhere, fussing with a pitiful little garden or something he's trying to develop there. Have you, Dr. Holmes ? " No badinage from the young lady this morning, observed Ellery to himself ; and a sudden suspicion leaped into his mind. Miss Forrest was a " guest," eh ? The probabilities were, now that he thought of it, that the girl was in some way connected with the mysterious society woman skulking in her bedroom upstairs. This explanation would account for her excessive nervousness of the night before, her pallor and unnatural actions this morning.

" No," said Dr. Holmes. " Waiting breakfast for the others, as a matter of fact."

" I see," murmured the Inspector. He stared out over the rocky ground for a moment and then rose. " Well, son, I think we'd better be using that telephone again. See how our little fire's getting along, and then we'll be on our way."

" Right."

They moved toward the foyer.

" Oh, but you'll stay breakfast, of course," said Dr. Holmes quickly, flushing. " Couldn't think of letting you go, you know, without a spot of something——"

" Well, well, we'll see," replied the Inspector with a smile. " We've troubled you people enough as it is——"

" Good morning," said Mrs. Xavier from the doorway. They turned all at once. Ellery could have sworn he detected anguished anxiety in the eyes of Miss Forrest.

The doctor's wife was attired in a crimson morning-gown ; her grey-touched glossy jet hair was piled in Spanish masses on her head and her olive skin was delicately pallid. She stared inscrutably from the Inspector to Ellery.

" 'Morning," said the Inspector hastily. " We were just going to call up Osquewa, Mrs. Xavier, and find out if the fire——"

" I have already telephoned Osquewa," said Mrs. Xavier in a toneless voice. For the first time Ellery detected something faintly foreign in her speech.

Miss Forrest said breathlessly : " And ? "

" Those people have made not the slightest progress in fighting the flames." Mrs. Xavier swept to the edge of the terrace and brooded out upon the dreary vista. " It is burning steadily and—gaining."

" Gaining, eh ? " murmured Ellery. The Inspector was deathly still.

" Yes. It is not yet out of control, however," said Mrs. Xavier with her maddening Mona Lisa smile, " so you need have no fears for your safety. It is really just a question of time."

" Then there's no way down yet ? " muttered the Inspector.

" I'm afraid not."

" Oh, lord," said Dr. Holmes, and flung his cigarette away. " Let's have breakfast ; shall we ? "

No one replied. Miss Forrest moved suddenly, shrinking back as if she had seen a snake. They bent forward. It was a long feathery ash drifting out of the sky. As they watched, fascinated, others settled down.

" Cinders," gasped Miss Forrest.

" Well, what of it ? " said Dr. Holmes in a strained high voice. " Wind's changed, Miss Forrest, that's all."

" Wind's changed," repeated Ellery thoughtfully. He

frowned all at once and dipped into his pocket for his cigarette-case. Mrs. Xavier had not stirred a muscle of her broad smooth back.

The silence was broken by the voice of Mark Xavier from the front door. " Good morning," he growled. " What's all this about cinders ? "

" Oh, Mr. Xavier," cried Miss Forrest, " the fire's worse ! "

" Worse ? " He tramped forward and stood beside his sister-in-law. His sharp eyes were dulled and glassy this morning, and the whites were shot with streaks of blood. He looked as if he had not slept, or had been drinking heavily.

"That's bad," he muttered, " that's bad," over and over again. " It doesn't seem as if——" Then he stopped and raised his voice ; it rang out harshly. " Well, what the devil are we waiting for ? The fire'll keep. How about breakfast ? Where's John ? I'm starved ! "

The tall shambling loose-jointed figure of Bones appeared from the side of the house, carrying a pick and an earth-stained shovel. In the light of the sun he was merely an emaciated old man in dirty overalls, with glaring eyes and a surly mouth. He pounded up the steps, looking neither to right nor to left, and disappeared through the front door.

Mrs. Xavier stirred. " John ? Yes, where is John ? " She turned and her black eyes smoked into the bloodshot eyes of her brother-in-law.

" Don't *you* know ? " said Mark Xavier with a sneer. Lord, what people ! thought Ellery.

" No," said the woman slowly. " I don't. He didn't come up to sleep last night." The black eyes flashed and flamed. " At least I didn't find him in bed this morning, Mark."

" Nothing strange about that," said Dr. Holmes hurriedly, with a forced laugh. " Probably tinkered about in the lab half the night. He's engrossed in an experiment——"

"Yes," said Mrs. Xavier. "He did say something last night about staying in the laboratory ; didn't he, Mr. Queen ? " and she turned her remarkable eyes suddenly upon the Inspector.

The Inspector was grim. He barely concealed his distaste. "He did, Madam."

"Well, I'll go fetch him," said Dr. Holmes eagerly, and plunged through one of the open French windows of the game-room.

No one spoke. Mrs. Xavier returned her brooding attention to the sky. Mark Xavier sat quietly down upon the rail of the terrace, a cigarette sending curls of smoke into his half-closed eyes. Ann Forrest twisted and untwisted a handkerchief in her lap. There was a step from the foyer and the stout figure of Mrs. Wheary appeared.

"Breakfast is waiting, Mrs. Xavier," she said nervously. "These gentlemen——" she indicated the Queens —" are they . . . ? "

Mrs. Xavier turned around. "Of course," she said in a furious voice.

Mrs. Wheary flushed and retreated.

Then suddenly they were staring at the French window through which Dr. Holmes had plunged a few moments before. The tall young Englishman was standing in the window, his white-blotched right hand clenched, his brown hair curiously dishevelled and sticking up into the air, his mouth working and his face as grey as his tweed knickerbockers.

He said nothing at all for an eternity, his lips opening and closing and no sounds coming from them.

Then he said in the hoarsest, most blurred voice Ellery had ever heard : " He's been murdered."

PART II

" Psychology never errs. The chief difficulty is knowing your subject. Psychology . . . is an exact science with infinite ramifications."—MINDS HUMAN AND INHUMAN *by* Stanley Whyte, D.Sc.

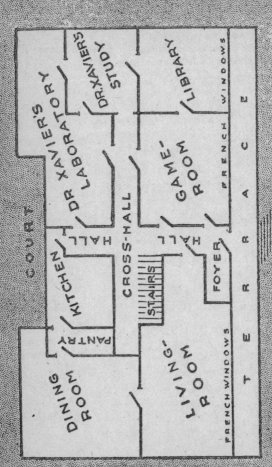

GROUND-FLOOR PLAN OF DR. XAVIER'S HOUSE

CHAPTER V

THE SIX OF SPADES

A RIPPLE starting from the neckline of Mrs. Xavier's low-cut gown flowed downward and disappeared in a flutter of crimson skirt. She was leaning against the terrace rail, her hands gripping the rail on each side of her strong body. The olive knuckles greyed, looking like lumps of cartilage. Her black eyes were washed cherries about to pop out. But she made no sound at all, and the expression on her face did not change. Even the horrible smile remained.

Miss Forrest's eyes rolled until only a shallow arc of pupil showed against the elliptical whites. She made a sick noise and started from her chair, only to fall back with a thud.

Mark Xavier crushed the red tip of his cigarette between his forefinger and thumb and lunged off the rail. He lurched by the motionless figure of Dr. Holmes into the house.

" Murdered ? " said the Inspector slowly.

" Oh, my God," whispered Miss Forrest, biting the back of her right hand and staring at Mrs. Xavier.

Then Ellery sprang after Xavier and they all stumbled after Ellery, across the game-room through a door into a book-lined library, through another door into . . .

Dr. Xavier's study was a small square room with two windows which overlooked the narrow fringe of rocky ground and the margin of trees at the right of the house. There were four doors : the one from the library ; a door sharply to the left, as they faced into the room, which led to the cross-hall ; a third on the same wall, but giving upon the surgeon's laboratory ; and a fourth directly across the room also leading into the laboratory. This last door was wide open, disclosing a segment of the white-walled, full-shelved laboratory beyond.

The study was modestly, even monastically, furnished. Three towering mahogany bookcases with glass windows, an old armchair, a lamp, a hard black-leather couch, a small cabinet, a silver cup in a glass case, a long poor group-picture jammed with dinner-jacketed men— framed, on the wall ; and in the centre of the room a wide mahogany desk facing the library door.

Behind the desk was a swivel-chair, and in the swivel-chair was Dr. Xavier.

Except for the fact that his rough tweed coat and red woollen necktie lay carelessly in a heap on the arm-hair, he was dressed as they had last seen him on the previous night. His head and breast lay limply on the desk top before him, left arm from the elbow down resting beside his head, long fingers rigidly outstretched, palm flat against the mahogany. His right arm below the shoulder was out of sight, hanging below the desk-level. His collar was unfastened and lay away from his grey-blue neck.

His head rested on the left cheek, mouth pursed and contorted, eyes glaring wide open. The upper part of his torso was half-twisted away from the surface of the desk ; a splatter of thick dark red was visible on the shirt-front at the right breast. In the coagulated welter of crimson were two blackish holes.

The top of the desk was bare of the usual desk-top accessories. Instead of a blotting pad and an ink-well and pen-tray and paper there were only scattered playing-cards, arranged in rather curious order. Most of them, in small piles, were concealed by the surgeon's body.

At the margin of the green rug which covered the

floor, in the corner near the closed door which led into the cross-hall, lay a long black revolver.

. . . .

Mark Xavier was leaning against the jamb of the library-door, glaring into the study at the quiet figure of his brother.

Mrs. Xavier, over Ellery's shoulder, said : " John," thickly.

Then Ellery said : " I think you had all better go away. Except Dr. Holmes. We'll need him. Please, now."

" *We'll* need him ? " echoed Mark Xavier harshly. Lids blinked over his bloodshot eyes. He swayed away from the jamb. " What d'ye mean—we ? Who the devil do you think you are, anyway ? "

" Now, Mark," said Mrs. Xavier mechanically ; she tore her eyes away from her husband's corpse and smothered her lips in a red cambric handkerchief.

" Don't Mark me, damn you ! " snarled Xavier. " Well, you—you—Queen——"

" Tut, tut," said Ellery mildly. " I think your nerves are a little shot, Mr. Xavier. This is no time for argument. Be a good chap and take the ladies away. There's work to be done."

The big man clenched his fist and stepped forward to glower in Ellery's face. " I've a good mind to smash you one ! Haven't you two butted in enough ? Best thing for both of you to do is beat it. Get out ! " Then a thought seemed to strike him ; it lit up his bloodstreaked eyes like a fork of lightning. " There's something damned queer about your two," he said slowly. " How do we know that you——? "

" Oh, you talk to the idiot, dad," said Ellery impatiently, and stepped into the study. He seemed fascinated by the cards on which the torso of Dr. Xavier rested.

The big man's face was reddening and darkening and his mouth worked soundlessly. Mrs. Xavier leaned against the door suddenly and covered her face with her hands. Neither Dr. Holmes nor Miss Forrest had so much as stirred a muscle ; both looked and looked and looked at the dead man's motionless head.

The old gentleman felt about in one of his inner pockets and produced a worn black case. He snapped the lid open and held up the case. Inside lay a round embossed gold shield.

The red drained slowly out of Mark Xavier's face. He stared at the shield as if he had been blind from birth and was seeing a thing of colour and three dimensions for the first time.

" Police," he said with difficulty, moistening his lips.

At the word Mrs. Xavier's hands fell away. Her skin was almost green and her ebony eyes a blazing black pain, the pain of naked agony. " Police ? " she whispered.

" Inspector Queen of the Homicide Squad, New York Police Department," said the old gentleman in a matter-of-fact voice. " I daresay it sounds like something out of a book or an old-time melodrama. But there you are and we can't change it. We can't change a lot of things." He paused to regard Mrs. Xavier fixedly. " At that I'm sort of sorry that I didn't announce last night that I'm a copper."

No one answered. They were all staring at him and at the shield with expressions of mingled terror and stupefaction.

He snapped the lid down and returned the case to his pocket. " Because," he said, and the old sharpness of the manhunt was glittering in his eyes, " if I had I'm dead certain Dr. John Xavier would be alive and kicking this morning." He turned slightly and looked into the study. Ellery was bent over the dead man, touching his eyes, the nape of his neck, the rigid left hand. The Inspector turned back and continued in conversational tones : " This morning. It's a beautiful morning, at that.

Too damned beautiful to be dead in." He searched them all impartially with eyes that were not only liquid with suspicion but weary with experience.

"B-but," stammered Miss Forrest, "I d-don't . . ."

"Well," said the Inspector dryly, "people don't generally commit murders when they know there's a policeman under the same roof, Miss Forrest. Too bad—for Dr. Xavier. . . . Now all of you listen to me." Ellery was moving quietly about the study now. The Inspector's voice tightened ; a whip-lash note sprang into it and the two women instinctively shrank back. Mark Xavier did not even stir. "I want Mrs. Xavier, Miss Forrest, and you, Xavier, to stay right here, in the library. I'm going to keep the door open, and I don't want any of you to leave the room. We'll attend to Mrs. Wheary and this fellow Bones later. Nobody can get away, anyway ; not with that handy little blaze down the mountain stopping up the exits. . . . Come in here with me, Dr. Holmes. You're the only one on the premises who can make himself useful."

The little old gentleman stepped into the study. Dr. Holmes shivered, closed his eyes, opened them again, and followed.

The others did not blink or move or make any outward sign that they had heard. They remained precisely where they were, as if they had been frozen to the floor.

.   .   .   .

"Well, El ? " murmured the Inspector.

Ellery rose from his knees behind the desk and absently lit a cigarette. "Very interesting. I think I've seen most of it already. Queer affair, dad."

"It would be with this bunch of lunatics mixed up in it." He scowled. "Well, whatever it is, it'll keep for a couple of minutes. A few things to do right off the bat." He turned to Dr. Holmes, who had paused before the desk and was gazing glassy-eyed at the body of his colleague. The Inspector shook the young Englishman's arm, not unkindly. " Snap out of it, Doc. I know he was your friend and all that, but you're the only medical man available and we've got to have medical help."

The staring look ebbed out of Dr. Holmes's eyes and he turned his head slowly. " Just what do you want me to do, sir ? "

" Examine the body."

The young man paled. " Oh, God, no ! Please. I can't ! "

" Come, come, youngster, get a grip on yourself. Don't forget that you're a professional man. You've handled plenty of stiffs in the lab, no doubt. I've had this happen before. Prouty, friend of mine in the Medical Examiner's office in Manhattan, once had to perform an autopsy on the body of a man he used to play poker with. He was a little sick afterward—but he did it."

" Yes," said Dr. Holmes hoarsely, licking his lips. " Yes, I understand." He shuddered. Then he set his jaw and said more quietly : " Very well, Inspector," and trudged around the desk.

The Inspector examined his squared shoulders for an instant, murmured : " Good boy," and flung a glance at the group beyond the door. They had not stirred from their positions.

" Here a moment, El," grunted the Inspector. Ellery, his eyes extraordinarily bright, drifted to his father's side. " We're in something of a funny position, son. We've got no proper authority at all, even to touch the body. We've got to notify Osquewa—I suppose that's where the jurisdiction lies."

" That had occurred to me, of course," frowned Ellery. " But if they can't break through the fire——"

" Well," said the Inspector a little grimly, " it won't be the first time we've handled a case ourselves—and on vacation, too." He jerked his head in the direction of the library doorway. "Keep an eye on those people. I'm going to the living-room and buzz Osquèwa. See if I can't get hold of the Sheriff."

"Right."

The Inspector trotted past the revolver on the rug as if he did not see it and disappeared through the doorway leading into the cross-hall.

Ellery eyed Dr. Holmes for an instant. The physician, white but composed, had undone the dead man's shirt, exposing the two bullet-wounds. The edges of the holes were blue beneath the dry blood. He peered at them intently without moving the position of the body, flashed a glance diagonally across the room toward the door by which the Inspector had just left the room, nodded, and began to finger the dead man's arms.

Ellery nodded and sauntered over to the same door. He stooped and picked up the revolver by its long barrel. He held it up to the light streaming in through the windows and shook his head.

"Even if we had some aluminium powder——" he muttered.

"Aluminium powder?" Dr. Holmes did not look up. "I suppose you mean to make a fingerprint test, Mr. Queen?"

"Scarcely necessary. This is a very nicely polished butt, and the trigger shines. As for the barrel——" He raised his shoulders and broke open the weapon. "Whoever used this exercised the usual care and wiped the gun clean of prints. Sometimes I think there should be a law against detective stories. Gives potential criminals too many pointers. Hmm. . . . Two chambers empty. I suppose there's no doubt this was the offending weapon. However, you might probe for the slugs, Doctor."

Dr. Holmes nodded. A moment later he rose, went into the laboratory, and returned with a shining instrument. He bent over the body again.

Ellery turned his attention to the small cabinet. It occupied a part of the wall which was pierced through for the library door, and stood between the library door and the door to the cross-hall. The top drawer was slightly open. He pulled it out. A scratched and discoloured leather holster, its belt missing, lay in the drawer; at the rear was a box of cartridges. The box contained only a few cartridges.

" Perfectly suicidal," he murmured, eyeing the holster and box. Then he shut the drawer. " I suppose, Doctor, this was Dr. Xavier's own revolver? I note from the holster and weapon itself that it's an old U.S. Army weapon."

" Yes." Dr. Holmes looked up briefly. " He was in the service during the War. Captain of infantry. He kept the gun, he once told me, as a memento. And now——" He fell silent.

" And now," remarked Ellery, " it's turned upon him. Odd how things work out. . . . Ah, dad. What's the news, if any? "

The Inspector closed the cross-hall door abruptly. " Managed by dumb luck to catch the Sheriff in town while he was back for forty winks. It's as we figured."

" Can't break through, eh? "

" Not a chance. Fire's getting worse. And even if he could, he said, he's too busy now. They need all the help they can get. Three people have been burned to death already, and from the way he sounded over the wire," said the Inspector grimly, " he couldn't get very excited about another corpse."

Ellery examined the silent figure of the tall blond man against the jamb. " I see. And so? "

" When I introduced myself over the wire he jumped at the chance and made me a special deputy with full authority to conduct the investigation and make the arrest. He'll get up here with the County coroner as soon as it's possible to break through the fire. . . . And so it's up to us."

The man in the doorway uttered a curious sigh—whether of relief, despair, or sheer fatigue Ellery could not decide.

. . . .

Dr. Holmes straightened ; his eyes were deadly dull. "Quite finished now," he announced in a flat voice.

"Ah," said the Inspector. "Good man. What's the verdict ? "

"Precisely what," demanded the physician, resting the knuckles of his right hand on the edge of the card-cluttered desk, " do you want to know ? " He spoke with difficulty.

"Shots cause death ? "

"Yes. No other marks of violence on the body, on superficial examination. Two bullets in the right breast, a little to the left of the *sternum*, one rather high. One smashed the third sternal rib and ricocheted into the summit of the right lung. The other was lower and passed between two ribs into the right *bronchus*, near the heart."

From beyond the doorway came a sick gulp. The three men paid it no attention.

"Hemorrhage ? " snapped the Inspector.

"Quite so. Bloody froth on the lips, as you can see."

"Death instantaneous ? "

"I should say not."

"I could have told you that," murmured Ellery.

"How ? "

"Get to it in a moment. You haven't had a really good look at the body, dad. Tell me, Doctor—what about the direction of the shots ? "

Dr. Holmes passed his hand over his mouth. " I scarcely think there's any mystery about that, Mr. Queen. The revolver——"

"Yes, yes," said Ellery impatiently. "We can see that

very clearly, Doctor. But do the angles of fire bear it out ? "

" I should say so. Yes, unquestionably. Both passages show the same angle of direction. The weapon was fired from approximately that spot on the rug where you picked up the revolver."

" Good," said Ellery with satisfaction. " A little to Xavier's right, but facing him. He could scarcely have been unaware of the presence of his murderer, then. By the way, you've no idea, I suppose, whether the weapon was in that drawer yesterday evening ? "

Dr. Holmes shrugged. " I'm sorry, no."

" It's not really important. Probably it was. All the indications point to a crime of impulse. At least as far as the question of preparations is concerned." Ellery explained to his father that the revolver had come from the cabinet-drawer, had belonged to Dr. Xavier, and had been wiped clean of fingerprints after the crime.

" It's easy enough, then, to figure out what happened," said the Inspector thoughtfully. " No way of telling through which of the four doors the murderer entered : chances are it was through the library or hall. But this much is clear : when the murderer came in here the doctor was playing cards with himself right where he is now. Murderer opened the drawer, took out the gun. . . . Was the gun kept loaded ? "

" I believe so," said Dr. Holmes dully.

" Took out the gun, standing just about at the cabinet there near the hall door, fired twice, wiped the gun clean, dropped it on the rug, and beat it into the cross-hall."

" Not necessarily," remarked Ellery.

The Inspector glared. " Why not ? Why cross the room and go out by a far door when there's one right behind you ? "

Ellery said mildly : " I merely said ' not necessarily.' "

I suppose that's what occurred. It still tells nothing. No matter which door the murderer used to enter the room and leave, there's nothing to be learned from specific determination. None of these doors leads into a room from which there is no other exit. All of them were accessible to anyone in the house who descended unobserved to this floor, say, from upstairs."

The Inspector grunted. Dr. Holmes said wearily : " If that's all you want me for, gentlemen. . . . The bullets are here." He indicated two battered slugs coated with blackish blood which he had tossed to the desk.

" The same ? " demanded the Inspector.

Ellery examined them indifferently. " Yes, same make as the ones in the revolver and cartridge-box. Nothing there. . . . Before you go, Doctor."

" Yes ? "

" How long has Dr. Xavier been dead ? "

The young man consulted his wrist-watch. " It's almost ten now. Death occurred, I should judge, no later than nine hours ago. Roughly at one a.m. this morning."

For the first time Mark Xavier in the doorway moved. He jerked his head up and drew in his breath with a whistling sound. As if this were a signal, Mrs. Xavier moaned and tottered back to a library chair. Ann Forrest, biting her lip, bent over her and murmured something sympathetic. The widow shook her head mechanically and leaned back, fixing her eyes upon the rigid left hand of her husband, just visible to her through the doorway.

" One a.m.," frowned Ellery. " It must have been a little past eleven when we retired last night. I see. . . . You omitted something, dad. No slightest sign of a struggle. That means he probably knew his murderer and didn't suspect foul play until it was too late."

" Fat lot of good that does us," grunted the Inspector.

" Sure he knew who bumped him. He knew everybody on this mountainside."

" You mean to say, of course," said Dr. Holmes in a strained voice, " in this house ? "

" You got me the first time, Doc."

.   .   .   .

The corridor door opened and Mrs. Wheary's neat grey head poked in. " Breakfast——" she began, and then her eyes widened and her jaw sagged ludicrously. She screamed once and almost fell through the doorway. The emaciated figure of Bones sprang into view from behind her, throwing out his long arms to catch her fat body. Then he, too, caught sight of Dr. Xavier's still figure and his grey wrinkled cheeks became greyer. He almost dropped the housekeeper's figure.

Ellery leaped forward and caught the woman in his arms. She had fainted. Ann Forrest stepped gingerly into the study, hesitated, swallowed hard, and ran forward to help. Between them they managed to drag the heavy old woman into the library. Neither Mark Xavier nor the widow moved.

Leaving the housekeeper in the young woman's charge, Ellery strode back into the study. The Inspector was scrutinising the haggard old man with impersonal minuteness. Bones was gaping at his employer's dead body, and he looked more like a corpse than the corpse itself. Snags of yellow teeth showed against the black of his open mouth. His eyes were glassy, goggling. Then sense came back into them, and a curious mounting rage. He worked his lips soundlessly for several moments until he forced a hoarse animal cry out of his wrinkled throat. Then he turned and plunged through the doorway. They heard him blundering along the cross-hall, repeating the senseless cry like a man stricken insane.

The Inspector sighed. " He takes it pretty, pretty," he muttered. " Attention, everybody ! "

He stalked to the library door and looked out at them. They looked back at him. Mrs. Wheary, revived, was sobbing quietly in a chair beside her mistress.

" Before we go ahead with a more thorough examination," said the Inspector coldly, " there are a few things need clearing up. I want the truth, mind. Miss Forrest, you and Dr. Holmes left the game-room last night just before we did. Did you go right up to your room ? "

" Yes," said the girl in a low voice.

" Right to sleep ? "

" Yes, Inspector."

" You, Dr. Holmes ? "

" Yes."

" Mrs. Xavier, did you go right to your room last night when we left you on the landing, and did you stay there all night ? "

The widow raised her extraordinary eyes ; they were dazed. " I—yes."

" Did *you* go right to bed ? "

" Yes."

" Didn't you discover during the night that your husband hadn't come up to sleep ? "

" No," she said slowly. " I did not. I slept through until morning."

" Mrs. Wheary ? "

The housekeeper sobbed : " I don't know anything at all about this, sir, as God is my judge. I just went to bed."

" How about you, Xavier ? "

The man licked his lips before replying. When he spoke his voice was cracked. " I didn't stir from my bedroom all night."

" Well, I might have expected it," sighed the Inspector. " So nobody here saw the doctor after Mr. Queen, Mrs. Xavier and I left him in the game-room last night, hey ? "

They shook their heads almost eagerly.

" How about the shots ? Anybody hear them ? "

Blank stares.

" It must be the mountain air," said the Inspector sarcastically. " Although at that maybe I'm a little harsh. I didn't hear them myself."

" These are soundproof walls," said Dr. Holmes lifelessly. " Specially constructed—the study and laboratory. We did a lot of experimenting with animals, Inspector. The noise, you know——"

" I see. These doors down here are always unlocked, I suppose ? " Mrs. Wheary and Mrs. Xavier nodded simultaneously. " Now how about the gun ? Anybody here who didn't know there was a weapon and ammunition in that little cabinet in the study ? "

Miss Forrest said quickly : " I didn't, Inspector."

The old gentleman grunted. Ellery smoked reflectively in the study, scarcely listening.

The Inspector eyed them for a moment, then he said briefly : " That's all for now. No," he added in a caustic tone, " don't move. There's a lot more. Dr. Holmes, you stay with us ; we may need you."

" Oh, for God's sake," began Mrs. Xavier, half-rising. She looked haggard and old. " Can't we——? "

" Stay where you are, please, Madam. There are a lot of things that have to be done. One of them," said the Inspector grimly, " is to get that hidden guest of yours, Mrs. Carreau, down for a little chin-chin." And he began to shut the door in their gaping, stricken faces.

" And," said Ellery gravely, " the crab. Please don't forget the crab, dad."

But they were too stupefied for speech.

.   .   .   .

" Now, Doctor," continued Ellery briskly, when the door was closed, " how about *rigor mortis* ? He looks stiff as a board to me. I've had some little experience examining dead bodies, and this one looks remarkably well advanced."

"Yes," muttered Dr. Holmes. "*Rigor* is complete. In fact, *rigor* has been complete for nine hours."

"Here, here," frowned the Inspector. "Are you sure of that, Doctor? It doesn't sound kosher——"

"I assure you it's so, Inspector. You see, Dr. Xavier was"—he licked his lips—"badly diabetic."

"Ah," said Ellery softly. "We meet the diabetic corpse once more. Remember Mrs. Doorn in the *Dutch Memorial Hospital*, dad?[1] Go on, Doctor."

"It's quite the usual thing," said the young Englishman with a weary shrug. "Diabetics may go into *rigor* as early as three minutes after death. Special blood condition, of course."

"I remember now." The Inspector took a pinch of snuff, inhaled deeply, sighed, and put the box away. "Well, it's interesting but not helpful. Just park yourself on that couch, Dr. Holmes, and try to forget this business for a while. . . . Now, El, let's see all this queer stuff you were gabbling about."

Ellery flung his half-smoked cigarette out the open window and went around the desk to stand beside the swivel-chair in which Dr. Xavier's body sat.

"Look at that," he said, pointing toward the floor.

The Inspector looked, and then, with a rather startled expression, squatted on his hams and grasped the hanging right arm of the dead man. It seemed made out of steel; he had the greatest difficulty moving it. He grasped the dead hand.

The hand was clenched. Three fingers—middle finger, ring-finger, and little finger—were curled tightly into the palm. Between the extended forefingers and the

---

[1] *The Dutch Shoe Mystery* by Ellery Queen (Victor Gollancz Ltd., 1931).

thumb the dead surgeon held a ragged fragment of stiff paper.

"What's this?" muttered the Inspector, and he tried to pull the fragment from between the two dead digits. The fingers held tenaciously. Grunting, the old gentleman grasped the thumb in one hand and the forefinger in the other and exerted all his wiry strength. After a struggle he managed to loosen the grip to the extent of perhaps a sixteenth of an inch. The stiff paper fluttered to the rug.

He picked it up and rose.

"Why, it's a torn piece of card!" he exclaimed, a note of disappointment in his voice.

"So it is," said Ellery mildly. "You sound fearfully disgruntled, dad. Needn't be. I've the feeling that it's considerably more significant than it looks."

It was half a six of spades.

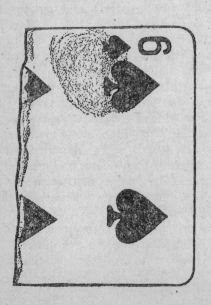

The Inspector turned it over ; the back was a gaudy red design of intertwined *fleur-de-lis*. He glanced at the cards on the desk ; their backs were of the same design.

He looked inquiringly at Ellery, and Ellery nodded. They stepped forward and tugged at the dead man. Managing to raise him a little from the surface of the desk they pushed the swivel-chair back a few inches and lowered the body again, so that only the head rested on the edge. Virtually the entire spread of cards was revealed.

" The six of spades came from this desk," murmured Ellery, " as you can see." He pointed to a row of cards. Dr. Xavier had apparently been playing, before his murder, the common type of solitaire in which thirteen cards are stacked in a pile as a source from which the player may draw, and then four cards are placed face up in a row, with a fifth card placed face up on a line by itself. The game was well advanced. The second card of the group of four was a ten of clubs. Beneath it, covering most of the ten, lay a nine of hearts ; beneath the nine, similarly placed, lay an eight of spades ; then a seven of diamonds ; then a considerable space ; and finally a five of diamonds.

" The six was between the seven of diamonds and the five of diamonds," muttered the Inspector. " All right. So he picked it out of that row. I don't see. . . . Where's the rest of this six of spades ? " he demanded suddenly.

" On the floor behind the desk," said Ellery. He circled the desk and stooped. When he stood up he held in his hand a crumpled ball of card. He smoothed it out and fitted it to the fragment from the dead man's right hand. It matched perfectly, beyond the remotest possibility of duplication.

As on the fragment from the dead man's hand, there was an oval finger-smudge on the crumpled piece. It was obviously the smudge of a thumb, like the other. When the halves were fitted together the two smudges

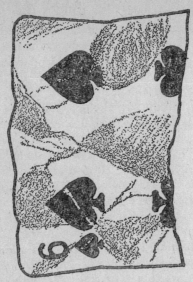

faced each other, each pointing diagonally upward to the line of tearing.

" Smudges are from his fingers when he tore the card, of course," went on the Inspector thoughtfully. He examined the dead man's thumbs. " Yes, they're dirty. That damned soot, I guess, from the fire ; it's all over everything. Well, El, I see now what you mean."

Ellery shrugged and turned to the window to stare out. Dr. Holmes was bent almost double on the black couch, holding his head between his hands.

" He was shot twice and the murderer beat it, leaving him for dead," continued the Inspector slowly. " But he wasn't dead. In his last conscious moments he picked that six of spades out of the solitaire game he'd been playing, deliberately tore off half the card, crumpled the other half and threw it away, and then passed out. Why the devil did he do that, now ? "

" You're asking an academic question," said Ellery

without turning. "You know as well as I do. You've observed, of course, that there's no paper or writing implements on the desk."

"How about in the top drawer there?"

"I looked. The cards came from there—the usual clutter of games inside. Paper, but no pen or pencil."

"None in his clothes?"

"No. It's a sports suit."

"And the other drawers?"

"They're locked. He hasn't the key on his person. I suppose it's in another suit, or if it's somewhere about he didn't have the strength to get up and look for it."

"Well, then," snapped the Inspector, "it's plain enough. He didn't have the means of writing the name of his murderer. So he left the card—the uncrumpled half of the card—instead."

"Exactly," murmured Ellery.

Dr. Holmes's head came up; his eyelids were angry-red. "Eh? He left——?"

"That's it, Doc. By the way, I take it Dr. Xavier was right-handed?"

Dr. Holmes stared stupidly. Ellery sighed. "Oh, yes. I checked on that the very first thing."

"You *checked*——?" began the old gentleman, astonished. "But how——"

"There are more ways," said Ellery wearily, "of killing a cat than one, as any exterminator will tell you. I looked through the pockets of his discarded coat there on the armchair. His pipe and tobacco-pouch are in the right-hand pocket. I patted his trouser pockets, too; there's change in the right pocket, and the left one is empty."

"Oh, he was right-handed, right enough," muttered Dr. Holmes.

"Well, that's good, that's good. Checks with the card found in his right hand and the direction of the smudge on the corner. Swell ! So we're as well advanced as we were before—not a jot more. What in the name of all that's holy did he mean by that piece of card ? Doc, do you know whom he might have had in mind, leaving a six of spades that way ? "

Dr. Holmes, still staring, started. " I ? No, no. I couldn't say, really I couldn't."

The Inspector strode to the library door and flung it open. Mrs. Wheary, Mrs. Xavier, the dead man's brother—they were exactly as he had left them. But Miss Forrest had disappeared.

" Where's the young woman ? " said the Inspector harshly.

Mrs. Wheary shuddered and Mrs. Xavier apparently did not hear ; she was rocking to and fro with a staccato motion.

But Mark Xavier said : " She went out."

" To warn Mrs. Carreau, I suppose," snapped the Inspector. " Well, let her. None of you can get away, glory be ! Xavier, come on in here, will you ? "

The man got slowly out of position, straightened, squared his shoulders, and followed the Inspector into the study. There he avoided looking at his dead brother, swallowing hard and shifting his gaze from side to side.

" We've an ugly job here, Xavier," said the old gentleman crisply. " You'll have to help, Dr. Holmes ! "

The Englishman blinked.

" You ought to be able to answer this. You know that we're all stuck up here until the Sheriff of Osquewa can get through to us, and there's no telling when that will be. In the meantime, in the case of a capital crime, although I've been deputised by the Sheriff to conduct an investigation I've no authority to bury the body of the victim. That must be held for the usual inquest and legal release. Do you understand ? "

" You mean," said Mark Xavier hoarsely, " he—he's got to be *kept* this way ? Good God, man——"

Dr. Holmes rose. " Fortunately," he said in a stiff tone, " we—there's a refrigerator in the laboratory. Used for experimental broths requiring frigid temperatures. I think," he said with an effort, " we—can make it."

" Good." The Inspector clapped the young man on the back. " You're doing fine, Doc. Once the body's out of sight I know you'll all feel better. . . . Now lend a hand, Xavier ; and you, Ellery. This is going to be a job."

. . . .

When they returned to the study from the laboratory, a vast irregularly shaped room crammed with electrical apparatus and a fantastic growth of weirdly shaped glass vessels, they were all pale and perspiring. The sun was very high now and the room was insufferably hot and stuffy. Ellery threw the windows up as far as they would go.

The Inspector opened the door to the library again. " And now," he said grimly, " we've got time to do a little real sleuthing. This, I'm afraid, is going to be good. I want every one of you to come upstairs with me and——"

He stopped. From somewhere at the rear of the house came the sounds of clashing metal and strident shouting. One of the voices, shrill with rage, belonged to the man-of-all-work, Bones. The other was a deep desperate bellow of vaguely familiar tone.

" What the devil," began the Inspector, whirling about. " I thought nobody could get——"

He tugged at his service revolver, dashed through the study, and plunged down the cross-hall in the direction of the furious sounds. Ellery was at his heels, and the rest followed with stumbling, bewildered eagerness.

The Inspector turned right where the cross-hall met the main corridor and darted to the far door at the rear which he and Ellery had glimpsed on their entrance to the house the previous night. He flung open the door, revolver raised.

They were in a spotless tiled kitchen.

In the centre of the kitchen, amid a clutter of dented pans and broken dishes, two men were struggling, locked in a desperate embrace.

One was the emaciated old man in overalls, eyes starting from his head, screaming curses and tugging at his adversary with maniacal strength.

Over Bones's shoulder, gross and monstrous, glared the fat face and froggy eyes of the man the Queens had encountered on the dark Arrow Mountain road the night before.

CHAPTER VI

SMITH

"Oh, so it's you," muttered the Inspector. "Stop it!" he said sharply. "I've got you covered and I mean business."

The fat man's arms dropped and he stared stupidly.

"Ah, our friend the motorist," chuckled Ellery, stepping into the kitchen. He slapped the fat man's hips and breast. "Not heeled. *Tsk!* Monstrous oversight. Well, what have you to say for yourself, friend Falstaff?"

A purple tongue slithered over the man's lips. He was stocky and enormous—a wide, wide bulwark of a man with a small round paunch. He took a step forward and his body wobbled like jelly. He looked for all the world like a dangerous, middle-aged gorilla.

Bones was glaring at him with a convulsive hatred that shook his whole angular frame.

"What have I—— ?" began the stranger in his unpleasant bass voice. Then cunning crept into his little eyes. "What's the meaning of this?" he boomed with heavy dignity. "This creature attacked me——"

"In his own kitchen?" murmured Ellery.

"He's lying!" shrieked Bones, trembling with rage. "I caught him sneaking into the house through the open front door and he snooped around till he found the kitchen! Then he——"

"Ah, the grosser appetite," sighed Ellery. "Hungry, eh? I thought you'd be back." He whirled suddenly and searched the faces of the group behind him. They were staring at the fat man with baffled eyes.

" Is *he* the one ? " said Mrs. Xavier huskily.

" Yes, indeed. Ever see him before ? "

" No, no ! "

" Mr. Xavier ? Mrs. Wheary ? Dr. Holmes ? . . . Strange," murmured Ellery. He stepped closer to the fat man. " We'll overlook the little raid just now ; certain allowances must be made for starving men if only out of sheer humanitarianism. And with *that* bulk to feed. . . . I daresay you were ravenous to have risked coming back to-day, after the frantic efforts you must have made all night to get through the fire. Eh ? "

The fat man said nothing. His little eyes flicked from face to face and his breathing came in hoarse gasps.

" Well," said Ellery sharply, " what were you doing on the mountain last night ? "

The fat man's barrel-chest surged suddenly. " And what's it to you ? "

" Still fractious, eh ? I might inform you that you're a damned live suspect for murder."

" *Murder !* " The jowls sagged and all the cunning vanished from the froggy eyes in a twinkling. " Who— who—— ? "

" Stop stalling," snapped the Inspector. The revolver was still in his hand. " Who, eh ? I thought a moment ago it didn't make any difference. . . . Who'd you like it to be ? "

" Well ! " The fat man sighed hugely, eyes never still. " Naturally. . . . Murder. . . . I don't know anything about this, gentlemen ; how could I ? I was wandering around half the night looking for a way—for a way out. Then I parked my car down the road a bit and slept until morning. How should I—— ? "

" Did you drive back to the house at all when you found you couldn't get past the road below ? "

" Why—no. No."

" Well, why the hell didn't you ? "

"I—I didn't think of it."

"What's your name?"

The fat man hesitated. "Smith."

"His name, he says," remarked the Inspector to the world at large, "is Smith. Well, well. What Smith? Just Smith? Or hasn't your imagination got to the point of picking a first name yet?"

"Frank—Frank Smith. Frank J. Smith."

"Where you hail from?"

"Why—ah, New York."

"Funny," muttered the Inspector. "I thought I knew every evil pan in the City. Well, what *were* you doing up here yesterday evening?"

Mr. Smith licked his purple lips again. "Why—I guess I lost my way."

"You *guess?*"

"I mean I lost my way, you see. When I—yes, when I got to the top here and saw I couldn't go any farther I turned round and drove down again. That's when you met me, you see."

"You sang a different tune then," said the old gentleman disagreeably. "And you sure were in one hell of a hurry. So you don't know anybody in this house, hey? When you were lost last night, you didn't think of stopping in here and asking your way, either, did you?"

"N-no." Mr. Smith's eyes fidgeted from the Queens to the silent company behind them. "But who, may I ask, was the unfort——"

"Unfortunate who was passed violently from the here to the hereafter?" Ellery squinted at him thoughtfully. "A gentleman named John Xavier, Dr. John S. Xavier. Name mean anything to you?"

The emaciated man-of-all-work began to make threatening sounds deep in his scrawny throat again.

"No," said Mr. Smith hastily. "Never heard of him."

" And you've never toiled up this Arrow Mountain road before, Mr.—ah—Smith ? Last night was the first time—your *début*, as it were ? "

" I assure you . . ."

Ellery bent and lifted one of the fat man's puffy paws. Mr. Smith growled in a startled way and snatched his hand back. " Oh, I'm not going to bite. Just looking for rings, you know."

" R-rings ? "

" But you haven't any." Ellery sighed. " I think, dad, we're—uh—blessed with another guest for some time. Mrs. Xavier—no, Mrs. Wheary might make the necessary arrangements."

" I guess so," said the Inspector glumly, putting his revolver away. " Got any duds in your car, Smith, or whatever your name is ? "

" Yes, of course. But can't I——? Isn't the fire——? "

" You can't, and the fire isn't. Get your things out of the car ; can't trust you to Bones—he's liable to chew your ear off. Good man, Bones. That's the spirit. Keep your eyes open." The Inspector tapped the silent old man on his bony shoulder. " Mrs. Wheary, show Mr. Smith to a room on the first floor. There's an empty, isn't there ? "

" Y-yes, sir," said Mrs. Wheary nervously. " Several."

" Then feed him. You stay put, Smith. No funny business." He turned to Mrs. Xavier, who had shrunken incredibly within herself ; her flesh looked withered. " Beg pardon, Madam," he said stiffly, " for taking charge of your household this way, but in murder cases we haven't got time to stand on ceremony."

" That's quite all right," she whispered. Ellery examined her with fresh interest. The vitriol seemed to have drained out of her since the discovery of her husband's corpse. The smoke and fire of her black eyes had been quenched ; they were lifeless. And behind them, in the glaze, he thought, lurked fear. She had altered completely—all but the dreadful half-smile. That clung to her lips with the stubborn vitality of physical habit.

" All right, folks," said the Inspector abruptly. " Now let's pay a little visit to the society lady upstairs. We'll all see Mrs. Carreau together and then I'll get the whole story straight without anyone trying to put one over or keep something back. Maybe we'll see daylight in this rotten business."

A low, musical, controlled voice startled them into whirling toward the corridor. " There's no need of that, Inspector. I've come down, you see."

And in the same flashing instant Ellery, spinning about, caught sight of Mrs. Xavier's eyes. They were hot rich black again.

CHAPTER VII

THE WEEPING LADY

SHE WAS leaning on tall Ann Forrest's arm—a dainty fragile beauty with the bloom of a delicate fruit. She looked no older than thirty—scarcely that. Her little figure was trim, graceful, slender, sheathed in some grey soft clinging material. Her hair was smoky black and she had two straight determined brows over brown eyes. There was sensitiveness in the thin flare of her nostrils and her little mouth. The lightest of touches had etched tiny wrinkles about her eyes. In her carriage, her poise, the way she stood and the way she held her head Ellery read breeding. A remarkable woman, he thought— quite as remarkable in her way as Mrs. Xavier. The thought swung him about. Mrs. Xavier had miraculously regained her youth. The fires had never been brighter in her extraordinary eyes, and all the drooping muscles had been revitalised. She was glaring with feline intensity at Mrs. Carreau. Fear has been displaced by the frankest, most naked hatred.

" You're Mrs. Marie Carreau ? " demanded the Inspector. If he still felt for her any of the admiration he had voiced to Ellery the night before, he did not show it.

" Yes," replied the small woman. " That's quite correct. . . . I beg your pardon." She turned to Mrs. Xavier, the queerest pain and compassion in the depths of her eyes. " I'm so sorry, my dear. Ann has told me. If there is anything I can do . . ."

The black pupils dilated ; the olive nostrils flared.

" Yes ! " cried Mrs. Xavier, taking a step forward. " Yes ! Get out of my house, that's what you can do ! You've made me suffer more . . . Get out of my house, you and your damned——"

" Sarah ! " rasped Mark Xavier, grasping her arm and shaking her roughly. " Don't forget yourself. Do you realise what you're saying ? "

The tall woman's voice rose to a scream. " She—she——" A trickle of saliva appeared at one corner of her mouth. Her black eyes were blazing pits.

" Here, here," said the Inspector softly. " What's all this, Mrs. Xavier ? "

Mrs. Carreau had not stirred ; bloodless cheeks were her only sign of emotion. Ann Forrest gripped her round arm more tightly. Mrs. Xavier shuddered and shook her head from side to side. She relaxed limply against her brother-in-law.

" That's all right, then," continued the Inspector in the same soft voice. He flashed a glance at Ellery. But Ellery was studying the face of Mr. Smith. The fat man had retreated to the farther side of the kitchen and was striving to hold his breath. He looked as if he were squeezing himself in some fantastic effort to achieve two dimensions. The wattled face was deathly purple. " Let's go into the living-room and talk."

.   .   .   .

" Now, Mrs. Carreau," said the old gentleman when they were all seated stiffly in the big room, the hot sunlight pouring in through the French windows, " please explain yourself. I want the truth, now ; if I don't get it from you I'll get it from the others, so you may as well make a clean breast of it."

" What would you like to know ? " murmured Mrs. Carreau.

" A lot of things. Let's get the practical answers first. How long have you been in this house ? "

" Two weeks." Her musical voice was barely audible ; she kept her eyes on the floor. Mrs. Xavier was lying in an armchair with closed eyes, deathly still.

" Guest here ? "

" You might—call it that." She paused, lifted her eyes, dropped them again.

" With whom did you come, Mrs. Carreau ? Or were you alone ? "

She hesitated again. Ann Forrest said swiftly : " No. I came with Mrs. Carreau. I'm her confidential secretary."

" So I've noted," said the Inspector coldly. " You'll please keep out of this, young woman. I've a score to settle with you for disobeying orders. I don't like my witnesses running off and passing the word along to— others." Miss Forrest flushed and bit her lip. " Mrs. Carreau, how long have you known Dr. Xavier ? "

" Two weeks, Inspector."

" Oh, I see. Didn't you know any of the others before, either ? "

" No."

" Is that right, Xavier ? "

The big man muttered : " That's right."

" Then sickness brought you up here, eh, Mrs. Carreau ? "

She shivered. " In—in a way."

" You're supposed to be travelling in Europe now, aren't you ? "

" Yes." Her eyes were raised now, pleading. " I—I didn't want my—it known."

" Is that why you hid last night when my son and I drove up, why these people were so nervous, covered you up ? "

She whispered : " Yes."

The inspector straightened and thoughtfully took snuff. Not particularly auspicious he thought. He glanced about, searching for Ellery. But Ellery had unaccountably disappeared.

"Then you never saw anyone here before ; just came for medical treatment ? For observation, maybe ? "

"Yes, Inspector, oh yes ! "

"Hmm." The old gentleman took a turn about the room. No one spoke. "Tell me, Mrs. Carreau—did you leave your room last night for any reason ? " He could scarcely hear her reply. "Eh ? "

"No."

"That's not true ! " cried Mrs. Xavier suddenly, opening her eyes. She sprang to her feet, tall and magnificently furious. "She did ! I saw her ! "

Mrs. Carreau paled. Miss Forrest half-rose, eyes snapping. Mark Xavier looked startled and extended his arm in a curious gesture.

"Hold everthing," murmured the Inspector. "And that means everybody. You say you saw Mrs. Carreau leave her room, Mrs. Xavier ? "

"Yes ! She slipped out of her room a little after midnight and hurried downstairs. I saw her enter my—my husband's study. They were there——"

"Yes, Mrs. Xavier ? For how long ? "

Her eyes wavered. "I don't know. I—didn't—wait."

"Is that true, Mrs. Carreau ? " asked the Inspector in the same soft tone.

Tears had sprung into the small woman's eyes. Her mouth quivered, and then she began to weep. "Yes, oh, yes," she sobbed, hiding her face on Miss Forrest's bosom. "But I didn't——"

"Just a moment." The Inspector regarded Mrs. Xavier with a faintly mocking smile. "I though you told us, Mrs. Xavier, that you retired at once last night and slept through the night ? "

The tall woman bit her lip and sat down suddenly.

" I know. I lied. I thought you would suspect——— But I saw her ! It was she ! She———" She stopped in confusion.

" And you didn't wait," said the Inspector mildly, " to see when she came out. My, my, what are our women coming to ! All right, Mrs. Carreau, why did you wait until you thought everyone was asleep to slip down for a chat with Dr. Xavier—after midnight ? "

Mrs. Carreau fumbled for a grey silk handkerchief. She dabbed at her eyes and set her little chin firmly. " It was stupid of me to lie, Inspector. Mrs. Wheary had come to my room before she retired to tell me that strangers—you gentlemen—were staying the night because of a fire below. She told me Dr. Xavier was downstairs. I was—worried," her brown eyes flickered, " and went down to talk to him."

" About my son and me, hey ? "

" Yes. . . . "

" And your—er—condition also, hey ? "

She reddened, but she repeated : " Yes."

" How'd you find him ? All right ? Spry ? Natural ? As usual ? Nothing on his mind ? "

" He was quite the same, Inspector," she whispered. " Kind, thoughtful—as ever. We talked a while, then I went back upstairs———"

" Damn you ! " shrieked Mrs. Xavier, on her feet again. " I can't, I won't stand it ! She's been off in corners with him every night—since she came—whispering, whispering with that cunning pretty false smile of hers —stealing him away from me—weeping crocodile tears —playing on his sympathies. . . . He never could resist a pretty woman ! Shall I tell you why, Inspector, why she's here ? " She pounced forward, levelling a shaking finger at the shrinking figure of Mrs. Carreau. " Shall I ? Shall I ? "

Dr. Holmes spoke for the first time in an hour. " Oh,

I say, Mrs. Xavier," he mumbled, " I shouldn't——"

" No, oh, no," moaned Mrs. Carreau, hiding her face in her hands. " Please, please. . . . "

" You contemptible she-devil ! " raged Ann Forrest, jumping to her feet. " You *would*, you—you wolverine ! I'll——"

" Ann," said Dr. Holmes in a low voice, stepping before her.

The Inspector watched them with bright, almost smiling eyes. He was very still ; barely moved his head from one face to another as they spoke. The big room was noisy with furious voices, heavy breathing. . . . " Shall I ? " screamed Mrs. Xavier, madness in her eyes. " Shall I ? "

The noise stopped as abruptly as if someone had sheared it off with a bolo. There was a sound from the corridor door.

" There's really no need, Mrs. Xavier," said Ellery cheerfully. " We know all about it, you see. Dry your eyes, Mrs. Carreau. This is far from a major tragedy. My father and I are eminently trustworthy people and you may be sure we shall keep your secret—longer, I fear," he said with a sad wag of his head, " than some of the others. . . . Dad, I take particular pleasure in introducing to you the—ah—the—what you saw last night, or thought you saw." The Inspector was gaping. " And, I might add, two of the brightest, nicest, best-mannered and friendliest lads who ever became irked at the necessity of skulking in a bedroom and decided to crawl out into a corridor for a little romantic peep at the terrible men who had blundered into their host's house. Meet—reading from left to right—Messrs. Julian and Francis Carreau, Mrs. Carreau's sons. I've just made their acquaintance and I think they're delightful ! "

Ellery was standing in the doorway, an arm about the

shoulder of each of two tall good-looking boys whose bright eyes investigated every detail of the tableau before them inquisitively. Ellery, who stood behind them smiling, nevertheless contrived to fix his father with an angry eye. The old gentleman stopped gaping, gulped, and came forward rather shakily.

The boys were perhaps sixteen—strong, wide-shouldered, with sunbrowned faces and pleasant regular features quite like their mother's, but in a masculine way. One might have been a brown plaster model of the other. In every detail of physique and facial feature they were identical. Even their clothes—grey flannel suits meticulously pressed, sunny blue neckties, white shirts, black grained shoes—were identical.

But it was not the fact that they were twins which had brought the Inspector's jaw to the half-mast. It was the fact that they slightly faced each other, that the right arm of the boy on the right was twined about his brother's waist, that the left arm of the boy on the left was out of sight behind his brother's back, that their smart grey jackets met and, incredibly, *joined* at the level of their breast-bones.

They were Siamese twins.

CHAPTER VIII

XIPHOPAGUS

THEY MET the Inspector with rather shy, if boyish, curiosity, each offering his free hand in turn for a hearty grip. Mrs. Carreau had magically revived ; she was erect in her chair now and smiling at the boys. What effort it was costing her, Ellery thought with admiration, no one except perhaps Ann Forrest could possibly know.

" Gosh, sir ! " exclaimed the twin on the right in a pleasant tenor voice. " Are you a real live Inspector of police, as Mr. Queen says ? "

" I'm afraid so, son," said the Inspector with a feeble grin. " And what's your name ? "

" I'm Francis, sir."

" And you, my boy ? "

" Julian, sir," replied the twin on the left. Their voices were one. Julian, the Inspector thought, was the graver of the two. He looked earnestly at the Inspector. " May we—may we see the gold badge, sir ? "

" Julian," murmured Mrs. Carreau.

" Yes, mother."

The boys looked at the beautiful woman. They both smiled at once ; it was uncanny and delightful. Then, with perfect grace and ease, they walked across the room in step and the Inspector saw their broad young backs swaying in practised rhythm. He also saw that Julian's left arm, resting against the small of his brother's back, was in a cast and strapped to his brother's body. The boys bent over their mother's chair and she kissed each one's cheek in turn. Whereupon they sat down on a divan with gravity and fastened their eyes upon the Inspector, to his immediate embarrassment.

"Well," he said, somewhat at a loss. "This puts a different complexion on things. I think I see now what this is all about. . . . By the way, youngster—you, Julian—what's the matter with your flipper?"

"Oh, I broke it, sir," replied the lad on the left instantly. "Last week. We had a little fall on the rocks outside."

"Dr. Xavier," said Francis, "set it for Julian. It didn't hurt much, did it, Jule?"

"Not much," said Julian manfully. And they both smiled again at the Inspector.

"Hrrmph!" said the Inspector. "I suppose you know that something's happened to Dr. Xavier?"

"Yes, sir," they said together, soberly, and their smiles faded. But they could not conceal the excited glint in their eyes.

"I think," said Ellery, stepping into the room and closing the corridor door, "that we may as well have a complete understanding. Whatever is told in this room, of course, Mrs. Carreau, goes no further."

"Yes," she sighed. "It's all a little unfortunate, Mr. Queen. I was hoping . . . I'm not very brave, you see." She brooded over her sons, eyeing their straight big bodies with the queerest mixture of pride and pain. "Francis and Julian were born a little over sixteen years ago in Washington. My husband was still alive at that time. My sons were born perfectly healthy, normal children except," she paused and closed her eyes, "for one thing, as you see. They were joined at birth. Needless to say, my family was—horrified." She stopped, breathing a little fast.

"The usual myopia of great families," said Ellery with an encouraging smile. "As you say, it wasn't very heroic. I assure you I should feel proud——"

"Oh, I am," she cried. "They're the *best* children—so strong and straight and—and patient. . . ."

"There's mother for you," said Francis, grinning. Julian contented himself by staring gravely at his mother.

"But they were too many for me," continued Mrs. Carreau in a low tone. "I was weak and—and a little frightened myself. My husband unfortunately thought —as they did. So . . ." She made a queer helpless gesture. It was not difficult to see what must have happened. The publicity-loathing family of aristocrats ; family conferences, lavish expenditures of hush money, the infants spirited away from the lying-in hospital, placed in charge of a capable and reliable nurse, an announcement to the newspapers that Mrs. Carreau had had a dead baby. . . . "I saw them often, on secret visits. As they grew older they came to understand. They never complained, dear boys, and were always cheerful and not the least bit bitter. Of course we had the best tutors and medical attention. When my husband died I thought—— But they were still too strong for me. And I wasn't, as I've said, particularly courageous. And all the while I wanted—my heart cried——"

"Sure, sure," said the Inspector, clearing his throat hastily. "I think we understand, Mrs. Carreau. I suppose it wasn't possible to do anything about it—medically, I mean ? "

"We can tell you about that," said Francis cheerfully.

"Oh, you can, son ? "

"Oh, yes, sir. You see, we're joined at the breastbone by a lig—lig——"

"Ligature," said Julian, frowning. "You *never* remember that word, Fran. I should think you would, you know."

"Ligature," said Francis, nodding at this severe criticism. "It's very strong, sir. Why, we can stretch it for about six inches ! "

" But doesn't it hurt ? " asked the Inspector, wincing.

" Hurt ? No, sir. Does your ear hurt when you stretch it, sir ? "

" Well," replied the old gentleman with a broad smile, " I guess not. I never thought of that."

" Cartilaginous ligature," explained Dr. Holmes. " What in teratology we call a xiphoid growth. Most amazing phenomenon, Inspector. Perfectly elastic and unbelievably strong."

" We can do tricks with it," said Julian soberly.

" Now, Julian," said Mrs. Carreau in a weak voice.

" But we can, mother ! You know we can. We prac- tised that trick the original Siamese twins used to do ; we showed it to you, remember ? "

" Oh, Julian," said Mrs. Carreau faintly, suppressing a smile.

Dr. Holmes's hard young cheeks shone with a sud- den professional glow of enthusiasm. " Chang and Eng —those were the Siamese twins' names—could support each other's dead weight by the ligature alone. These lads are very acrobatic about it. Lord, they can do more things than I can ! "

" That's because you don't exercise enough, Dr. Holmes," said Francis respectfully. " Why don't you try punching the bag ? We——"

The Inspector was grinning by this time and the atmosphere of the room had cleared miraculously. The entirely normal conversation of the boys, their bright intelligent air and utter lack of bitterness and self- consciousness dispelled any awkward feeling their presence might theoretically have been expected to arouse. Mrs. Carreau was smiling fondly at them.

" Anyway," continued Francis, " it would be all right, I guess, if the doctors had only *that*," he pointed to his chest, " to worry about, you see, But——"

" Perhaps you'd better let me explain, old boy," said

Dr. Holmes gently. " You see, Inspector, there are three common—common as they are !—types of so-called Siamese twins, all three of which are exemplified by rather medically famous cases. There's the pyogopagus type—back to back—case of renal juncture ; that is, kidneys joined. Probably the best-known example were the Blascek twins, Rosa and Josepha. There was an attempt to sever them surgically——" He stopped, his face darkening. " Then there's the——"

" Was the attempt successful ? " asked Ellery quietly.

Dr. Holmes bit his lip. " Well—no. But then we didn't know as much——"

" That's all right, Dr. Holmes," said Francis earnestly. " We know all about these things, you see, Mr. Queen. Naturally our own cases interested us. The Blascek girls died as a result of the attempt. But then Dr. Xavier wasn't around——"

Mrs. Carreau's cheeks were paler than the whites of her eyes. The Inspector hurled a furious glance at Ellery and signalled Dr. Holmes to continue.

" Then," said Dr. Holmes with difficulty, " there's the xiphopagus—twins joined by the xiphoid process of the *sternum*. That's the most famous case of all, of course —the original Siamese twins, Chang and Eng Bunker. Two healthy, normal individuals . . . "

" Died in 1874," announced Julian, " when Chang contracted pneumonia. They were sixty-three years old ! They were married and had loads of children, and everything ! "

" They weren't really Siamese," added Francis, smiling, " sort of three-quarters Chinese and one-quarter Malay, or something. They were horribly smart, Inspector Queen. And very rich. . . . That's the kind *we* are." He said hastily : " Xiph-xiphopagus, not rich."

" We are rich," said Julian.

" Well, you know what I mean, Jule ! "

" Finally," said Dr. Holmes, " there's the so-called side-to-side type. The boys, as I said, are front-to-front—joined livers. And, of course, a common blood-stream." He sighed. " Dr. Xavier had the complete case-history. Mrs. Carreau's personal physician supplied it."

" But what," murmured Ellery, " was the purpose of bringing these husky young brutes to *Arrow Head*, Mrs. Carreau ? "

There was a little silence. The atmosphere thickened again. Mrs. Xavier was staring dully at Mrs. Carreau.

" He said," whispered the small woman, " that perhaps——"

" He gave you hope ? " inquired Ellery slowly.

" Not that—exactly. It was just the barest, faintest chance. Ann—Miss Forrest had heard he was doing experimental work. . . . "

" Dr. Xavier," interrupted the young physician tonelessly, " had been occupying his time here in rather—bizarre experiments. I shouldn't say bizarre. Unorthodox, perhaps. He was, of course, a very great man." He paused. " He expended a good deal of time and money on the—experiments. There was some publicity ; not a good deal, because he detested it. When Mrs. Carreau wrote——" He stopped.

The Inspector looked from Mrs. Carreau to Dr. Holmes. " I take it, then," he murmured, " you didn't share Dr. Xavier's enthusiasm, Doctor ? "

" That, replied the Englishman stiffly, " is beside the point." He glanced at the Carreau twins with the oddest mixture of affection and pain.

There was another silence. The old gentleman took a turn about the room. The boys were perfectly quiet, but alert.

The Inspector halted. " Did you boys like Dr. Xavier ? " he said abruptly.

"Oh, yes!" they said in instant unison.

"Did he ever—well, hurt you?"

Mrs. Carreau started, alarm flooding her soft eyes.

"No, sir," replied Francis. "He just examined us. Made all kinds of tests. With X-rays and special foods and injections and things."

"We're used to *that* sort of thing, all right," said Julian darkly.

"I see. Now about last night. Slept well, did you?"

"Yes, sir." They were very solemn now and breathing a little more rapidly.

"Didn't hear any peculiar sounds during the night, I suppose? Like guns going off?"

"No, sir."

The old gentleman rubbed his chin for a moment. When he spoke again he was grinning. "Had your breakfast, both of you?"

"Yes, sir. Mrs. Wheary brought it up to us early this morning," said Francis.

"But we're hungry again," added Julian quickly.

"Then suppose you two young men trot out into the kitchen," said the Inspector amiably, "and get Mrs. Wheary to rustle you some grub."

"Yes, *sir*!" they exclaimed in chorus and rose, kissed their mother, excused themselves, and left the room with the peculiarly graceful rhythm imparted to their bodies by the act of walking.

CHAPTER IX

THE MURDERER

A BENT figure appeared on the terrace beyond one of the French windows, and peered into the living-room.

" Oh, Bones," called the Inspector ; the man started. " Come on in here. I want you in on this."

The old man slipped through the window. His lugubrious face was set in even more savage lines than before and his long skinny arms dangled and jerked, the fingers curling and uncurling.

Ellery studied his father's bland face thoughtfully. There was something up. An idea, a suddenly snatched and half-formed idea, was stewing in the Inspector's brain.

" Mrs. Xavier," began the old man in a mild voice, " how long have you lived here ? "

" Two years," said the woman lifelessly.

" Your husband bought this house ? "

" He built it." Fear had begun to creep back into her eyes. " He retired at that time, purchased the summit of Arrow Mountain, had it cleared and the house constructed. Then we moved in."

" You've been married only a short time, haven't you ? "

" Yes." She was startled now. " About six months before—before we came here to live."

" Your husband was a wealthy man, wasn't he ? "

She shrugged. " I have never inquired deeply into his finances. He gave me, always, the best of everything." The feline glare returned for an instant as she added : " The best of material things."

The Inspector took a pinch of snuff elaborately ; he seemed very sure of himself. " I seem to recall that your husband had never been married before, Mrs. Xavier. How about you ? "

She tightened her lips. " I was a widow when I—met him."

" No children from either marriage ? "

She sighed queerly. " No."

" Hmm." The Inspector crooked his finger at Mark Xavier. " You ought to know something about your brother's financial condition. Well off, was he ? "

Xavier started out of a profound reverie. " Eh ? Oh, money ! Yes. He was well-cushioned."

" Tangible assets ? "

The man lifted his shoulders. " Some of it in real estate, and you know what realty values are to-day. Most of it, however, in solid government securities. He had some money from our father when he began practising medicine—as I did—but he's made most of what he has . . . had . . . in his profession. I was his attorney, you know."

" Ah," said the Inspector. " Glad you mentioned that. I was wondering how we'd jump the testamentary hurdle all bottled up this way. . . . So you're an attorney, hey ? He left a will, of course."

" There's a copy in his bedroom safe upstairs."

" Is that right, Mrs. Xavier ? "

" Yes." She was oddly quiet.

" What's the combination ? " She told him. " All right. Please remain where you are. I'll be back shortly." He buttoned his jacket with nervous fingers and hurried from the room.

.   .   .   .

He was gone a long time. The living-room was very quiet. From the rear came the cheerful shouts of

Julian and Francis, apparently applying themselves to the cream of Mrs. Wheary's larder with gusto and enthusiasm.

Once there was a heavy step in the hall and they all turned to the door. But it remained shut, and the step continued to tramp toward the foyer. A moment later they spied the gorilla-like figure of Mr. Smith on the terrace ; he was staring out over the bleak rocky ground before the house.

Ellery sulked in a corner and sucked a fingernail. For some reason too nebulous to grasp he felt disturbed. What on earth was his father up to ?

Then the door opened and the Inspector appeared. His eyes were sparkling. In his hand he held a legal-looking paper.

" Well," he said benevolently, closing the door. Ellery studied him, frowning. There was something in the wind. When the Inspector became benevolent during the progress of an investigation, there was something decidedly in the wind. " I've found the will, all right. Short and sweet. By your husband's will, Mrs. Xavier, I find that you're practically his sole beneficiary. Did you know that ? " He waved the document.

" Of course."

" Yes," continued the Inspector briskly, " except for a small bequest to his brother Mark and a few to various professional societies—research organisations and such— you inherit the bulk of his estate. And, as you said, Xavier, it's considerable."

" Yes," muttered Xavier.

" I see too that there won't be any trouble about probating the will and settling the estate," murmured the old gentleman. " No chance for a legal contest ; eh, Xavier ? "

" Of course not ! There's no one to contest. I certainly shan't, even if I had grounds—which I haven't—and

I'm John's only blood-relative. As a matter of fact, although it isn't pertinent, my sister-in-law has no living relatives, either. We're the last on both sides."

"That makes it very cosy, I must say," smiled the Inspector. "By the way, Mrs. Xavier, I suppose you and your husband had no real differences ? I mean—you didn't quarrel about the various things that split up late marriages ? "

"Please." She put her hand to her eyes. And *that's* very cosy, too, thought Ellery grimly. He kept watching his father, alive in every nerve now.

Unexpectedly the man Bones rasped : "That's a lie. She made his life one long hell ! "

"Bones," gasped Mrs. Xavier.

"She was always nagging him," went on Bones, the cords of his throat taut ; his eyes were blazing again. "She never gave him a minute's peace, damn her ! "

"That's interesting," said the Inspector, still smiling, "and *you're* an interesting sort of coot to have around the house, Bones, old boy. Go on. I take it you were pretty fond of Dr. Xavier ? "

"I'd have died for him." His bony fists tightened. "He was the only one in this rotten world ever lent a hand when I was down, the only one ever treated me like a white man, not some—some scum. . . . She treated me like dirt ! " His voice rose to a scream. "I tell you she——"

"Right, right, Bones," said the Inspector with a touch of sharpness. "Hold it. Now listen to me, all of you. We found in Dr. Xavier's dead hand a torn half of playing-card. He'd evidently found strength enough before he died to leave a clue to his murderer's identity. He tore off half a six of spades."

"Six of spades ! " panted Mrs. Xavier ; her eyes were protruding from their shadowed sockets.

"Yes, Madam, a six of spades," said the Inspector,

regarding her with some satisfaction. " Let's do a little figuring. What could he have meant to tell us ? Well, the cards came from his own desk ; so it isn't a question of ownership. Now, he didn't use a whole card ; only a half. That means the card as a card wasn't the import- ant thing ; it was the piece, or what was on the piece."

Ellery stared. There was something in association, after all. You *could* teach an old dog new tricks. He chuckled silently.

" On the piece," continued the Inspector, " was the number 6, in the border of the card, and a few—what d'ye call it ? "

" Pips," said Ellery.

" Pips—spades. Spades mean anything to any of you ? "

" Spade ? " Bones licked his lips. " *I* use a spade——"

" Whoa," grinned the Inspector. " Don't let's get into fairy tales. That would be too much. No, he didn't mean you, Bones."

" Spade," said Ellery briefly, " if it meant anything at all, which I doubt, signified death. It always has, you know." His eyes were narrowed and he was paying at- tention only to his father.

" Well, whatever it meant it's not the main thing. The main thing is the number 6. Number 6 mean any- thing to any of you ? "

They stared at him.

" Evidently not," he chuckled. " Well, I didn't think it would. As a number I don't see how it could refer to anyone here. Might in one of these, now, detective stories with secret societies and such tripe ; but not in real life. Well, if 6 as a number doesn't mean anything to you, how about 6 *as a word* ? " He stopped grinning and his face hardened. " Mrs. Xavier, you have a middle name, haven't you ? "

Her hand was at her mouth. " Yes," she said faintly. " Isère. My maiden name. I am French. . . ."

" Sarah Isère Xavier," said the Inspector grimly. He whipped his hand into his pocket and produced with a flourish a small sheet of delicately tinted personal stationery, monogrammed at the top with three capital letters. " I found this piece of writing-paper in your desk in the big bedroom upstairs, Mrs. Xavier. Do you admit it's yours ? "

She was on her feet, swaying. " Yes. Yes. But——"

He held the paper high, so that all their wide eyes could see it. The monogram read : *S I X*. The Inspector dropped the sheet and stepped forward. " Dr. Xavier in his last living moment accused *S I X* of murdering him. I saw the light when I remembered that two of your initials were *S X*. Mrs. Xavier, consider yourself under arrest for the murder of your husband ! "

For one horrible moment Francis's merry laugh rang faintly in their ears from the kitchen. Mrs. Carreau was white as death, her right hand on her breast. Ann Forrest was trembling. Dr. Holmes was blinking at the tall woman swaying before them with disbelief, nausea, mounting rage. Mark Xavier was rigid in his chair, only the muscles of his jaw working. Bones stood like a mythological figure of vengeance, glaring with awful triumph at Mrs. Xavier.

The Inspector snapped : " You knew that on the death of your husband you would come into a pot of money, didn't you ? "

She took a small backward step, breathing thickly. " Yes——"

" You were jealous of Mrs. Carreau, weren't you ? Insanely jealous ? You couldn't stand seeing them together conducting what you thought was an affair right before your nose, could you ?—when all the time they were just discussing Mrs. Carreau's sons ! " He advanced steadily, never taking his hard eyes from hers, a little grey nemesis.

" Yes, yes," she gasped, retreating another step.

" When you followed Mrs. Carreau downstairs last night and saw her slip into your husband's study and after a while slip out again, you were mad with jealous rage, weren't you ? "

" Yes," she whispered.

" You went in, snatched the revolver from the drawer, shot him, killed him, murdered him ; didn't you, Mrs. Xavier ? *Didn't you ?* "

The edge of the chair stopped her. She tottered and fell into the seat with a thud. Her mouth was working soundlessly, like the mouth of a fish seen through the glass window of an aquarium.

" Yes," she whispered. " Yes."

Her glazedly black eyes rolled over once ; then she shuddered convulsively and fainted.

CHAPTER X

LEFT AND RIGHT

It was a terrible afternoon. The sun was overpowering. It poured its fierce liquefying strength upon the house and the rocks and turned both into infernos. They wandered about the house like materialised ghosts, scarcely speaking, avoiding each other, physically wretched from the dampness of their clothing and the heaviness of their limbs, mentally sick and exhausted. Even the twins were subdued ; they sat quietly by themselves on the terrace and watched their elders with round eyes.

The unconscious woman had been turned over to the mercies of Dr. Holmes and Miss Forrest ; that surprising young woman, it developed, having had considerable professional experience as a nurse in the years preceding her employment by Mrs. Carreau. The men carried the heavy figure of Mrs. Xavier upstairs to the master—now masterless—bedroom.

" You'd better give her something to keep her asleep for a while, Doc," said the Inspector thoughtfully as he gazed down upon the handsome recumbent figure. There was no triumph, only distaste in his eyes. " She's the nervous type. They go off the handle at the least emotional disturbance. Might try to do away with herself when she comes to. Not that it wouldn't be the best thing for her, poor devil. . . . Give her a hypo or something."

Dr. Holmes nodded silently ; he went down to the laboratory and returned with a filled hypodermic. Miss

Forrest fiercely banished the men from the bedroom. She and the physician alternated at the sleeping woman's bedside for the remainder of the afternoon.

Mrs. Wheary, informed of the culpability of her mistress, wept briefly and not convincingly ; she had always known, she informed the Inspector through squeezed tears, that " it couldn't turn out well ; she was too jealous. And him such a kind, good, handsome man, poor lamb, who didn't even look at other women ! I was his housekeeper before his marriage, sir, and when *she* came to live with us she started right away. Jealous ! She was just crazy."

The Inspector grunted and became practical. None of them had had a mouthful of food since the previous night. Could Mrs. Wheary so compose herself as to scrape together a passable luncheon ? He personally was on the verge of starvation.

Mrs. Wheary sighed, wiped away the last arid tear, and turned back to her kitchen-cabinet.

" Though I will say," she moaned as the Inspector turned to go, " that there isn't any too much food in the house, sir, begging your pardon."

" What's that ? " said the Inspector sharply, halting.

" You see," sniffed Mrs. Wheary, " we've got some canned goods and things, sir, but the more perishable vittles—milk and eggs and butter and meats and fowl— we've about run out of 'em, sir. The grocer at Osquewa delivers once a week, sir ; terrible long trip it is on these blessed mountain roads. He was due yesterday, but with this awful fire and all——"

" Well, do the best you can," said the old gentleman mildly, and went away. In the gloom of the corridor, where he was unobserved, his mouth drooped. Things looked far from promising, despite the solution of the case. He bethought himself of the telephone and trotted with rising hope to the living-room.

He put the instrument down after a while, his shoulders sagging. The line was dead. The inevitable had occurred ; the fire had reached the telephone poles and brought the wires down. They were completely cut off from the outside world.

No use getting the others in more of a state than they were, he thought, stepping out on to the terrace and smiling mechanically at the twins. He cursed the fate that had induced him to take his vacation. As for Ellery . . .

He came to with a start just as Mrs. Wheary plodded out of the foyer to announce luncheon.

Where *was* Ellery ? thought the Inspector. He had disappeared not long after they had taken Mrs. Xavier upstairs.

He went to the edge of the porch and squinted over the tumbled rocks in the devastating sunlight. The place was as barren and ugly and grim as the surface of another and lifeless planet. Then he caught a glimpse of white beneath the nearest tree off the left side of the house.

Ellery was sprawled full-length in the shade of an oak, hands behind his head, staring intently up at the green leaves above him.

" Lunch ! " yelled the Inspector, cupping his hands.

Ellery started. Then he wearily picked himself up, brushed off his clothes, and trudged toward the house.

. . . .

It was a dismal meal, eaten for the most part in silence. The fare was poor and wonderfully diversified, but it seemed to make little difference, for they all munched away without appetite, scarcely noticing what they were putting into their mouths. Dr. Holmes was missing ; still upstairs with Mrs. Xavier. When Ann Forrest finished, she rose quietly and went away. A few moments later the young physician appeared, sat down, and began to eat. No one said anything.

After luncheon they dispersed. Mr. Smith, who could be called a ghost only by the most generous stretch of the imagination, nevertheless contrived to look like one. He had not joined the others in the dining-room, having already been fed by Mrs. Wheary. He kept strictly to himself and no one ventured near him. He spent most of the afternoon tramping heavily about the terrace chewing a damp cigar as gorilla-like as himself.

" What's eating you ? " demanded the Inspector when he and Ellery retired to their room after luncheon for a shower and fresh clothing. " You'll crack your jaw pulling that long face ! "

" Oh, nothing," muttered Ellery, flinging himself on the bed. " I just feel annoyed."

" Annoyed ! At what ? "

" At myself."

The Inspector grinned. " For not spotting that sheet of stationery ? Well, you can't have the luck all the time."

" Oh, not that. That was very clever, and you needn't be so modest about it. It's something else."

" What ? "

" That," said Ellery, " is what annoys me. I don't know." He sat up nervously, rubbing his cheek. " Call it intuition—it's a convenient word. But something is trying to crawl past my conscious defences and make contact. The merest wraith of a something. And what it is I'm blessed if I know."

" Take a shower," said the Inspector sympathetically. " Maybe it's just a headache."

When they had redressed Ellery went to the rear window and scowled out over the abyss. The Inspector moved about, hanging his clothes on hooks in the wardrobe.

" Getting set for a long stay, I see," murmured Ellery, without however turning.

The Inspector stared. " Well, it gives me something to do," he grunted at last. " I have a hunch we won't be so damn' idle in a few days."

" Meaning ? "

The old man did not reply.

After a while Ellery said : " We may as well be thoroughly technical about this affair. Did you lock that study downstairs ? "

" The study ? " The Inspector blinked. " Why, no. What the deuce for ? "

Ellery shrugged. " You never can tell. Let's amble down there ; I've a yen anyway to soak in a little of the gory atmosphere. Maybe that wraith will materialise."

They went downstairs through an empty house. Except for Smith on the terrace no one was about.

They found the scene of the crime as they had left it ; Ellery, obsessed by the vaguest twinges of alarm, went over the room thoroughly. But the desk with the cards on it, the swivel-chair, the cabinet, the murder-weapon, the cartridges—everything was untouched.

" You're an old lady," said the Inspector jovially. " Although it *was* dumb to leave that gun around. And the cartridges. I think I'll get 'em in a safer place."

Ellery was regarding the top of the desk gloomily. " You might put those cards away, too. After all, they're evidence. This is the *craziest case*. Corpse has to be stuffed into a refrigerator, evidence held for the proper officials, nice little blaze toasting—figuratively—our toes. . . . Pah ! ",

He shoved the cards together, went through them to get all their faces turned the same way, stacked them together and handed them to his father. The torn piece of card with the six of spades showing, and the crumpled remainder, he tucked after a moment of hesitation into his own pocket.

The Inspector found a Yale key sticking into the lock on the laboratory side of one study door, closed the doors and locked them from the study, locked the library door with an ordinary steel key of the skeleton type from his own key-ring, and used the key again on the outside of the cross-hall door.

" Where are you going to cache the evidence ? " murmured Ellery as they began to mount the stairs.

" Don't know. Have to get a fairly safe place."

" Why didn't you leave it in the study ? You took plenty of trouble to lock the three doors."

The Inspector grimaced. " Doors from the hall and library any kid could open. I locked 'em just for effect. . . . What's this ? "

A little knot of people was crowded about the open door of the master bedroom. Even Mrs. Wheary and Bones were there.

They pushed their way through to find Dr. Holmes and Mark Xavier bending over the bed.

" What's the trouble ? " snapped the Inspector.

" She's come out of it," panted Dr. Holmes, " and I'm afraid she's a bit violent. Hold her, Xavier, will you ! Miss Forrest—get my hypo. . . ."

The woman was struggling desperately in the men's grip, her arms and legs threshing like flails. Her eyes were glaring at the ceiling, wide open and blind.

" Here," muttered the Inspector. He leaned over the bed and said in a crackling clear voice : " Mrs. Xavier ! "

The threshing ceased and sense crept back into her eyes. She brought her chin down and looked about her rather dazedly.

" You're acting very foolishly, Mrs. Xavier," the Inspector went on in the same sharp tone. " It won't get you anywhere, you know. Snap out of it ! "

She shuddered and closed her eyes. Then she opened them and began very softly to weep.

The men straightened up with deep sighs of relief, Mark Xavier wiping his damp brow and Dr. Holmes turning away with dejected, drooping shoulders.

" She'll be all right now," said the Inspector quietly. " But I shouldn't leave her alone, Doctor. As long as she's tractable, you understand. If she gets fractious again, put her to sleep."

He was startled to hear the woman's voice, husky but controlled, from the bed. " I shall not make any more trouble," she said.

" That's fine, Mrs. Xavier, that's fine," said the Inspector heartily. " By the way, Dr. Holmes, you'd probably know. Is there any place in the house here where I can put something for safekeeping ? "

" Why, the safe in this room, I should think," replied the physician indifferently.

" Well . . . no. It's the—evidence, y'see."

" Evidence ? " growled Xavier.

" Those cards from the doctor's desk in the study."

" Oh."

" There's an empty steel cabinet in the living-room, sir," ventured Mrs. Wheary timidly from the group in the corridor. " It's a sort of safe, but the doctor never kept anything in it."

" Who knows the combination ? "

" No combination, sir. It's got some kind of funny locks and things, with just one funny key. Key's in the big table-drawer."

" Fine. The very thing. Thanks, Mrs. Wheary. Come along, El." And the Inspector strode out of the bedroom followed by a battery of eyes. Ellery sauntered after, frowning. When they were on the stairs descending to the ground floor he glanced at his father with a quizzical eyebrow.

" That," he murmured, " was a mistake."

" Hey ? "

" Mistake, mistake," repeated Ellery patiently. " Not that it makes a particle of difference. *I've* got the important evidence right here in my pocket." He tapped the pocket which held the halves of playing-card. " At that it may be interesting. Sort of baited trap. Is that what you had in mind ? "

The Inspector looked sheepish. " Well . . . not exactly. Hadn't thought of it that way. Maybe you're right."

They went into the deserted living-room and sought out the cabinet. It was imbedded in one of the walls near the fireplace, its face painted to match the wooden panelling of the wall, but frankly a hiding-place. Ellery found the key in the top drawer of the big table ; he regarded it for a moment, shrugged, and tossed it to his father.

The Inspector caught the key, hefted it with a frown, and then unlocked the cabinet. The mechanism worked with a convincing series of complex clicks. The deep recess inside was empty. He took the loose pack of cards from his pocket, regarded it for a moment, sighed, and then slapped it down on the floor of the recess.

Ellery swung on his heel at a slight sound from the terrace. The gross figure of Mr. Smith appeared beyond a French window, bulbous nose flattened against the glass, frankly spying upon them. He started guiltily at Ellery's movement, jerked upright, and disappeared. Ellery heard his elephantine step resound on the wooden flooring of the terrace.

The Inspector took the murder-weapon from his pocket and the box of cartridges. He hesitated, then returned them to his pocket. " No," he muttered. " That's too chancy. I'll keep 'em on me. Have to find out if this is the only key to the cabinet. Well, here goes," and he slammed the door shut and locked it. The key he put on his own key-ring.

. . . .

Ellery was increasingly silent as the afternoon wore on. The Inspector, yawning, left him to his own devices and trudged upstairs to their room for a nap. As he passed the door of Mrs. Xavier's bedroom he saw Dr. Holmes standing at one of the front windows, hands clasped behind his back, and the woman lying wide-eyed and quiet in bed. The others had disappeared.

The Inspector sighed and went on.

When he emerged an hour later, feeling distinctly refreshed, the bedroom door was closed. He opened it softly and peered in. Mrs. Xavier lay as he had last seen her. Dr. Holmes had apparently not stirred from his position by the window. But Miss Forrest now had made her appearance; she lay in a *chaise-longue* near the bed, eyes closed.

The Inspector closed the door and went downstairs.

Mrs. Carreau, Mark Xavier, the twins, and Mr. Smith were on the terrace. Mrs. Carreau was making a pretence of reading a magazine; but her eyes were cloudy and her head did not move from side to side. Mr. Smith was still patrolling the terrace chewing the ragged end of his cigar. The twins were engrossed in a game of chess, which they were playing on a magnetised pocket-board with metal pieces. Mark Xavier half-lay on a chair, head on his breast, apparently asleep.

" Have you seen my son around ? " asked the Inspector of the world at large.

Francis Carreau looked up. " Hullo there, Inspector ! " he said cheerfully. " Mr. Queen ? I think I saw him go down there under the trees about an hour ago."

" He was carrying a pack of cards," added Julian.

" Come on, Fran, it's your move. I think you're going to be licked."

" Not," retorted Francis, " when I can give you a bishop and take your queen, I won't ! How d'ye like that ? "

" Shucks," said Julian disgustedly. " I give up. Let's have another."

Mrs. Carreau looked up, smiling faintly. The Inspector smiled back at her, looked up at the sky, and then descended the stone steps to the gravel path.

He turned left and made for the trees, in the direction of the spot where Ellery had reclined before luncheon. The sun was low, and the air was still and sticky. The sky was like a brazen disc gleaming in coloured lights. He sniffed suddenly and stopped short. A feeble breeze had conveyed an acrid odour to his nostrils. It was— yes, the smell of burning wood ! Startled, he glanced at the sky just above the trees. But he could see no smoke. The direction of the wind had changed, he thought moodily, and now they would probably smother with the foul smell of the resinous fire until the wind changed direction again. As he strode on a large flake of ash settled softly upon one of his hands. He brushed it off quickly and went on.

He gained the shady cover of the marginal trees and peered into the gloom, his eyes tingling after the brilliance of the open terrain. Ellery was nowhere to be seen. The Inspector remained quietly where he was until his pupils adjusted themselves to the shadows, and then stepped forward listening with cocked ears. The trees closed in over him, stifling him with their hot green odour.

He was about to shout Ellery's name when he heard an odd tearing sound from his right. He tiptoed in that direction and cautiously peeped around the trunk of a large tree.

Fifteen feet away Ellery leaned against a cedar, occupied with a curious business. He was surrounded by a scattering of ripped and crumpled playing-cards. His hands were raised before him at the instant the Inspector caught sight of him, forefinger and thumb of each hand delicately gripping the top edge of a card. His eyes were trained earnestly upon the topmost branch of the tree opposite. Then he ripped the card, almost negligently. In the same motion he crumpled one of the pieces and threw it away. He lowered his eyes at once to study the torn half remaining in his hand, grunted, tossed it to the ground, dipped his hand into one of his coat-pockets, drew out another card, and began to repeat the whole incredible process of gripping, looking away, tearing, crumpling, examining, and so on.

The Inspector watched his son with bunched brows for some time. Then his foot moved and a twig snapped. Ellery's head darted round in the direction of the sound.

" Oh, it's you," he said, relaxing. " That's bad business, pater. Get you a bullet some time."

The Inspector glowered. " What in time are you doing ? "

" Worthy research," replied Ellery, frowning. " I'm on the trail of that ectoplasm I spoke about this afternoon. It's beginning to take recognisable shape. Here ! " He thrust his hand into his pocket and produced another card. The Inspector noted that it came from a deck he had observed in the game-room the night before. " Do something for me, will you, dad ? " He thrust the pasteboard into his father's astonished hand. " Tear this card in two, crumple one of the pieces and throw it away."

" What the devil for ? " demanded the old gentleman.

" Go on, go on. This is a new form of relaxation for tired sleuths. Tear it and crumple one piece."

Shrugging, the Inspector obeyed. Ellery's eyes

remained fixed upon his father's hand. "Well?" growled the Inspector, surveying the fragment he was holding.

"Hmm. Interesting. I *thought* it would work; but then I couldn't be sure, being conscious of what I was striving for. That's the hell of making tests when you know what you want to achieve. . . . Here, wait a moment. If that's true, and it looks like a Euclidean axiom now, there's only one other problem. . . ." He sank to the card-cluttered ground at the foot of the cedar, squatting on his heels, sucking his lower lip and gazing abstractedly on the ground.

The Inspector began to fume, thought better of it, and waited more patiently for the result of his son's profound and no doubt esoteric meditations. Experience had taught him that Ellery rarely acted mysterious without purpose. There was evidently something important going on behind the wrinkles of that tanned forehead. Reflecting over the possibilities, the Inspector was even beginning to see a faint glimmer of light when he was startled by Ellery's springing to his feet with a wild gleam in his eye.

"Solved!" shouted Ellery. "By George, I might have known. *That* was child's play compared with the other. Yes, stands to reason on reconsideration. . . . Must be right. Shining vindication of the sadly abused observational and ratiocinative process. *Skoal!* Come along, sire. You are about to witness the materialisation of a wraith. Somebody's going to be grateful for the persistence of that little ghost that haunted my brain-pan this morning!"

.   .   .   .

He hurried toward the clearing, sober-faced, but quite plainly triumphant. The Inspector pattered along behind, with the merest suggestion of a sinking feeling in the pit of his stomach.

Ellery bounded up the steps of the porch and looked about, his breath coming a little quickly. "Would you people mind coming upstairs with us for a moment? We've something rather important to go over."

Mrs. Carreau rose, startled. "All of us? Important, Mr. Queen?" The twins dropped their miniature chess-board and jumped up, mouths open.

"Of a surety. Ah—Mr. Smith, you too, please. And Mr. Xavier, we'll need you. Francis and Julian, of course."

Without waiting he dashed into the house. The woman, the two men, and the twins looked in some trepidation and bewilderment at the Inspector, but the old gentleman was grimly—and not for the first time—playing his rôle. He had set his features in very stern and omniscient lines. He followed them into the house, inwardly wondering what it was all about. The sickness in his stomach was distressing.

"Come in, come in," said Ellery cheerfully, as they paused doubtfully in the doorway of Mrs. Xavier's bed-room. The confessed murderess was propped on her elbows in bed, staring with a sort of fascinated fear at Ellery's non-committal back. Miss Forrest had risen, pale and obviously alarmed. Dr. Holmes was studying Ellery's profile with enigmatic eyes.

They trooped in, all of them awkwardly avoiding the woman on the bed.

"Nothing formal about this," continued Ellery in the same light tone. "Sit down, Mrs. Carreau. Ah, you prefer to stand, Miss Forrest? Well, I shan't weary you. Where's Mrs. Wheary? And Bones? We must have Bones." He strode into the corridor and they heard him shouting for the housekeeper and the man-of-all-work. He returned and a moment later the stout woman and the emaciated old man appeared, apprehensively pale. "Ah, come in, come in. Now, I believe, we're ready for a little demonstration of the niceties of criminal planning. To err is human ; thank God we're dealing with flesh and blood ! "

This remarkable speech had an immediate effect. Mrs. Xavier slowly sat up in bed, black eyes staring and hands clutching the sheet.

" What——" she began, and licked her dry lips. " Aren't you finished with—me ? "

" And the divine quality of forgiveness . . . of course you remember that," continued Ellery rapidly. " Mrs. Xavier, compose yourself, This may prove slightly shocking."

" Come to the point, man," growled Mark Xavier.

Ellery fixed him with a cold eye. " You will please permit me to conduct this demonstration without interference, Mr. Xavier. I should like to point out that guilt is a large and comprehensive term. We are all a tribe of stone-throwers—first-stone throwers, I might add. You will kindly remember that."

The man looked puzzled.

" And now," said Ellery quietly, " for the lesson. I'm going," he went on, digging his hand into his pocket, " to show you a card-trick." He produced a playing-card.

" Card-trick ! " gasped Miss Forrest.

" A very unusual card-trick, to be sure. This is one that immortal Houdini did *not* include in his repertoire. Please observe." He held the card up before them, his fingers holding the back, his two thumbs pointing toward each other as they held the face of the card. " I am going to treat this card as if I wanted to tear it in half, and then I am going to crumple one of the halves and throw it away."

They held their breaths, eyes fixed on the card in his hands. The Inspector nodded to himself and uttered a noiseless sigh.

His left hand holding steady, Ellery made a quick movement of his right hand, ripping off half the card. This, remaining in his right hand, he immediately crumpled and threw away. Then he held up his left hand ; in it was the other half of the card.

"You will please observe," he said, "what has happened. I wanted to tear this card in two. How did I accomplish this simple and yet marvellous digital feat ? By exerting force with my *right* hand, by crumpling with my *right* hand, by throwing away the unwanted piece with my *right* hand. This left my right hand empty, and my left hand occupied. Occupied," he said sharply, "with the piece I had gone through the whole process for. *My left hand*, which did no work whatever except to counterbalance the exertions of my right, *becomes the repository of the uncrumpled half.*"

He swept their dazed faces with a stern glance. There was no levity in his demeanour now.

"What is the significance of all this ? Simply that I am a dextrous individual ; that is, upon my right hand I throw the burden of all manual work. I use my right hand to do manual work *instinctively*. It is one of the integral characteristics of my physical make-up. I can never achieve left-handed gesture or motion without a distinct effort of will. . . . Well, the point is that Dr. Xavier was right-handed, too, you see."

And then realisation flooded into their faces.

"I see you grasp my meaning," continued Ellery grimly. "We found the uncrumpled half of the six of spades in Dr. Xavier's right hand. But I have just demonstrated that a right-handed individual in going through the process of tearing, crumpling, throwing away one half and retaining the other half will retain the other half in his left hand. Since both halves of a playing-card are substantially identical it is not a question of mentally preferring one half to the other.

Consequently the half retained will always be retained, as I say, in the hand that didn't do the work. Consequently, we found the retained half of playing-card *in Dr. Xavier's wrong hand*. Consequently, Dr. Xavier did not tear that card. Consequently, someone else did tear that card and *placed it in Dr. Xavier's hand*, making the pardonable mistake of concluding without complete consideration that since Dr. Xavier was right-handed the card should be found in his right hand. Consequently," and he paused and a look of pity crossed his face, " we all owe Mrs. Xavier the profoundest apology for putting her in excruciating mental distress, for accusing her wrongly of having committed murder ! "

Mrs. Xavier's mouth was open ; she blinked like a woman coming out of darkness into dazzling sunlight.

" For, you see," went on Ellery quietly, " if someone else placed the uncrumpled half of the six of spades in the dead man's hand, then someone else—not the dead man—was accusing Mrs. Xavier of having murdered her husband. But if the dead man was not the accuser, the whole case collapses. Instead of a guilty woman, we have a wronged woman, a *framed* woman ! Instead of a murderess, we have an innocent victim of the well-known frame-up. And who could the framer be except the real murderer ? Who would have motive to throw suspicion of murder upon an innocent person except the murderer himself ? " He stooped and picked up the crumpled half of card. Then he put both pieces into his pocket. " The case," he said slowly, " far from being solved, has just begun."

There was a cutting silence for some time, and the most silent of all was Mrs. Xavier. She sank back upon the pillow, hiding her face in her hands. The others began quickly and surreptitiously to examine each other's faces. Mrs. Wheary groaned and leaned weakly against the jamb. Bones glared from Mrs. Xavier to Ellery, utterly stupefied.

" But—but," stammered Miss Forrest, staring at the woman in bed, " why did she—why—— ? "

" A very pertinent question, Miss Forrest," murmured Ellery. " That was the second of the two problems I had to solve. Once I had solved the first and concluded that Mrs. Xavier was innocent, the question naturally arose : If she was innocent, why had she confessed to the crime ? But that," he paused, " becomes self-evident with a little thought. Mrs. Xavier," he said softly, " why did you confess to a crime of which you are innocent ? "

The woman began to sob with hacking heaves of her breast. The Inspector turned and went to the window to stare out. Life seemed very dismal at the moment.

" Mrs. Xavier ! " murmured Ellery. He leaned over the bed and touched her hands. They fell away from her face and she stared up at him with streaming eyes. " You are a very great woman, you know ; but we really can't permit you to make the sacrifice. *Whom are you shielding ?* "

PART III

" It is as if you batter away at a stubborn door with all your strength and after exhaustive effort break it down. For a moment the light blinds you and you think you are seeing reality. Then your eyes become inured and you see that the details had been wispiest illusion, that it is merely an empty compartment with another stubborn door on the opposite side. . . . I daresay that every investigator of crime has experienced this same feeling on a case which has more than the average subtlety."—From RAMBLES IN THE PAST (p. 233) *by* Richard Queen.

CHAPTER XI

THE GRAVEYARD

THE CHANGE which came over the face of Mrs. Xavier was remarkable. It was as if her features, one by one, were turning to stone. Her skin hardened first, and then her mouth and chin ; the skin smoothed and flattened like poured concrete and the whole woman filled out like a mould. In a twinkling, with the alchemy of instant readjustment peculiar to her, she regained the agelessness of her youth.

She even smiled, the old half-smile of the Gioconda. But she did not reply to Ellery's head-cocked question.

The Inspector turned slowly to survey the faces of the customary puppets. They were always puppets, he reflected—damned wooden-faced ones, when they wanted to keep something back. And they all wanted to keep something back in a murder investigation. There was nothing to be learned from all those guilty countenances. But guilt, he knew from the bitter wisdom of experience, was only a comparative quality of the human animal. It was the heart, not the face, which told the guilty tale. He sighed and almost wished for the lie-detecting apparatus of his friend the Columbia University professor. In one case notably . . .

Ellery straightened and removed his *pince-nez*. " So we are to meet with silence on the single item of importance, eh ? " he said thoughtfully. " I suppose you realise, Mrs. Xavier, that by refusing to speak you're making yourself an accessory after the fact ? "

" I do not know what you are talking about," she said in a low impassioned voice.

"Indeed? At least you comprehend the obscure fact that you're no longer held for murder?"

She was silent.

"You won't talk, Mrs. Xavier?"

"I have nothing to say."

"El." The Inspector moved his head shortly and Ellery, with a shrug, retreated. The old gentleman stepped forward and eyed Mrs. Xavier with an odd antagonism. After all, she *had* been his catch. "Mrs. Xavier, the world is full of funny people, and they do all sorts of cussed things and generally it's hard to tell why they do 'em. Human beings are inconsistent. But a copper can tell you why some people do certain things, and standing the gaff for somebody else's capital crime is one of them. Shall I tell you why you were willing to accept the blame for a murder you didn't commit?"

She pressed back against the pillows, her hands shoving hard on the bed. "Mr. Queen has already...."

"Well, maybe I can take it a little further, you see." The Inspector rubbed his jaw. "I'm going to be brutal, Mrs. Xavier. Women of your age——"

"What about women of my age?" she demanded, her nostrils flaring.

"*Tch, tch*, there's the female for you! I was going to say that women of your age will make the greatest personal sacrifices for one of two reasons—love or passion."

She laughed hysterically. "You distinguish between them, I see."

"I certainly do. I had a definite difference in mind. By love I mean the highest kind of spiritual—ah—feeling...."

"Oh, rubbish!" She half-turned away.

"You say that as if you mean it," muttered the Inspector. "No, I suppose you wouldn't be capable of sacrificing yourself for, say, your children——"

" My children ! "

" But you haven't any, and that's why I've come to the conclusion, Mrs. Xavier," his voice crisped, " that you're protecting a—lover ! "

She bit her lip and began to pluck at the sheet.

" I'm sorry if I have to make a speech about it," continued the old gentleman calmly, " but as an old bull with plenty of experience I'd sort of bet on it. Who is he, Mrs. Xavier ? "

She glared at him as if she would gladly strangle him with her own white hands. " You're the most despicable old man I've ever met ! " she cried. " For God's sake, let me alone ! "

" You refuse to talk ? "

" Get out, all of you ! "

" That's your last word ? "

She was working herself up to a pitch of empurpling passion. " *Mort' dieu*," she whispered, " if you don't get out . . ."

" Duse," said Ellery with a scowl and, turning on his heel, stalked out of the room.

.   .   .   .

They stifled in the evening heat. From the terrace, to which they had repaired by common consent after a dinner of tinned salmon and silence, the whole of the visible sky was peculiarly red, a rubaceous backdrop framing the mountainous scene and made dull and illusory by the clouds of smoke which soared from the invisible burning world below. It was a little difficult to breathe. Mrs. Carreau's mouth and nose were muffled by the flimsiest of grey veils, and the twins succumbed to a depressing tendency to cough. Specks of orange light whirled into the sky from below on the wings of the updraught of wind, and their clothes were grimy with cinders.

Mrs. Xavier, marvellously restored to health, sat by herself, a deposed empress, at the far western end of the terrace. Swathed in black satin, she merged with the evening and became a disturbing presence felt rather than seen.

" Good deal like old Pompeii, I should imagine," remarked Dr. Holmes at last, after the steepest of silences.

" Except," said Ellery savagely, swinging his leg against the terrace rail, " that it and we and the whole world are slightly cock-eyed. The crater of Vesuvius is where the town ought to be, and the Pompeiians—meaning this brilliantly conversational company—are where the crater ought to be. Quite a spectacle ! Lava flowing upward. I think I shall write to the National Geographic Society about it when I get back to New York." He paused ; he was in the bitterest of moods. " If," he added with a dry smile, " I ever do. I'm beginning seriously to doubt it."

" So," said Miss Forrest with a quiver of her capable shoulders, " am I."

" Oh, there's really no danger, I'm sure," said Dr. Holmes quickly, hurling an irritated glance at Ellery.

" No ? " drawled Ellery. " And what shall we do if the fire gets worse ? Take wing and fly away, like good little pigeons ? "

" You're making a mountain out of a molehill, Mr. Queen ! "

" I'm making a fire—which is already burning satisfactorily—out of a mountain. . . . Come, come. This is stupid. No sense in arguing. I'm sorry, Doctor. We'll be frightening the ladies half to death."

" I've known it now," said Mrs. Carreau quietly, " for hours."

" Known what ? " muttered the Inspector.

" That we're really in the most frightful position, Inspector."

" Oh, nonsense, Mrs. Carreau."

" It's chivalrous of you to say so," she smiled, " but there's no sense trying to disguise our predicament, now, is there ? We're trapped like—like flies in a bottle." Her voice was a little tremulous.

" Now, now, it isn't as bad as all that," said the Inspector with a hearty attempt at raillery. " Just a matter of time, Mrs. Carreau. This is a pretty tough old mountain."

" Covered by singularly inflammable trees," said Mark Xavier in mocking tones. " After all, maybe there's such a thing as divine justice. Maybe this entire affair has been arranged from on high for the express purpose of smoking out a murderer."

The Inspector flung him a sharp glance. " There's a thought," he growled, and turned to stare out upon the grey-red sky.

Mr. Smith, who had not uttered a word all afternoon, kicked back his chair suddenly, startling them. His elephantine bulk loomed disgustingly in shadows against the white walls. He thundered to the edge of the steps, descended a step, hesitated, and turned his huge head toward the Inspector.

" I suppose there's no harm in my walking around the grounds for a while ? " he rumbled.

" If you want to break a leg over these stones in the dark, that's up to you," said the old gentleman disagreeably. " *I* don't care a whoop. You can't get away, Smith, and that's all that concerns me."

The fat man began to say something, smacked his thin lips together, and tramped heavily down the steps. They heard his large feet crunching against the gravel on the drive long after he was no longer visible.

Ellery, in the act of lighting a cigarette, by chance caught a glimpse of Mrs. Carreau's face in the glow that fell upon the terrace through the foyer doorway. Its expression froze him into immobility. She was staring, straining, after the vast back of the fat man, a humid terror in her soft eyes. Mrs. Carreau and the unknown quantity, Smith ! . . . The match burned down to his fingertips and he dropped it, swearing beneath his breath. He *thought* he had noticed something there in the kitchen. . . . And yet he would have sworn that Smith had been afraid of this charming *petite dame* from Washington. Why should there be terror in *her* eyes ? It was preposterous to believe that they were afraid of each other ! This gross hostile creature with the trace of a lost culture in his manner and speech, and this gentlewoman from the land of misfortune. . . . Not impossible, to be sure. Strange lives mingled in the waters of the past. He wondered, with a certain rising excitement, what the secret might be. Did the others——? But the most searching scrutiny of the faces about him failed to detect an expression of recognition or secrecy. Except perhaps in the case of Miss Forrest. Peculiar young woman. Her eyes fluttered as she tried to avoid looking at Mrs. Carreau's set face. Did she know too, then ?

They heard Smith's ponderous step on the gravel, returning. He mounted the steps and sat down in the same chair, his froggy eyes inscrutable.

" Find what you were looking for ? " grunted the Inspector.

" Eh ? "

The old gentleman waved his hand. " Never mind. This is one lay-out that doesn't call for the services of a police patrol." And he chuckled rather bitterly.

" I was merely taking a walk," said the fat man in an offended rumble. " If you think I'm trying to get away——"

" Perish the thought ! Though I shouldn't blame you if you did."

" By the way," remarked Ellery, squinting at the tip of his cigarette, " I'm correct, I take it, in assuming that you and Mrs. Carreau, Smith, are old acquaintances ? "

The man sat still. Mrs. Carreau fumbled with the wisp of veil over her mouth. Then he said : " I don't understand. Why the devil should you assume that, Queen ? "

" Oh, an idle fancy. Then I'm wrong ? "

Smith fished a fat brown cigar, of which he seemed to have an inexhaustible supply, from the caverns of his clothes and stuck it very deliberately into his mouth. " Why not," he said, " ask the lady ? "

Ann Forrest jumped to her feet. " Oh, this is intolerable ! " she cried. " Aren't we ever to have any rest from this endless questioning ? Sherlock, let's do something. Bridge, or—or anything. I'm sure Mrs. Xavier won't mind. We'll go crazy just sitting here tormenting one another this way ! "

" Bully idea," said Dr. Holmes eagerly, rising. " Mrs. Carreau—— ? "

" I should love to." Mrs. Carreau rose and hesitated. " Mr. Xavier, you play a stirring game, I've noticed." Her voice was very light. " Will you be my partner ? "

" I suppose I may as well." The lawyer got to his feet, tall and uncertain in the dim light. " Anybody else ? "

The four waited a moment and then, when no one replied, they shuffled through the French windows into the game-room. The lights flashed on and their voices, pitched a little unnaturally, came to the ears of the Queens on the terrace.

Ellery was still squinting at his cigarette ; he had not stirred. Neither had Mr. Smith. Watching him covertly, Ellery could have sworn that there was relief on the man's lunar face.

Francis and Julian Carreau suddenly appeared in the

glow from the foyer. " May we——" began Francis with a quaver. The twins looked frightened.

" May you what ? " asked the Inspector kindly.

" May we go in, too, sir ? " said Julian. " It's a little —sort of—dull out here. We'd like to play some billiards, if you don't mind."

" Of course. Why should I mind ? " smiled the Inspector. " Play billiards, eh ? I shouldn't think——"

" Oh, we can do m-most everything," stammered Julian. " I usually use my left arm, but to-night I guess I'll have to squirm about a bit and use my right. We're rather good, you know, sir."

" Don't doubt it for a moment. Go ahead, youngsters. Have a good time. Lord knows there's little enough for you to do around here."

The boys grinned gratefully and disappeared through the French windows, moving with their graceful rhythm.

The Queens sat in silence for a long time. From the game-room came the sound of shuffling cards, restrained voices, the click of billiard balls. Mrs. Xavier, shrouded in darkness, might not have existed. Smith, cold cigar stuck between his lips, seemed to be dozing.

" There's something," remarked Ellery at last in a low tone, " I really want to see, dad."

" Hey ? " The old gentleman started out of a reverie.

" I've been meaning to have a peep at it for some time now. The laboratory."

" What in time for ? We saw it when——"

" Yes, yes. That's what gave me the notion. I think I saw something. . . And then Dr. Holmes made a rather significant remark. Coming ? " He rose and flicked the cigarette away into the darkness.

The Inspector got to his feet with a groan. " Might as well. Oh, Mrs. Xavier ! "

There was a baffling little sound from the murk at the end of the terrace.

" Mrs. Xavier ! " repeated the Inspector, alarmed. He went quickly to where the invisible woman was sitting and peered down at her. " Oh, I'm sorry. You really shouldn't do that, now."

She was sobbing. " Oh ... please. Haven't you tormented me enough ? "

The old gentleman was distressed. He patted her shoulder awkwardly. " I know. It's all my fault and I apologise for it. Why don't you join the others ? "

" They—they don't want me. They all think ... "

" Nonsense. It's your nerves. A little chatter will do you good. Come on, now. You don't want to be out here alone."

Under his fingers he felt her shiver. " No. God, no."

" Come along, then."

He assisted her to her feet and a moment later they drifted into the light. Ellery sighed. The tall woman's face was wet with tears and her eyes were red. She paused and fumbled for a handkerchief. Then she dabbed at her eyes, smiled, and sailed from the terrace.

" What a woman ! " murmured Ellery. " Remarkable. Any female is who cries her eyes out and then neglects to powder the ravaged countenance. ... Coming ? "

" Go on, go on," said the Inspector irritably. " Less gab and more action. I'll live to see the end of this business yet ! "

" Let us sincerely hope so," said Ellery, moving toward the foyer. There was no levity in his tone.

¹ . . . .

Avoiding the game-room, they walked down the main corridor to the cross-hall. Through the open door of the kitchen ahead they caught a glimpse of Mrs. Wheary's broad back and the motionless figure of Bones, who was standing at one of the kitchen windows staring out at the Stygian night.

The Queens turned right and stopped before a closed

door midway between the crossing of the halls and the
door of Dr. Xavier's study. The Inspector tried the door;
it gave. They slipped into the black room.

" Where the devil's the switch? " grumbled the
Inspector. Ellery found it and the laboratory blazed with
light. He closed the door and set his back against it,
looking around.

Now that he was at leisure to inspect the laboratory,
he felt a stronger recurrence of the impression of scientific modernism and mechanical efficiency which had
struck him earlier in the day when he had been party
to the gruesome business of stowing Dr. Xavier's body
away. The place bristled with awe-inspiring apparatus.
To his untrained eye it was the last word in research
laboratories. Notoriously unscientific, ignorant of the
application of most of this glittery and queerly shaped
equipment, he surveyed the array of cathode-ray tubes,
electric furnaces, twisted retorts, racks of giant test-
tubes, bottles of evil-looking broths, microscopes and
chemical jars and odd tables and X-ray machines with
vast respect. Had he seen an astronomical telescope he
should have not felt surprise. The variety and complexity of the equipment meant little more to him than
that Dr. Xavier had been conducting chemical and
physical, as well as biological, researches.

Both father and son avoided that corner of the room
which housed the refrigerator.

" Well? " growled the Inspector after a time. " *I*
don't see anything for us here. Most likely the murderer
never even set foot in this room last night. What's
bothering you? "

" Animals."

" *Animals?* "

" I said," repeated Ellery firmly, " animals. Dr.
Holmes earlier to-day mentioned something about experiments with diverse creatures, and their capacity for

noise, in connection with the soundproofing of these rooms. Now I'm very curious about experimental animals, have an unscientific horror of vivisection."

" Noise ? " frowned the Inspector. " I don't hear any."

" Probably mildly anæsthetised. Or sleeping. Let's see. . . . The partition, of course ! "

At the rear of the laboratory there was a boarded-off cubicle which reminded Ellery vaguely of a butcher's icebox. A heavy door with a chromium latchet provided entrance. He tried the door ; it was unlocked. Opening it, he went in, groped for an overhanging bulb, turned on the switch, and blinked about him. The compartment was shelved ; on the shelves stood cages of various sizes. And in the cages was the queerest assortment of creatures he had ever seen.

" Lord ! " he gasped. " It's—it's colossal ! Make the fortune of a Coney Island freak-show impresario. Dad ! Look at this."

The light roused them. Ellery's last word was drowned in a torrent of animal voices : squeaks and tiny barks and the raucous screeching of fowl. The Inspector, faintly alarmed, pushed into the small compartment and his eyes widened even as his nose wrinkled in disgust.

" Pfui ! Smells like the Zoo. Well, I'll be bedevilled ! "

" More," corrected Ellery dryly, ' like the Ark. All we need now is an old gentleman with a flowing beard and patriarchal robes. In pairs ! I wonder if they're consistently male and female ? "

Each cage housed two creatures of the same species. There were two queer-looking rabbits, a pair of rufflefeathered hens, two pinkish members of the guinea-pig tribe, two solemn-faced marmosets. . . . The shelves were full, and upon them were cages inhabited by the weirdest collection of creatures outside an animal trainer's nightmare, many of which they failed to recognise.

But the miscellaneous nature of the collection was not what startled them. It was the fact that, as far as they could see, each pair of creatures was composed of twins —Siamese twins of the animal kingdom.

And some of the cages were empty.

. . . .

They quit the laboratory rather in haste, and when the Inspector closed the corridor-door behind them he heaved a sigh of relief. " What a place ! Let's get away from here." Ellery did not reply.

When they reached the juncture of the two corridors, however, he said quickly : " Just a second. I think I'm going to gabble a little with friend Bones. There's something . . ." He hurried toward the open kitchen door, the Inspector trotting wearily behind.

Mrs. Wheary whirled at the sound of Ellery's step. " Oh ! . . . Oh, it's you sir. Gave me a turn."

" I shouldn't wonder," said Ellery cheerfully. " Ah, there, Bones. I'm panting to ask you a question."

The emaciated old man glowered. " Go ahead and ask," he said sullenly. " I can't stop your asking."

" Indeed you can't. Bones," said Ellery, leaning against the jamb, " are you by chance a horticulturist ? "

The man stared. " A what ? "

" A devotee of Mother Nature, with special reference to the old lady's flowers. I mean to say, are you trying to cultivate a garden in that stony soil outside ? "

" Garden ? Hell, no."

" Ah," said Ellery thoughtfully, " I judged not, despite what Miss Forrest said. And yet this morning you appeared from the side of the house carrying a pickaxe and spade. I have since investigated that side of the house and there is no sign of the simple aster, the exalted orchid, or the lowly pansy. *What the devil were you burying this morning, Bones ?* "

The Inspector gave voice to an astonished grunt.

"Burying?" The old man did not seem perturbed; rather more surly than before, that was all. "Why, those animals."

"Bull's eye," murmured Ellery over his shoulder. "Empty cages are empty cages, eh? ... And why did you have to bury animals, my good Bones?—Ah, that name! I've solved it! You were Dr. Xavier's keeper of the ossuary, as it were. Eh? Well, why did you have to bury animals? Come, come, speak up!"

The yellow snags of teeth showed in a grin. "There's a smart question. They were dead, that's why!"

"Quite right. Stupid question! Yet one never knows, Bones. ... They were the twin-animals, weren't they?"

For the first time something frightened twitched across the man's wrinkled face. "The twin—the twin-animals?"

"I'm sorry if I speak indistinctly," said Ellery gravely. "The twin-animals—t-w-i-n, twin. Eh?"

"Yes." Bones glared at the floor.

"You buried yesterday's quota to-day?"

"Yes."

"But no longer Siamese, eh, Bones?"

"Don't know what you mean."

"Ah, but I'm afraid you do," said Ellery sadly. "I mean this: Dr. Xavier has for some time been experimenting upon Siamese-twin creatures of the lower species—where in the name of heaven did he get them all?—in an earnest, quite unfiendish, and very scientific attempt to sever them surgically without loss of life to either. Is that right?"

"I don't know anything about that," muttered the old man. "You'll have to ask Dr. Holmes about all that."

"Scarcely necessary. Some—most—perhaps all of these experiments have been unsuccessful. Whereupon we find you in the unique rôle of animal undertaker. How much of a graveyard have you out there, Bones?"

"Not much. They don't take up much space," said Bones sullenly. "Only once, though, there was a big pair—cows. But mostly little ones. It's been going on, on and off, for over a year. The doctor did do some good ones, I know that."

"Ah, some were successful? That was to have been expected from a man of Dr. Xavier's reputed skill. And yet—— Well, thank you, old timer. Good night, Mrs. Wheary."

"Wait a minute," growled the Inspector. "If he's been *burying* things out there . . . How do you know it isn't something——?"

"Something else? Nonsense." Ellery pulled his father gently out of the kitchen. "Take my word for it, Bones is telling the truth. No, it isn't that that interests me. It's the appalling possibility . . ." He fell silent and walked on.

"How's that for a shot, Jule?" came the ringing voice of Francis Carreau from the game-room. Ellery stopped, shook his head, and went on. The Inspector followed, biting his moustache.

"It does look queer," he muttered.

They heard the heavy tread of Smith on the terrace.

" It's like Swift's island in the sky," muttered Ellery.
Looks bad, eh ? "

" Bad enough, son."

Without another word they went downstairs.

The house was dipped in silence ; no one was about.
The crisp chill of a mountain morning strove vainly to
get at their damp cheeks as they stood on the terrace and
gazed moodily at the sky. Ash and cinders rained
steadily now ; and although from their vantage-point
they could see nothing of the world below, the whirling
débris of the fire brought up by the winds that incessantly spiralled the mountain told them that the blaze
had made alarming progress.

" What the devil are we going to do ? " complained the
Inspector. " This is getting so damn' serious I'm afraid
to think about it. We're in one hell of a jam, El."

Ellery cupped his chin in his hands. " I'll admit that
the death of one human being doesn't seem cosmically
important, under the circumstances. . . . What the
deuce was that ? "

They both started up, straining their ears. From
somewhere at the east of the house came a series of
metallic sounds, muffled and baffling.

" I thought nobody could——" The old gentleman
stopped growling. " Come on."

They hurried down the steps and sped along the
gravel drive in the direction of the sounds. Rounding
the left side of the house, they stopped short. The drive
branched off here and the branch led to a low rambling
wooden building, the garage. The two wide doors were
open, and from the interior of the garage came the noise.
The Inspector darted forward and cautiously peered
into the dim interior. He beckoned to Ellery, who tiptoed along the margin of vegetation flanking the gravel
and joined his father.

There were four cars in the garage, neatly lined up.

CHAPTER XII

BEAUTY AND THE BEAST

IT WAS the most stifling night either man had experienced. They tossed side by side for three hou a hell compounded of sticky darkness and acrid air, then by mutual consent gave up the effort to woo sl Ellery crawled out of bed, groaning, and snapped light on. He groped for a cigarette, pulled a chair one of the rear windows, and smoked without savou The Inspector lay flat on his back, cropped moustac moving up and down in a champing mutter, staring the ceiling. The bed, their night-clothes, were soake in perspiration.

At five o'clock, with the black sky lightening, they took turns under the shower. Then they dressed listlessly.

Morning dawned brazenly. Even the first faint streaks were dipped in molten heat. Ellery, at the window, blinked out over the valley.

" It's worse," he said gloomily.

" What's worse ? "

" The fire."

The old gentleman put his snuff-box away and went quietly to the other window. From the perpendicular edges of the back of Arrow Mountain thick streamers, mile-long lengths of fluttering grey flannel, curved and lifted to the sun. But the smoke was no longer at the base of the Arrow ; it had advanced with silent menace so much farther upward that it seemed to both men to be tickling the summit. The valley was almost invisible. They were floating in air—the summit, the house, themselves.

One of then was the low-slung Duesenberg belonging to the Queens. The second was a magnificent black limousine with a long hood—unquestionably the property of the late Dr. Xavier. The third was a powerful sedan with foreign lines ; it could only have belonged to Mrs. Carreau. The fourth was the battered Buick which had borne the dead weight of Mr. Frank J. Smith of New York City up the steep Arrow Mountain road.

From the rear of Smith's car came the deafening din of metal upon metal. The author of the din was hidden by the body of the car.

They edged between the Buick and the foreign automobile and pounced forward upon the stooping figure of a man who was wielding a rusty hand-axe on the gasoline tank of the fat man's car. The metal was already slashed in several places and the rich dark odorous liquid was gushing to the cement floor in streams.

The man uttered a frightened squeal, dropped the axe, and came up fighting. It took the Queens several minutes of rough work to subdue him.

It was old Bones, glaring sullenly as usual.

" What on earth," panted the Inspector, " do you think you're doing, you crazy fool ? "

His bony shoulders sagged, but he said defiantly : " Taking his gas away from him ! "

" Sure," snarled the Inspector. " We can see that. But why ? "

Bones shrugged.

" And why didn't you drain if off, instead of trying to make scrap iron out of the tank ? "

" He couldn't refill it this way."

" You're a rotten Nihilist," said Ellery sadly. " He could take one of the other cars, you know."

" I was going to put *them* out of commission, too."

They stared. " Well, I'll be damned," said the Inspector after a moment. " I believe you would, at that."

"But it's so silly," protested Ellery. "He can't get away, Bones. Where would he go?"

Bones shrugged again. "It's safer this way."

"But why so anxious to impede the departure of Mr. Smith?"

"I don't like his damn' fat face," rasped the old man.

"Now there," cried Ellery, "is a reason! Look here, my friend; you let us catch you fiddling around these cars again and, by thunder, we'll—we'll annihilate you!"

Bones shook himself, lifted his withered lips in a sneer, and shuffled rapidly out of the garage.

The Inspector threw up his hands and followed, leaving Ellery to dip his toe into the gasoline thoughtfully.

.   .   .   .

"As long as we're frying," growled the Inspector after breakfast, "we may as well fry working as idling. Come along."

"Working?" echoed Ellery blankly. He was smoking his sixth cigarette of the morning and gazing upon vacancy. He had been frowning for an hour.

"You heard me."

They left the game-room, where the others were apathetically congregated under the hot breeze of an electric fan, and the Inspector led the way down the hall to the door of Dr. Xavier's study. He used the skeleton-key from his key-ring and opened the door. The room looked exactly as they had last seen it the day before.

Ellery closed the door and leaned against it. "Now what?"

"I want to look at his papers," muttered old Queen. "You never can tell."

"Oh." Ellery shrugged and went to one of the windows.

The Inspector went through the study with the practised ruthlessness of a lifetime of experience. The cabinet,
the desk, the bookcase—he explored each nook and
cranny, glancing hastily over memoranda, old letters, a
gibberish of medical notations, receipted bills—the usual
mess. Ellery contented himself with staring at the trees
wavering in the fierce heat outdoors. The room was a
furnace and both men were wet to the skin.

"Nothing," announced the old gentleman glumly.
"Nothing but a lot of junk, that is."

"Junk? Now, that's something else again. I'm always
interested in the scrap-heap of a man's property."
Ellery strolled to the desk where the Inspector was
going through the last drawer.

"It's a scrap-heap, all right," grunted the Inspector.
The drawer was full of odds and ends. Stationery
supplies, a broken and rusty surgical instrument, a box
of checkers, a score or more of pencils of varying size,
most of them with broken points; a solitary cuff-link
with a tiny pearl inset in the centre—apparently the
sole survivor of a pair; at least a dozen tie-clips and
stick-pins, most of them tarnished green; shirt-studs of
rather bizarre design, an old fraternity pin with two
diamond chips missing, two watch-chains, an elaborate
silver key, a polished animal-tooth yellow with age, a
silver tooth-pick. . . . The drawer was the tomb of a
man's accumulated trinkets.

"Gay sort of chap, wasn't he?" murmured Ellery.
"Lord, how can a man amass such a mess of perfectly
useless adornments! Come, come, dad, we're wasting
time."

"I s'pose," grumbled the Inspector. He slammed the
drawer shut, sat annoying his moustache for a moment,
and then with a sigh rose.

He locked the door behind them and they trudged
down the hall.

"One minute." The old gentleman suddenly peered into the game-room through the cross-hall door. He withdrew his head at once. "It's all right ; she's in there."

"Who's in there ? "

"Mrs. Xavier. Gives us a chance to sneak up to her bedroom for a quiet little look-see."

"Oh, very well. But I can't imagine what you hope to find."

They toiled upstairs, sweltering in the heat. Across the hall from the landing they could see Mrs. Wheary's broad back bent over the bed in Mrs. Carreau's room. She neither saw nor heard them. They went quietly into Mrs. Xavier's room and shut the door.

It was the master bedroom, the largest chamber on the floor. It was predominantly feminine in character —a tribute, as Ellery remarked dryly, to the overpowering personality of its mistress. Very little of Dr. Xavier struck the eye.

"No wonder the poor fellow spent his days and nights in the study. I'll wager he's slept many a night away on that battered old couch downstairs ! "

"Stop jabbering and keep an ear on the hall," grunted the Inspector. "Rather not have her catch us in here."

"You will save a lot of time and perspiration if you tackle that chiffonier. All the other pieces are unquestionably filled with Parisian fripperies of the *genus* female."

The massive piece in question was, like the other furniture, of French design. The Inspector went through its compartments and drawers like an agéd Raffles.

"Shirts, socks, underwear, the usual junk," he reported, "*and* gewgaws. Lord, what gewgaws ! Whole top drawer crammed full of 'em. Only these look new, not like those relics downstairs. Who says a medical man can't be frivolous ? Didn't that poor fool know that stick-pins went out of style fifteen years ago ? "

"I told you it was a waste of time," said Ellery irritably. Then a thought struck him. "No rings?"

"Rings?"

"I said rings."

The Inspector scratched his head. "Now, by ginger, that *is* queer. You'd think a man with his fondness for trinkets would at least have one ring, wouldn't you?"

"That was in my mind. I don't recall any on his hands, do you?" said Ellery with a sharp note in his voice.

"No."

"Hmm. This business of the rings is the oddest feature of the whole affair. We'd better watch our own or we'll be losing them one of these fine days. Not that they're worth anything, but then that's what someone's apparently after—rings that aren't worth anything. Pshaw! It's nutty. . . . How about Mrs. Xavier? Do a Jimmy Valentine and go through her jewel-box, will you?"

The Inspector obediently rifled Mrs. Xavier's dressing-table until he found the box. Both men examined its contents with practised eyes. And although it contained several diamond bracelets and two necklaces and a half-dozen pairs of earrings, all of them clearly expensive, there were no rings at all, not even cheap ones.

The Inspector closed the box thoughtfully and put it back where he had found it. "What's it mean, El?"

"I wish I knew. It's queer, deucedly queer. No rhyme nor reason really. . . ."

A step outside caused them simultaneously to whirl and race noiselessly towards the door. They pressed close to each other behind it, scarcely breathing.

The knob moved a little, and stopped. There was a click as it moved again, and then the door very slowly pushed inward. It stopped half-ajar and they could hear someone's hoarse breath through the crack. Ellery squinted through it and stiffened.

Mark Xavier was standing with one foot in his sister-in-law's room and the other in the corridor. He was pale and his body rigid with tension. He stood there that way without stirring for a full minute, as if he were debating whether to go in or go back. How long he would have remained that way Ellery was never to know ; for of a sudden he whirled, hastily closed the door, and from the sound of his footsteps made off on a run down the hall.

The Inspector pulled the door open and peered out. Xavier was padding along the carpeted corridor toward the farther end, where his room lay. He fumbled with the knob for a moment, pulled his door open, and vanished.

" Now what did that mean ? " murmured Ellery, emerging from Mrs. Xavier's room and closing the door behind his father. " What scared him, and why did he want to sneak in there at all ? "

" Somebody coming," whispered the Inspector. The two men sped across the hall to their own room. They wheeled and walked leisurely back again, as if they were just going downstairs.

Two neatly-brushed young heads appeared from below. It was the twins coming upstairs.

" Ah, boys," said the Inspector genially. " Going in for a nap ? "

" Yes, sir," said Francis ; he seemed startled. " Uh—you been up here long, sir ? "

" We thought——" began Julian.

Francis paled ; but something must have flashed between him and his brother, for Julian stopped.

" A little while," smiled Ellery. " Why ? "

" Did you see anybody—come up sir ? "

" No. We've just come out of our bedroom."

The boys grinned rather feebly, shuffled their feet for a moment, and then went into their own room.

"Proving," murmured Ellery as they descended the staircase, "that boys will be boys."

"What d'ye mean?"

"Oh, it's most obvious. They saw Xavier make for the upper floor and followed him out of sheer curiosity. He heard them coming up and ran. Did you ever know a normal boy who didn't love to wallow in mysteries?"

"Hunh," said the Inspector, compressing his lips. "That may be, but how about Xavier? What devilment was *he* up to?"

"What devilment was he up to," said Ellery soberly, "indeed."

.   .   .   .

The house wilted under the noon sun. Everything was hot to the touch and slithery with ash-grime. They lolled about in the comparative coolness of the game-room, too listless to talk or play. Ann Forrest sat at the grand piano and fingered a meaningless tune; her face was moist with perspiration and her fingers were wet upon the keys. Even Smith had been driven from the furnace of the terrace; he sat by himself in a corner near the piano, sucking a cold cigar and blinking his froggy eyes from time to time.

Mrs. Xavier for the first time in over a day awakened to her responsibilities as a hostess. For hours now she had seemed to be emerging from a bad dream; her face was softer and her eyes not so agonised.

She rang for the elderly housekeeper. "Luncheon, Mrs. Wheary."

Mrs. Wheary was visibly distressed. She wrung her hands and paled. "Oh, but, Mrs. Xavier, I—I can't serve," she whispered.

"And why not?" demanded Mrs. Xavier coldly.

"I mean I can't serve a formal luncheon, Mrs. Xavier," wailed the old lady. "There—there isn't really enough variety . . . enough to eat, you see."

The tall woman sat up straight. " Why—— You mean we've run out of provisions ? " she said slowly.

The housekeeper was surprised. " But you must have known, Mrs. Xavier ! "

She passed her hand over her forehead. " Yes, yes, Mrs. Wheary. Perhaps I—I didn't notice. I've been a little upset. Isn't there—anything ? "

" Just some canned things, Mrs. Xavier—salmon and tuna and sardines ; there's plenty of *that* ; and just a few tins of peas and asparagus and fruit. I've baked bread this morning—there's still a little flour and yeast—but the eggs and butter and potatoes and onions are gone, and the—— "

" Please. Make up some sandwiches. Is there any coffee left ? "

" Yes, Madam, but no cream."

" Tea, then."

Mrs. Wheary flushed and went away.

Mrs. Xavier murmured : " I'm so sorry. We were a little short to begin with, and now that the grocer's missed the weekly delivery, and the fire—— "

" We quite understand," said Mrs. Carreau with a smile. " This isn't the usual situation and we shouldn't stand on the usual ceremony. Don't distress yourself—— "

" We're all good soldiers, anyway," said Miss Forrest gaily.

Mrs. Xavier sighed ; she did not look directly at the small woman across the room.

" Perhaps if we went on short rations," began Dr. Holmes hesitantly.

" It looks as if we'll have to ! " cried Miss Forrest, banging out a horrible chord, and then she blushed and fell silent.

No one said anything for a long time.

Then the Inspector said softly : " Look here, folks.

We may as well face the facts. We're in one devil of a fix. Up to now I'd hoped those people down there might do something with the fire." They were regarding him furtively, striving to mask their alarm. He added in haste : " Oh, they undoubtedly will yet. . . ."

" Did you see the smoke this morning ? " said Mrs. Carreau quietly. " *I* saw it from my bedroom balcony."

There was another silence. " At any rate," said the Inspector hurriedly, " we mustn't give up. As Dr. Holmes suggests, we'll have to go on a very strict diet." He grinned. " That ought to suit the ladies, eh ? " They smiled feebly at that. " It's the sensible thing to do. It's just a question of holding out as long—I mean, until help comes. Just a question of time, you see."

Ellery, buried in the depths of a big chair, sighed noiselessly. He felt horribly depressed. This slow, slow waiting. . . . And yet his brain would not give him rest. There was a problem to be solved. The persistent wraith was annoying him again. There was something . . .

" It's very bad, isn't it, Inspector ? " said Mrs. Carreau softly. Her eyes strayed to the twins sitting quietly opposite her, and the queerest pain came into them.

The Inspector made a helpless little gesture. " Yes, it's—— Well, it's bad enough."

Ann Forrest's face was as white as her sports dress. She stared at him and then looked down and clasped her hands to conceal their trembling.

" Damn ! " exploded Mark Xavier, springing from his chair. " I'm not going to sit here and be smoked out like a rat in a hole ! Let's do something ! "

" Take it easy, Xavier," said the old gentleman mildly. " Don't let it get you. I was just going to suggest that— action. Now that we all know where we stand there's no sense dawdling around, as you say, and doing nothing. We've not really *looked*, you know."

" Looked ? " Mrs. Xavier was startled.

" I mean we haven't even gone over the ground. How about that cliff at the back of the house—is there any way down, even a dangerous way ? Just," he added hurriedly, " in case it comes to that. I always like to have an emergency exit. Ha-ha ! "

No one responded to his feeble laugh. Mark Xavier said grimly : " A mountain goat couldn't get down that declivity. Get *that* out of your head, Inspector."

" Hmm. It was just a thought," said the old gentleman weakly. " Well, then ! " He rubbed his hands with a false briskness. " There's only one thing to be done. After we've had a sandwich, we're going on a little tour of exploration."

They watched him with a rising of hopes, and Ellery in his chair felt a sick helplessness in the pit of his stomach. Ann Forrest's eyes began to sparkle.

" You mean—go into the woods, Inspector ? " she asked eagerly.

" There's a smart young woman ! That's exactly what I do mean, Miss Forrest. The ladies, too. Everybody get into the roughest clothes you have—knickers, if you've got 'em, or a riding habit—and we'll split up and search these woods from rim to rim."

" That'll be jolly ! " cried Francis. " Come *on*, Jule ! "

" No, no, Francis," said Mrs. Carreau. " You—you mustn't, you two——"

" And why not, Mrs. Carreau ? " said the Inspector heartily. " There isn't a particle of danger and it will be fun for the lads. Fun for all of us ! Get some of this gloom out of our bones. . . . Ah, Mrs. Wheary, that's fine ! Dig in, everybody ! Sooner we get started the better. Sandwich, El ? "

" I suppose so," said Ellery.

The Inspector stared at him, then shrugged and bustled about chattering like an old monkey. In a few moments they were all smiling and chatting amiably,

even gaily, with one another. They ate very fastidiously
and carefully, savouring each mouthful of the butterless
fish sandwiches. Ellery, watching them, felt the sickness in his stomach increase. Everybody seemed to have
forgotten the crisp cold corpse of Dr. Xavier.

.   .   .   .

The Inspector marshalled his forces like a latter-day
Napoleon, making a game of their proposed explora-
tions and at the same time shrewdly planning their
movements so that not a yard of the silent smoky woods
below them would go unsurveyed. Even Mrs. Wheary
was impressed into the ranks, and the saturnine Bones.
He placed himself on the extreme west of the semi-
circle of forest, Ellery on the extreme east, and the
others at spaced intervals between them. Mark Xavier
took the halfway position ; between him and the Inspector were Miss Forrest, Dr. Holmes, Mrs. Xavier, and
the twins ; between Xavier and Ellery were Mrs.
Carreau, Bones, Smith, and Mrs. Wheary.

" Now remember," shouted the Inspector when they
were all in their places except himself and Ellery. " Keep
going straight down, straight as you can. Naturally
you'll keep getting farther and farther away from one
another as you go down—mountain widens the farther
you go from the top. But keep your eyes open. When
you get close to the fire—don't go too close—peel a
sharp eye for a way through. If you find anything that
even looks promising, yodel and we'll all come running.
All set ? "

" All set ! " yelled Miss Forrest, very handsome in a
pair of knickerbockers which she had borrowed from Dr.
Holmes. Her cheeks were glowing and she was more
naturally effervescent than the Queens had ever seen her.

" Then *go* ! " And *sotto voce* the Inspector added :
" And may God help the lot of you."

They plunged into the woods. The Queens heard the Carreau boys whooping like young Indians as they crashed through the underbrush and vanished.

For a moment father and son measured each other in silence.

" How now, old Roman ? " murmured Ellery. " Satisfied ? "

" Well, I had to do something, didn't I ? And," the Inspector added defensively, " how do you know we won't find a way down ? It's not unlikely ! "

" It's most unlikely."

" Let's not argue about it," snapped the old gentleman. " Reason I placed you at the east and myself opposite is that those are the two likeliest places, no matter *what* you say. Keep as close to the edge of the cliff as you can. That's where the trees grow thinnest, probably, and that's where there'll be a way out, if any." He fell silent for a moment, and then he shrugged. " Well, get going. Good luck."

" Good luck," said Ellery soberly, and turned and made for the rear of the garage. He looked back before he rounded the house and saw his father clumping dejectedly along toward the west.

Ellery loosened his necktie, wiped his streaming forehead with a damp handkerchief, and went on.

He started at the lip of the precipice to the side of the house, behind the garage, and made his way into the woods as closely to the edge of the cut as he could. The hot foliage closed over his head and instantly he felt new beads of perspiration spring out of his pores all over his body. The air was stifling, unbreathable. It was filled with an impalpable smoke, invisible but choking. His eyes soon began to stream. He lowered his head and plunged on doggedly.

It was hardy going. Although he had dressed himself in jodhpurs and soft riding boots, the underbrush was so thick and treacherous underfoot that the leather was soon scratched in hundreds of places and tiny tears appeared in the tough material above his knees. The dry brush cut like knives. He gritted his teeth and tried to ignore the sharp assaults on his thighs. He began to cough.

It seemed to him that he slipped and slid and scratched his hands and face and stepped into mould-filled pits for a century. Each sliding step downward brought him into thicker, fouler atmosphere. He kept repeating to himself that he must be very careful, for there was no telling what vagary of the jagged side of the cliff which he was skirting under the trees might sheer the cliff off beneath his feet and topple him into the abyss below. Once he stopped and leaned against a tree to catch his breath. Through a rift in the leaves he could see over the next valley—remote and tantalising as a dream. Only occasionally could he descry details ; the smoke was dirty wool in the valley now, or at least between the valley and his vantage-point ; and even the strong hot winds which swirled about the mountain could not dissipate its stubborn layers.

He became conscious all at once of a dull earth-shaking boom.

It was difficult to determine its direction or distance. There it was again ! At a different point. . . . He wiped the sweat off his face, puzzling a little dazedly over the phenomenon. Then he had it. Blasting ! They were dynamiting sections of the woods in a desperate effort to check the conflagration.

He went on.

He staggered downward, it seemed to him, endlessly —a blundering figure condemned like Ahasuerus to wander alone in his especial hell of smoke, heat, and cinders. The heat was raw, searing, unendurable ; he gasped and choked under the fierce intensity of it.

How long, O Lord ? he thought with a tortured smile ; and plunged on.

And then he saw it.

He thought at first that it was an optical illusion, that his streaming eyes were peering through a fourth dimension into a grotesque unearthly pit in some fantastic etheric plane. Then he knew that he had reached the fire.

It was crackling and blazing steadily below him, a monstrous orange thing constantly changing shape like a phantasmagorical creature out of a madman's dream. It crept insidiously upward, feeding upon the lorn waterless drooping woods, sending out advance guards—feelers of flame which licked quickly at the undergrowth and then raised themselves like pseudopods with uncanny intelligence along dry boles and lower branches to ignite them in a flash, leaving glowing lines of fire, red Neon tubes, behind. And then came the main column of the fire itself to consume with irresistible ferocity what was left.

He staggered back, shielding his face. For the first time the full horror of their predicament struck him. The remorseless advance of the flames. . . . It was Nature in her most rapacious mood, awful and nauseating. He felt the impulse to turn and run blindly—anywhere—away from the conflagration ; he had to dig his nails into his palms to control himself. Then the heat blasted into his face again and with a gasp he scrambled back, slipping on the crumbling leaf-mould.

He made for the south, laterally along the line of fire, toward the spot where the side of the declivity must lie. There was desperation in his heart now, a cold leaden lump striving to burst from the internal pressure of fear. There must be a way. . . . Then he stopped, clutching at a slender trunk of birch to keep himself from falling. He had reached the cut.

For a long time he stood there, blinking with smarting

eyes over the smoke-filled valley. He might have been standing on the lip of an active volcano staring into the crater.

The trees grew to the margin of the jagged stone. And a little below, where the precipice cropped out in an arc so that he could see it, those trees were burning as furiously as the others.

By this road, at least, there was no escape.

.   .   .   .

He never knew how long it took him to climb the Arrow and return to the summit. The ascent was worse than the descent had been ; it was back-breaking, heart-bursting, lung-shattering work. His legs in their protecting boots felt petrified, and his hands were raw messes of bleeding skin. He crept upward with a blank brain, breathing in hoarse short gasps, eyes half-closed, refusing to think of the horror below. It took him, he knew later, hours.

Then at last he could breathe more easily and could see the last dense clump of trees at the summit. He struggled to the edge of the woods and collapsed against a cold bole with dumb gratitude. His bloodshot eyes lifted to the skies. The sun was low. It was not so hot as it had been. Water, a blessed bath, iodine for his wounds. . . . He closed his eyes and strove to muster sufficient strength to negotiate the last few yards to the house.

He opened them reluctantly. Someone was crashing through the underbrush not far to his right. One of the party returning. . . . And then he crouched and very swiftly slipped into the thicker protection of the trees behind, all his fatigue and soreness of heart vanishing in a tingling alertness.

The gross head of the fat man, Smith, was protruding from the fringe of woods a little to the west, cautiously surveying the summit. He was dishevelled, grey, and

even from the distance as scratched and torn as Ellery.
But it was not the fact that the mysterious and elderly
gorilla was returning, wounded and tired, from the
hunt, that caused Ellery to conceal his presence.

It was rather the fact that beside him, her delicate
face as drawn and scratched as her companion's, was
Mrs. Carreau.

. . . .

The odd pair searched the open terrain about the
house for a moment with provocative furtiveness. Then,
apparently assured that they were the first to return,
they stepped out of the woods boldly and tramped over
to a flat-topped boulder, upon which Mrs. Carreau sank
with an audible sigh. She clasped her chin in one small
fist and gazed inscrutably up at her colossal companion.
The big bulging man leaned against the nearest tree,
his little eyes roving.

The woman began to speak. Ellery, straining, could
see her lips move ; but he was too far away to hear what
she said, and he silently cursed the fate which had
brought him near the pair but not near enough to over-
hear their conversation. The man was restive, shifting
ponderously from foot to foot, collapsed against the tree
and, it seemed to Ellery, squirming under the lash of
the woman's tongue.

She spoke rapidly for some time, and not once did he
open his mouth to respond. Then suddenly she rose,
the picture of scornful dignity, and extended her right
hand.

For a moment Ellery thought that Smith meant to
strike her. He bounced away from the tree, his massive
jaws twitching and his jowls vibrating as he rumbled
something at her. His paw was half-raised. The woman
did not stir, nor did her hand fall. All the while he
spoke it was extended, motionless.

And finally his rage collapsed like a pricked balloon and he fumbled in the breast-pocket of his limp jacket. He produced a wallet with shaking fingers, took something out of it—Ellery could not see what—and slammed it into her small white red-streaked palm. Without another glance at her he lurched off toward the house.

Mrs. Carreau stood still for a long time, not looking at her clutched hand, pale and stiff as a statue. Then her left hand came up and met the right, and her fingers uncurled, and with a deliberate motion she began tearing what Smith had so unwillingly thrust upon her. She tore it into tiny pieces, savagely, and finally hurled the fragments violently away from her, toward the woods. Then she turned and stumbled after Smith, and Ellery could see her shoulders shake. She went blindly on, her face hidden in her hands. . . .

After a while Ellery sighed, straightened, and strode over to the spot the man and woman had just deserted. He looked around quickly. Both had disappeared in the house and the clearing was empty of life. So he stooped and proceeded to pick up every fragment he could find. They were of paper, as he had guessed, and one glance at a single scrap told him part of what he wished to know. He spent ten minutes crawling about, and when he had finished he went into the woods, sat down on the ground, took an old letter from his pocket, and using the outspread sheet as a table began to piece the fragments together.

For some time he sat with narrowed eyes scrutinising the result of his labour. It was a cheque on a Washington bank, dated the day on which the Queens had encountered the fat man in the Buick on the narrow Arrow road. It was made out to *Cash* and in a spidery feminine hand was signed *Marie Carreau.*

The cheque had been drawn to the amount of ten thousand dollars.

CHAPTER XIII

THE TEST

ELLERY, outstretched on his bed, perfectly naked, luxuriating in the cool sheets, a smouldering cigarette in his hand, stared up at the white ceiling in the deepening gloom of evening. He had bathed and treated his numberless cuts and scratches with iodine from the lavatory medicine chest, and physically he felt refreshed. But through his brain flashed stubbornly recurring pictures. One was of a deck of playing cards. Another was of a finger-smudge. And dominating the two, despite all his efforts to dislodge its lurid details, was the flickering vision of the hellfire raging below.

As he lay there at ease, thinking and smoking, he heard from time to time the weary steps in the corridor outside of the returning members of the household. The tonal quality of the sounds told their story with laconic eloquence. There was no sound of human voices. The steps were heavy, dragging, hopeless. Doors snicked laboriously shut. At the far end of the hall . . . that would be Miss Forrest, no longer the ebullient creature embarking on a gay adventure. Soon after steps across the corridor—Mrs. Xavier. Then the slow shuffling of four rhythmic feet—the twins ; no shouting now. Finally Dr. Holmes and Mark Xavier, and lagging behind them yet continuing after the others had ceased, two pairs of plodding feet . . . Mrs. Wheary and Bones bound for their rooms on the attic floor.

There was a long interval of complete silence then and Ellery wondered, through the maze of his thoughts, where his father was. Still hoping against hope, no doubt ; still searching for a way out which did not exist. A new thought struck him and he forgot everything as he pursued it with fierce concentration.

He was roused by a slow dragging step outside the door. He covered himself hastily with the sheet. The door opened and the Inspector appeared on the threshold, a ghost with dead eyes.

The old man said not a word. He shuffled into the lavatory and Ellery heard him bathing his face and hands. Then he shuffled out and sat down in the arm-chair and stared at the wall with the same haggard eyes. There was a long angry red scratch on his left cheek, and his wrinkled hands were pricked with wounds.

" Nothing, dad ? "

" Nothing."

Ellery could barely hear his voice ; it was cracked with fatigue.

And then the old man muttered : " You ? "

" Lord, no. . . . It was horrible, wasn't it ? "

" It was—that."

" Hear the booming on your side ? "

" Yes. Blasting. Puny scum ! "

" Now, now, dad," said Ellery gently. " They're doing their best."

" How about the others ? "

" I heard them all returning."

" Nobody said anything ? "

" The sound of their footsteps spoke for them. . . . Dad."

The Inspector raised his head a trifle. " Hey ? " he mumbled lifelessly.

" I saw something damned significant."

Hope flared into the old man's eyes ; he jerked around. " The fire——? " he cried.

" No," said Ellery quietly, and the grey head drooped

again. " I'm afraid we'll have to put ourselves into—
other hands for that. If we're lucky. . . ." He shrugged.
" One becomes resigned to what appears to be the
inevitable. Even when the inevitable is the end of all
things. I suppose you realise that our chances——"

" Slim."

" Yes. We may as well keep our heads. There's nothing
we can do, really. The other thing——"

" The murder ? Pah ! "

" Why not ? " Ellery sat up, hugging his knees. " It's
the only decent—well, the only sane thing, at any rate.
Normal occupation keeps men—and women—out of
the insane asylums." The Inspector grunted feebly.
" Yes, dad. Don't let it put you under. The fire's taken
something out of us, addled us a bit. I've never believed
in, always scoffed at what I thought was bilge-water
—that ' Carry on ! ' spirit of the romanticised Englishman. But there's something in it. . . . There are two
things I must tell you. One is what I saw when I was
coming back to the house."

A sparkle of interest crept into the old man's eye.
" Saw ? "

" Mrs. Carreau and Smith——"

" Those two ! " The Inspector started from the chair,
eyes snapping.

" That's better," chuckled Ellery. " Now you're yourself again. They had a secret confab when they thought
they were unobserved. Mrs. Carreau demanded something from Smith. Smith was defiant, the big ape, and
then something she said took all the bluster out of him.
He gave her what she demanded like a lamb. She tore
it into bits and threw it away. It was a cheque for ten
thousand dollars made out to cash and signed by Marie
Carreau. I've the pieces in my pocket."

" Good lord ! " The Inspector jumped up and began
to pace the floor.

" It's fairly clear, I think," mused Ellery. " Explains a lot of things. Why Smith was so anxious to leave the mountain the other night, why he was so reluctant to face Mrs. Carreau when he had to come back, why they met in secret this afternoon. Blackmail ! "

" Sure. Sure."

" Smith came up here, having trailed Mrs. Carreau, and managed to see her alone, or possibly with the Forrest girl present. He soaked her for ten thousand dollars. No wonder he was anxious to get away ! But when the murder occurred and we popped into the scene, and no one could leave, events took a different turn. Don't you see ? "

" Blackmail," muttered the Inspector. " It might be the kids. . . ."

" What else ? So long as the fact that she was the mother of Siamese twins remained unknown, she was glad to pay any amount of hush-money to keep Smith's mouth shut. But with a murder, an investigation, the certainty that when the road was open and the official police came upon the scene the story would come out— well, there was no longer any reason to pay Mr. Frank J. Smith for silence. Consequently she has just mustered up enough courage to demand the return of the cheque. Smith sees the light, returns it . . . and there you are."

" I wonder——" began the Inspector thoughtfully.

" Oh, there are all sorts of possibilities," murmured Ellery. " But that's not the important thing, dad. There's something else. I've been thinking——"

The Inspector grunted.

" Yes, thinking, and after an exhaustive bout with my memory I've come to a certain conclusion. Let me go over it for you——"

" About the murder ? "

Ellery reached for the fresh underclothes draped over

the footboard. " Yes," he said, " very decidedly about the murder."

   •   •   •   •   •   •   •   •

It was a fire-scarred and woebegone company which assembled in the game-room after Mrs. Wheary's mandatory dinner of tinned tuna, preserved plums, and withered tomatoes. They all showed signs of their frightful passage through the woods, and a more patched and iodine-stained assembly of human creatures Ellery had never seen. But it was the internal wounds which depressed the corners of their mouths and brought the glint of desperation into their eyes. Even the twins were subdued.

The Inspector began abruptly. " I've called you people together for two reasons. One is to take stock, and the other will come in a moment. First, did anybody find anything down there ? "

The misery on their faces was answer enough.

" Well, there's nothing to do then but sit and wait. Meanwhile," continued the Inspector in a sharp voice, " I want to remind you that the same state of affairs exists now as existed before. There's a corpse in this house, and a murderer."

Ellery saw that most, if not all, of them had quite forgotten. The pressure of their own danger had banished it from their minds. Now the old restraints came back and an instant readjustment of facial expressions. Smith sat very still. Ann Forrest flashed a warning glance at Mrs. Carreau. Mark Xavier nervously snapped a cigarette in two. Mrs. Xavier's black eyes glittered. The twins breathed more quickly, Dr. Holmes paled, and Mrs. Carreau twisted her handkerchief into a crumpled ball.

" We assume," the Inspector went on shortly, " the best, not the worst. By that I mean that I'm taking for granted that somehow we'll all get out of this mess. Consequently, we're going to proceed as if there were no fire but just a delay in the arrival of the regular officer having jurisdiction over this patch of mountain-side. Do you understand ? "

" The old line," sneered Mark Xavier. " Going to put one of us on the cat-o'-nine tails, I suppose. Why don't you confess that you're stumped, that someone's put it over you and the rest of us, and that you're just acting officious to surprise one of us into giving himself away ? "

" Ah," murmured Ellery, " but it's not a question of blundering in the dark, old chap. Not at all. We *know.*"

The man's fair skin went slowly grey. "You—know?"

" I see you're no longer quite so certain," drawled Ellery. " Dad, I think we understand each other ? . . . Ah, Mrs. Wheary. Come in. And you, Bones. We mustn't neglect you two."

They all turned mechanically to the foyer door ; the housekeeper and the man-of-all-work were hesitating on the threshold.

" Come in, come in, good folk," said Ellery briskly. " We want a full cast. Sit down. That's better."

The Inspector leaned on one of the open bridge-tables, glaring from one face to another. " You'll remember that Mr. Queen here bilked that pretty plan to have Mrs. Xavier accused of her husband's murder. She was framed, and whoever framed her murdered Dr. Xavier. You'll remember that ? "

Unquestionably they remembered that. Mrs. Xavier lowered her eyes, paling, and the others after a quick glance at her looked away. Mark Xavier's eyes were nearly closed, so intently was he watching the Inspector's lips.

" Now we're going to put you people through a test——"

" A test ? " said Dr. Homes slowly. " I say, Inspector, isn't——"

" Hold your horses, Doc. I said a test, and a test I mean. When it's all over and the smoke's cleared away," he paused grimly, " we'll have our man. Or," he added after another pause, " our woman. We're not particular so long as we get the guilty party."

No one answered ; their eyes were trained upon his unsmiling lips. Then Ellery stepped forward, and the eyes twitched to his. The Inspector retreated and took up his stand near the French windows. They were open to admit what little air there was. His erect little figure was framed in the blackness of the night outside.

" The revolver," said Ellery sharply, and extended his hand to his father. The Inspector produced the long-barrelled revolver which they had found on the floor of Dr. Xavier's study ; he snapped it open, inspected its empty chambers, snapped it shut again, and placed it without comment into Ellery's hand.

They watched this silent play in breathless bewilderment.

Ellery hefted the weapon with an enigmatic smile and then dragged the bridge-table to the foreground and a chair, placing the chair behind the table in such a position that whoever might sit in it would be facing the company.

" Now I want you to pretend," he said crisply, " that this is Dr. Xavier's study, that the table is Dr. Xavier's desk, and the chair his chair. Clear so far ? Very well." He paused. " Miss Forrest ! "

Under the whip of her sharply enunciated name the young woman jumped, her eyes widening with apprehension. Dr. Holmes half-rose in protest and then sank back, watching with narrowed eyes.

" M-me ? "

" Precisely. Stand up, please."

She obeyed, clutching the back of her chair. Ellery crossed the room to the far side, placed the revolver on the grand piano, and returned to his position beside the table.

" B-but what—? " the girl whispered again, blanching.

He sat down in the chair. " I want you, Miss Forrest," he said in a matter-of-fact tone, " to re-enact the shooting."

" Re-enact the sh-shooting ! "

" Please. You must pretend that I'm Dr. Xavier—a consummation no doubt devoutly to be wished. I want you to go into the cross-hall through that door behind you. When I give the signal, please come in. You will be standing a little to my right, facing me. I'm Xavier, and I shall be at my desk playing solitaire. When you enter, you are to reach over to the piano, pick up the revolver, face me squarely, and pull the trigger. I might add that the revolver is not loaded. Please see that it—ah—remains that way. Understand ? "

The girl was sickly pale. She tried to speak, her lips trembling, then abandoned the effort, nodded quickly, and left the room by the door Ellery had indicated. It clicked shut behind her, leaving staring eyes and silence.

The Inspector stood by the French windows, grimly watching.

Ellery folded his arms on the edge of the table before him, and called out : " Now, Miss Forrest ! "

The door opened slowly, very slowly indeed, and Miss Forrest's white face appeared. She hesitated, came in, closed the door behind her and her eyes at the same moment, shuddered and opened them and went reluctantly to the piano. For an instant she stared down with loathing at the revolver and then, seizing it, she pointed it in the general direction of Ellery, cried : " Oh, this is ridiculous ! " and snapped the trigger back. She dropped the weapon, sank into the nearest chair, and began to weep.

"That," said Ellery briskly, rising and making his way across the room, "was really excellent. All except the gratuitous remark, Miss Forrest." He stooped, retrieved the revolver, and said to his father: "You caught that, of course?"

"I did."

Their mouths were open now and Miss Forrest forgot to weep as she raised her head to join in the general staring.

"Now," continued Ellery, "Mr. Smith."

The united battery instantly focused upon the fat man's face. He sat still, blinking and working his jaws like a stupid cow.

"Stand up, please." Smith struggled to his feet and stood shifting his weight from one foot to the other. "Take this!" snapped Ellery, and thrust the revolver toward him. He blinked again, drew a billowing breath, and took it. It hung loosely from his fingers.

"What do I do?" he asked huskily.

"You're a murderer——"

"A *murderer!*"

"Only for purposes of our little experiment. You're a murderer and you've just shot—let's say Dr. Xavier. The smoking weapon is still in your hand. The weapon belonged to Dr. Xavier, so there is no point in your attempting to dispose of it. Still, you naturally don't care to leave fingerprints. So—you take out your handkerchief, wipe the gun clean, and then very carefully drop it to the floor. Got that?"

"Y-yes."

"Then do it."

Ellery stepped back and watched the fat man with cold eyes. Smith hesitated and then became very busy, as if his sole concern was to get his part of the proceedings over with as soon as possible. He gripped the butt firmly, whipped out a napkin-like handkerchief, polished butt and barrel and trigger and guard very expertly indeed, and then, holding the weapon in his swathed hand, dropped the gun. He stepped back, sat down, and wiped his forehead with slow swoops of his vast arm.

"Very good," murmured Ellery. "Very good indeed." He picked up the fallen weapon, shoved it in his pocket, and retraced his steps. "Now you, Dr. Holmes." The Englishman stirred uneasily. "Once more, in my miraculous way, I am a corpse. Your rôle in our little drama is to enact the med'co examining my cold and outraged corpse. I believe you understand without necessity of further explanation." Ellery sat down in the bridge-chair, slumped forward on the table, his left hand flat against the tabletop, his right arm dangling to the floor, his left cheek resting on the table. "Come on, old chap, come on ; I don't relish this characterisation, you know ! "

Dr. Holmes rose and stumbled forward. He stooped over Ellery's motionless figure, felt the nape of his neck, the muscles of his throat, rolled his head to examine the eyes, grasped and felt the arms and legs . . . went through a rapid expert examination.

"Is that quite enough ? " he asked at last in a strangled voice. "Or is there more to this ghastly farce ? "

Ellery jumped up. "No, that's sufficient, Doctor. But please don't be careless with your terms. This is, far from a farce, the most dreadful sort of tragedy. Thanks. . . . Mrs. Wheary ! "

The housekeeper clutched her bosom. "Y-yes, sir ? " she faltered.

"I want you to rise, cross the room, and turn off that electric-light switch near the foyer door."

"T-turn it off ? " she stuttered, getting to her feet.

" But won't—won't it be dark, sir ? "

" I should think so," said Ellery grimly. " Quickly, Mrs. Wheary."

She licked her lips, looked at her mistress as if for guidance, and then shuffled forward toward the foyer. At the wall she hesitated and Ellery signalled her impatiently to proceed. She shuddered and fumbled with the switch. The room was suddenly drenched in darkness, a darkness thick as chocolate syrup. What starlight there was above Arrow Mountain could not penetrate the weaving clouds of smoke outside. They might have been buried five miles beneath the sea.

Then, after an age, Ellery's clear voice crackled through the silence. " Bones ! Have you a match ? "

" Match ? " croaked the old man.

" Yes. Strike one, please, at once. Hurry, man, hurry ! "

They heard the scratch of a match and a tiny light flared up, revealing Bones's ghostly hand and part of his wrinkled sullen face. No one said anything until the light flickered and went out.

" All right, Mrs. Wheary. You may switch the lights on again," murmured Ellery.

The lights blazed on. Bones was sitting where he had been sitting, staring at the blackened stump of wood in his hand. Mrs. Wheary quickly returned to her chair.

" And now," continued Ellery equably, " for you, Mrs. Carreau."

She rose, pale but self-controlled.

Ellery opened the shallow drawer of the table and brought out a brand-new deck of cards. He ripped off the seal, crumpled and threw to one side the glassine envelope, and thumped the deck down on the table.

" You play solitaire, I suppose ? "

" I know the game," she replied in an astonished voice.

" You play simple solitaire ? I mean—thirteen closed cards, four open cards in a row, and the eighteenth card above them to build on ? "

" Yes."

" Superb. Please take these cards, Mrs. Carreau, sit down at this table, and play a game ! "

She stared at him as if she doubted his sanity, and then came quietly forward and sat down at the table. Her fingers groped for the deck. She shuffled the cards slowly, dealt thirteen, placed them face down in a pile, laid out the next four cards face up and side by side, and the next card above them. Then she took the remainder of the deck and began to play, exposing every third card and searching the ones above. . . .

She played quickly now, nervously, her fingers flashing and hesitating in stops and starts. Twice she made mistakes, and Ellery silently pointed these out before she proceeded. They watched with bated breath. What was coming ?

It was a fortuitous arrangement of cards and the game seemed endless. The cards above the four staggered piles grew. . . . Suddenly Ellery put his hand over the woman's fingers.

" That's enough," he said gently. " The gods are kind. I thought we should have to try more than one game before the desired effect would be achieved."

" Effect ? "

" Yes. You see, Mrs. Carreau, that in the fourth staggered row appears—between a red five and a red seven—the tell-tale six of spades ! "

Mrs. Xavier uttered a plangent sound.

" Now, now, don't be alarmed, Mrs. Xavier. This isn't another frame-up." Ellery smiled at Mrs. Carreau. " That's all for you, please. . . . Mr. Xavier ! "

For some time the tall lawyer had not been in the sneering mood. His hands were quivering and his mouth slack. Chap needs a stiff hooker of red-eye, thought Ellery with satisfaction.

" Well ? " said Xavier hoarsely, coming forward.

" Well ! " smiled Ellery. " We've a *very* interesting little experiment for you, Mr. Xavier. Will you please pick the six of spades out of the exposed cards ? "

He started. " Pick——? "

" Please."

He obeyed with fingers that shook. " What—what now ? " he said with a sickly attempt at smiling.

" Now," said Ellery sharply, " I want you to tear that card in two—quickly ! Yes, now ! Don't hesitate ! Tear it ! " Startled, Xavier obeyed before he could think. " Throw away one of the halves ! " He dropped a piece as if it burned his fingers.

" Well ? " he muttered, licking his lips.

" Just a moment," came the Inspector's dry impersonal voice from behind. " Stay where you are, Xavier. El, come here."

Ellery went to his father's side and they conversed in an earnest undertone for some minutes. Finally Ellery nodded and turned back to the company.

" I must announce after proper consultation a most successful set of tests," he said cheerfully. " Mr. Xavier, you might sit down at the table here. This may take a few minutes." The lawyer sank into the bridge-chair, still clutching the piece of pasteboard. " Good. Now listen carefully, all of you."

It was an unnecessary injunction ; they were sitting forward, enthralled spectators at a gripping play.

" If you will recall my little lecture on legerdemain not long ago," continued Ellery, taking off his *pince-nez* and polishing the lenses, " no doubt you remember that I demonstrated several things of importance. I demonstrated for one thing that since Dr. Xavier was right-handed the piece of card we found in his right hand was wrongly placed ; that had he torn the card the fragment would have remained in his left hand, since his right hand would have done all the work of tearing, crumpling, and throwing away. I concluded from this, too, that since the card was in the wrong hand Dr. Xavier had not torn the card ; consequently, it was not he who left a ' clue ' to the identity of the murderer. The card pointed to Mrs. Xavier as the murderer. But if the victim had not left the clue, then the clue is not authentic, is not evidence, and in effect becomes merely the inspired machination of one who attempted to frame Mrs. Xavier for the murder of her husband, trying to make it appear that he had accused her by this fantastic method. Who, I said in conclusion, could that one be—who but the murderer himself ? You recall ? "

They recalled. The evidence of their fascinated eyes answered.

" The problem resolved itself, then, into this : Find the person who *really* tore that six of spades in half, and we should have our murderer."

Mr. Smith astounded them all, including the Queens, by rumbling at this point in a mocking *basso profundo* : " That's a good trick—if you can do it."

" My dear Mr. Smith," murmured Ellery, " it has been done ! "

.   .   .   .

Mr. Smith shut his mouth very abruptly.

" Yes," continued Ellery with a dreamy survey of the ceiling, " there was a nice clue pointing to the murderer's identity, you know. It was before my eyes for so long that I blush now to think of my blindness. But I suppose one can't see everything." He lit a cigarette deliberately. " However, it is now very clearly seen indeed. The clue, needless to say, is on the card—the torn card, the torn *half* of the card crumpled by the murderer and thrown to the floor near the dead body of Dr. Xavier. What is the clue ? Well, we must thank the fire for its existence. The finger-smudge on the card, caused by the universal soot."

" The smudge," muttered Xavier.

" Precisely. Now how was the smudge placed ? How had the murderer torn the card ? How does any one tear a card ? Well, you demonstrated one of the two methods a moment ago, Mr. Xavier ; I've been doing it for hours now, and I think we may say that in tearing a card in half one of two methods is used. The more common method is to place the tips of the thumbs together on the edge to be torn, so that the thumb-tips meet and the thumbs are at an acute angle to each other ; the other fingers are on the other side of the card. Now we tear—with our thumbs fortunately sooty. What happens ? The pressure of the thumbs in tearing—or rather of one thumb in holding the card firm and the other in exerting the pull or push—leaves oval thumb-marks : one in the upper right-hand corner of the left half, which is to say the print of the left thumb ; the other in the upper left-hand corner of the right half, which is to say the print of the right thumb. In designating right and left I am imagining, of course, that I am holding the card squarely before me and that what I call the left half of the card is on *my* left, you see." He puffed thoughtfully for a moment. " The other method is virtually the same as the first, except that the thumbs at the top of the card point diagonally *downward* toward each other, rather than diagonally upward. The oval thumbmarks remain in the same corners I have just described, except of course that they point down toward each other, not up. In any event, the effect—the effect I am about to describe—is substantially the same. What have we ? "

They were hanging intently on every word.

"Well," drawled Ellery, "let's re-examine the crumpled half found on the floor of Dr. Xavier's study. Let's smooth it out, turn it around so that the thumb-print is at the top. Why at the top? Because every one tears from the top down, not from the bottom up. That's why I said the second method doesn't substantially differ in effect from the first. The thumbprint, despite the difference in angle, is still relatively in the same corner of the card, and it's the thumbprint of the same hand. Now, holding the smoothed piece in the position it must have taken when the card was torn, what do we see?" He puffed again. "That the torn edge of the card is on the *right*, that the thumbprint is pointing diagonally upwards toward the upper *right-hand* corner or, to express it in other words, that it was the *left* thumb which left its smudge there, and consequently the left hand which held that torn and crumpled half of the card!"

"You mean," whispered Miss Forrest, "that a left-handed person——"

"You're sharp, Miss Forrest," smiled Ellery. "That's exactly what I do mean. The murderer's left hand had held that half. The murderer, then, had crumpled that half in his left hand and thrown it away with his left hand. The left hand, then, *did all the work. Ergo,* as you say, the murderer of Dr. Xavier and the framer of Mrs. Xavier was left-handed." He paused briefly to study their puzzled faces. "The problem resolved itself, therefore, into discovering which of you ladies and gentlemen, if any, was left-handed." The puzzlement vanished, to be replaced by alarm. "That was the purpose of our slightly grotesque tests to-night."

"A trick," said Dr. Holmes indignantly.

"But an extremely essential one, Doctor. As a matter of fact, it was not so much a test to acquire knowledge as a little research into the psychology of guilt. I knew before we conducted the tests who was right-handed and who was not, purely from recollected observations. I knew, too, from the same source that none of you is ambidextrous. Now there were three people whom we've neglected to test to-night : Mrs. Xavier and the Carreau boys." The twins started. " But Mrs. Xavier, aside from the fact that she was framed and would scarcely have framed herself, is also right-handed, as I've had occasion to note many times. As for the twins, preposterous as even the theoretical notion of their guilt is, Francis on the right is naturally right-handed, as I've also observed ; and Julian on the left, who is left-handed, has his left arm broken and in a cast, making digital manipulation impossible. And," he added dryly, " since I'm thorough in all things, I've proved to my own satisfaction that the only way the lads could have achieved the effect of those thumbprints under the circumstances would have been by crossing their adjoining hands and tearing—a procedure so pointless that it need not be considered. . . . Well, now ! " His eyes glittered. " Who among the rest of you is left-handed ? Do you recall what you did to-night, all of you ? "

They stirred uneasily, biting their lips, frowning.

" I'll tell you what you did," continued Ellery softly. " Miss Forrest, you picked up the revolver and attempted to discharge it with your right hand. Mr. Smith, you held the revolver in your left hand but polished it clean with your right. Dr. Holmes, you conducted your mock-examination of my theoretically dead body, I am happy to report, with your right hand almost exclusively. Mrs. Wheary, you snapped the switch with your right hand, and you, Bones, struck a match with your right hand. Mrs. Carreau held the deck of cards in her left hand and dealt with the right——"

" Hold up," grunted the Inspector, coming forward

again. "We've got just what we want now. I might explain that Mr. Queen conducted these experiments for my benefit, to prove who was right-handed and who wasn't. I hadn't noticed before." He produced a pencil and paper from one of his pockets and suddenly slapped them down upon the bridge-table before the astonished lawyer. "Here, Xavier, I want you to act as our recording secretary. This is a little memorandum to the Sheriff of Osquewa, Winslowe Reid—if and when he gets here." He continued irritably without pausing : "Come, come, man, don't sit there dreaming. Write, will you ? "

It was all so neat and smooth and noiselessly efficient. The whole psychological effect had been calculated to the last nice detail. The irritability of the Inspector, impersonally directed at his head, caused Xavier to snatch up the pencil, his lips working, and poise it above the sheet.

"Write this now," growled the Inspector, pacing up and down. " ' My brother, Dr. John S. Xavier——' " the lawyer wrote quickly, with brutal jabs of the pencil, his face pale as death, " ' murdered in his study on the ground floor of *Arrow Head*, his residence situated on Arrow Mountain in Tuckesas County, fifteen miles from the nearest seat of jurisdiction, Osquewa, met his death by shooting at the hand of——' " the Inspector paused, and the pencil in Mark Xavier's left hand trembled, " ' at the hand of *myself !* ' Now sign your name, damn you ! "

For a suspended moment, an interval without duration, there was utter silence. They sat forward in their chairs bleakly, without movement, struck dumb.

The pencil dropped from Xavier's fingers and his shoulders humped with an instinctive defensive contraction of his muscles. His blood-shot eyes were glassy. Then before any of them could stir he was out of the chair, a co-ordinated organism of terrified nerves and unmanned flesh. The table turned over as he leaped. He bounded the few steps to the French window nearest the table and crashed out upon the terrace.

The Inspector woke up. " Stop ! " he shouted. " Stop, I tell you ! Or I'll stop you with a bullet ! "

But Xavier did not stop. He scrambled over the terrace rail, landing with a crunching thud on the gravel below. His figure began to fade out as he receded farther from the light shining from the game-room.

They rose in unison, without moving from their places, and craned out into the darkness, mesmerised. Ellery stood very still, cigarette checked an inch before his lips.

The Inspector uttered a curious sigh, reached into his hip pocket, drew out his service revolver, snapped the safety-catch off, leaned against the side of one of the tall windows, aimed at the ghostly dodging figure, and deliberately fired.

CHAPTER XIV

CHEATER CHEATED

THEY WERE all to carry the ghastly memory of that fantastic scene for the remainder of their lives. Themselves turned to stone, the grey little old gentleman leaning against the window, revolver incredibly in hand, the snort of flame and smoke, the crashing report, the staggering of the almost invisible man running for cover . . . and then his single scream, sharp and unpleasant as a harpy's, ending in a thick bubbling gurgle as abruptly as it had begun.

Xavier vanished.

The Inspector adjusted the safety-catch, stowed the weapon in his hip pocket, brushed his lips with the same deadly hand in a queer gesture, and then trotted out on to the terrace. He clambered over the rail and with difficulty lowered himself to the ground below.

Ellery awoke, then, and darted out of the room. He vaulted the terrace rail and sped past his father into the darkness.

Their movement broke the spell. In the game-room Mrs. Carreau swayed and steadied herself on Francis's shoulder. Miss Forrest, wholly colourless, uttered a choked little cry and sprang forward at the same time that Dr. Holmes, with a gasp, urged his leaden legs toward the window. Mrs. Xavier sank into her chair, her nostrils fluttering. The twins remained rooted to the floor, stricken.

They found the crumpled figure of Xavier on the rocks outside, prone and still. Ellery was on his knees, feeling for the man's heart.

" Is he—is he——? " panted Miss Forrest, stumbling up.

Ellery looked up at his father, who was staring down. " He's still alive," he said tonelessly, " and there's blood on the tips of my fingers." Then he got slowly to his feet and examined his hands in the quarter-light.

" Take care of him, Doc," said the Inspector quietly.

Dr. Holmes was on his knees, fingers probing. He looked up almost at once. " Can't do anything here. You must have touched his back, Queen, because that's where he's wounded. He's still conscious, I think. Help me, please, quickly."

The man on the ground groaned once and from his lips came another bubbling gurgle. His limbs twitched spasmodically. The three men raised him gently and carried him up the steps of the porch, across the terrace and into the game-room. Miss Forrest followed hastily, with one sick glance over her shoulder into the darkness.

In silence they deposited the wounded man on a sofa near the piano, face down. In the full light of the room his broad back became the focal point of their eyes. A little to the right below the shoulder-blade there was a dark round hole raggedly circled by a dark red stain.

His eyes on the stain, Dr. Holmes was stripping his coat off. As he rolled up his sleeves he murmured : " Mr. Queen. My surgical kit on one of the tables in the laboratory. Mrs. Wheary, a large pan of hot water at once, please. The ladies had better go away."

" I can help," said Miss Forrest swiftly. " I've been a nurse—Doctor."

" Very well. The others please go. Inspector, have you a knife ? "

Mrs. Wheary blundered from the room and Ellery went out of the doorway leading into the cross-hall, opened the corridor door to the laboratory, stumbled about until he found the switch, and immediately saw upon one of the laboratory tables a small black bag with the initials *P. H.* lettered upon it. He avoided looking in the direction of the refrigerator. Snatching up the bag he ran back to the game-room.

None of them had moved, despite Dr. Holmes's admonition. They seemed fascinated by the physician's deft fingers, the low groans of Xavier. Dr. Holmes was ripping the lawyer's coat up the back with the keen blade of the Inspector's pen-knife. When he had severed the coat he slit the wounded man's shirt and undershirt, revealing the naked bullet-hole.

Ellery, stonily watching Xavier's face, saw his left cheek twitch. There was a bloody foam on his lips and his eyes were only half-closed.

Dr. Holmes opened his bag as Mrs. Wheary stumbled in with a huge pan of steaming water. Ann Forrest took this from the old lady's shaking hands and deposited it upon the floor near the physician's kneeling figure. He ripped a large piece of absorbent cotton from a roll, dipped it into the water. . . .

The eyes opened full suddenly and glared without seeing anything. Twice the jaws worked soundlessly, and then they heard him gasp : " I didn't do it. I didn't do it. I didn't do it," over and over and over, as if it were a lesson he had learned which must be repeated endlessly in some dim schoolroom of his imagination.

The Inspector started. He leaned over Dr. Holmes and said in a whisper : " How bad is he ? "

" Bad enough," replied Dr. Holmes shortly. " Looks like the right lung." He was bathing the wound quickly but gently, wiping the blood away. A strong odour of disinfectant rose.

" Can we—talk to him ? "

" Ordinarily, I should say no. What he needs is absolute quiet. But in this case——" The Englishman shrugged his slim shoulders without pausing in his work.

Hastily the Inspector went to the head of the sofa and dropped to his knees in front of Xavier's white face. The lawyer was still mumbling : " I didn't do it, I didn't do it," with a sort of dull persistence.

" Xavier," said the Inspector urgently. " Can you hear me ? "

The slurred syllables stopped and the head jerked. His eyes shifted ever so little to focus upon the Inspector's face. Intelligence came into them and a swift spasmodic pain. He whispered : " Why did you—shoot me, Inspector ? I didn't do it. I didn't——"

" Why did you run ? "

" Lost my—head. I thought—— Went to pieces. Stupid. . . . I didn't do it, I didn't ! "

Ellery's fingertips cut into his palms tightly. He bent forward and said sharply : " You're a very sick man, Xavier. Why lie now ? We know you did. You're the only left-handed person in the house who could possibly have torn that six of spades as it was torn."

Xavier's lips trembled. " I didn't—do it, I tell you."

" You tore that six of spades and put it into your brother's dead hand to frame your sister-in-law ! "

" Yes . . ." gasped Xavier. " That's—true. I did. I framed her. I wanted—but——"

Mrs. Xavier rose slowly, horror in her eyes. She put her hand to her mouth and kept it there, staring at her brother-in-law as if she were seeing him for the first time.

Dr. Holmes was working quickly now, with the silent assistance of white-lipped Miss Forrest. The cleansed wound kept oozing blood. The pan of water was crimson

Ellery's eyes were mere slits ; his own lips were working and there was the oddest expression on his face. " Well, then——" he said slowly.

" You don't understand," panted Xavier. " I couldn't sleep that night. I tossed around. There was a book

I wanted in the library downstairs. . . . What's—that pain in my back?"

"Go on, Xavier. You're being fixed up. Go on!"

"I—put my dressing-gown on and went down to the——"

"What time was this?" demanded the Inspector.

"Two-thirty. . . . I saw light from the study when I got to the library. The door was closed but the cracks —I went in, found John—cold, stiff, dead. . . . So—so I framed her, I framed her——"

"Why?"

He tossed about, writhing. "But I didn't do it, I didn't kill John. He was dead when I got there, I tell you, sitting at the desk, dead as a stone——"

There was a dressing on the wound now, and Dr. Holmes was filling a hypodermic.

"You're lying," rasped the Inspector.

"I'm telling God's own truth! He was dead—when I got there. . . . I didn't kill him." His head lifted an inch, the cords of his neck white and ropy. "But—I know now who—did. I know who—did. . . ."

"You do?" roared the Inspector. "How do you know? Who was it? Speak up, man!"

There was a rich stillness in the room. It was as if all breathing had ceased and time had stopped flowing and they stood suspended in the vast dark reaches of interstellar space.

Mark Xavier tried very hard. He made a superhuman effort. It was sickening to watch him try. His left arm bulged with the strain of raising himself. The red glare in his eyes became redder, hotter, wilder.

Dr. Holmes gripped the skin of Xavier's naked left arm, hypodermic poised—an impersonal automaton.

"I——" It was the sole result of his effort. His white face went grey, a bubble of blood materialised between his lips, and he sank back unconscious.

The needle bit into his arm.

Then they breathed and stirred again, and the Inspector struggled to his feet and stood wiping his moist cheeks with his handkerchief.

" Gone ? " said Ellery, licking his lips.

" No." Dr. Holmes had risen, too, and was gazing moodily down upon the still figure. " Just out. I've given him morphine. Just enough to relax his muscles and keep him quiet."

" How bad is he ? " asked the Inspector huskily.

" Dangerous. I should say he has a chance. It's all a matter of his condition. The bullet is lodged in his right lung——"

" Didn't you get it out ? " cried Ellery, appalled.

" Probe for it ? " The physician raised an eyebrow. " My dear chap. That would be almost certainly fatal. As I say, his chances depend upon his condition. Offhand I should say his condition is none too good, although I've never given him a physical examination. He's a rather greedy toper, you know, and he runs a little to flesh. Seedy. Well ! " He shrugged and turned to Miss Forrest, his expression softening. " Thank you—Ann. You were very helpful. . . . And now, gentlemen, please help me get him upstairs. Be very careful. We don't want to induce hemorrhage."

The four men—Smith stood stupefied in a corner—raised the limp body and bore it upstairs to the bedroom in the western corner of the house overlooking the drive. The others trooped behind, huddled together as if for protection. No one seemed to relish being left alone. Mrs. Xavier was dazed ; the horror had not left her eyes.

The men undressed him and got him after delicate work into his bed. Xavier was breathing hoarsely now, but he no longer twitched and his eyes were closed.

Then the Inspector opened the door. " Come on in

and don't make any noise. I've got something to say and I want all of you to hear it."

They obeyed mechanically, their eyes drawn to the quiet figure beneath the sheet. A lamp on a night-table beside the bed shed a glow over Xavier's left cheek and the contour of his left side under the bedclothes.

"We seem," said the Inspector quietly, "to have pulled another boner. I'm not sure yet, and I haven't really made up my mind whether Mark Xavier was lying or not. I've seen men lie three seconds before they passed out. There's no assurance that because a man knows he's dying he's going to tell the truth. At the same time there was something—well, convincing in what he said. If he merely framed Mrs. Xavier and didn't kill Dr. Xavier, then there's still a murderer on the loose in the house. And I want to tell you," his eyes glittered, "that the next time there *won't* be any mistake!"

They continued to stare.

Ellery snapped : "Do you think he'll regain consciousness, Doctor ? "

"Possible," murmured Dr. Holmes. "When the effects of the morphine have passed off, he may come out of it without warning." He shrugged. "Or he may not. There are all sorts of considerations. As to death, as well. He may get a hemorrhage after several hours, or he may linger and contract an infection—although I've cleansed and disinfected the wound—or succumb to disease."

"Pleasant," grunted Ellery. "Aside from that, he has a chance, eh ? But what I'm interested in is the fact that he'll probably regain consciousness. When he does——" He glanced significantly about.

"He'll *tell*," cried the twins suddenly and then, abashed by the sound of their own voices, shrank back against their mother.

"Yes, my lads, he'll tell. A most intriguing prospect.

Consequently I think, dad, that it would be best to leave nothing to chance."

" I was just thinking that myself," replied the Inspector grimly. " We'll take turns watching him to-night—you and I. And," he added after a pause, " no one else." He turned sharply to Dr. Holmes. " I'll take the first watch, Doctor, until two a.m., and then Mr. Queen will relieve me until morning. If we should want you——"

" At the first sign of returning consciousness," said Dr. Holmes stiffly, " notify me at once. At once, please ; every second may be important. My room is at the other end of the corridor, you know, next to yours. There's nothing you can do for him, really, now."

" Except protect whatever life he's got left in him."

" We'll notify you," said Ellery. He eyed the others for a moment and added : " For the benefit of anyone who may be contemplating desperate measures, I should like to announce that the man on watch beside this bed to-night will be armed with the same weapon which brought poor Xavier down. . . . That's all."

.   .   .   .

When they were alone with the unconscious man the Queens felt a curious restraint. The Inspector sat down in a comfortable bedroom chair and loosened his collar, becoming very busy doing nothing of consequence. Ellery smoked gloomily by one of the windows.

" Well," he said at last, " this is a fine mess we're in." The Inspector grunted. " Old Dead-Eye Dick himself," continued Ellery bitterly. " Poor chap ! "

" What *are* you talking about ? " grumbled the Inspector uneasily.

" Your propensity for quick, straight, and thoughtless shooting, esteemed sire. It really wasn't necessary, you know. He couldn't have escaped."

The Inspector looked uncomfortable. " Well," he muttered, " maybe not, but when a man's charged with murder and promptly takes a run-out powder, what the devil is a poor dumb cop to think ? That's as good as a confession. Naturally I warned him, and then took a potshot at him——"

" Oh, you're very good at that," said Ellery dryly. " The heavy years haven't impaired your eagle's eye and your marksmanship in the slightest. But still it was a reckless and unwarranted thing to do."

" Well, suppose it was ! " exploded the Inspector, red with exasperation. " It's as much your fault as mine. You led me to believe——"

" Oh, hell, dad, I'm sorry," said Ellery contritely. The old gentleman sank back, mollified. " You're quite right. As a matter of fact, it was more my fault than yours. I assumed—damn my cocksureness !—that because someone had framed Mrs. Xavier for her husband's murder that that someone must have been the murderer. Of course, on inspection, that's a wholly unwarranted assumption. Yes, it's rather far-fetched, but then fantastic facts are no excuse for fantastic logic."

" Maybe he did lie——"

" I'm sure he didn't." Ellery sighed. " But there I go again. I'm not sure. I can't be sure. Of that or anything. This affair hasn't found me precisely shining. . . . Well ! Keep a sharp eye out. I'll be back at two."

" Don't worry about me." The Inspector glanced at the wounded man. " In a way, this is a sort of penance. If he doesn't come out of this I guess . . ."

" If he or you or anyone," said Ellery cryptically, his hand on the door-knob.

" Now what do you mean by *that* ? " muttered the Inspector.

" Take a peep outside through that lovely window," said Ellery dryly, and left the room.

The Inspector stared at him, rose, and went to the window. He sighed at once. The sky above the tree-tops was a ruddy dark glow. He had quite forgotten the fire in the excitement of the evening.

.   .   .   .

The Inspector turned the shade of the lamp on the night-table to direct more light upon the wounded lawyer. He gazed gloomily down upon the parchment of Xavier's skin and then with another sigh returned to his armchair. He shifted it so that by merely a half-turn of his head he could see both the single door and the man on the bed. After a moment he thought of something, made a wry face, and took his service revolver from his hip pocket. He looked at it soberly for a moment and placed it in the right-hand pocket of his jacket.

He slumped back in the chair in the half-light and folded his hands on his flat stomach.

For more than an hour there were intermittent sounds —doors closing, people walking up the corridor, the murmur of low voices. Then silence, gradually, in a subsidence of dull familiar noises, which soon became so complete that the Inspector might have fancied himself a thousand miles from the nearest conscious human being.

He lay in the chair, relaxed, but alert as he had never been in his life. He realised with the penetration of a life-time's study of human desperation where the danger lay. A man was dying, and in the power of that feeble tongue lay the danger. No measure, no matter how rash, would be too much for a murderer. . . . He half-wished, as he sat there, that he might have the freedom now to steal into all those darkened rooms about him and surprise someone still awake, or crouching in the gloom. But he would not leave the dying man for an instant. A sudden qualm made him tighten his grip on the weapon in his pocket ; then he rose and went to the windows. But access to the bedroom was impossible from that source. Reassured, he returned to his chair.

Time dragged. Nothing changed. The man on the bed lay still.

Once, long after, the little grey man thought he detected a sound from the corridor outside. It was almost, he thought as he sat up tingling in every fibre, as if someone had closed or opened a door. With the thought he sprang noiselessly from the chair, switched off the lamp on the night-table, and in the darkness sped to the door. Revolver in hand, he turned the knob without sound, pulled quickly, leaped aside, and waited.

Nothing happened.

He closed the door softly, switched on the lamp again, and returned to his chair. He was not particularly surprised. Even trained nerves were prone to jangle in the black reaches of the night. The sound had probably existed only in his imagination, an echo of his own fears.

Nevertheless, because he was a practical man in all things, he did not put the revolver back into his pocket. Instead, he let it lie loosely in his lap, ready to be snatched up the split-second after an alarm.

The night deepened without further sound or incident. His lids began to feel monstrously heavy and from time to time he shook himself awake. It was less hot now than it had been, but it was still stifling enough and his clothes stuck miserably to his body. . . . He wondered what the hour was and dragged out his heavy gold watch.

It was twelve-thirty. He put the watch away, sighing.

Almost precisely at one—he consulted his watch again the instant after it occurred—his nerves were tingling again. But this time not from real or fancied sounds outside. This sound came from the bed a few feet away. It emanated from the dying man.

Jamming his watch back, the Inspector jumped up and bounded across the rug to the bed. Xavier's left arm was stirring, and the sound was the thick burble he had heard hours before downstairs. There was even a movement of the head. The burble rose in volume, ending in a raucous cough. The Inspector thought the whole house must be aroused, it ripped out so harshly and loudly. He bent over Xavier, whose face was turned away from the light, and gently tugged until he worked his right arm under the man's neck. With his left arm he managed to turn Xavier over without permitting the wounded back to touch the bed ; so that finally, when he straightened, the recumbent figure lay on its left side, face to the light. The eyes were still closed, although the sounds continued.

Xavier was slowly regaining consciousness.

The Inspector hesitated. Should he wait, make the man talk ? Then he remembered Dr. Holmes's admonition, and the thought that delay might well deal the wounded man his death-blow made him hurry to the chair, snatch up the revolver, and run to the door. He could not leave Xavier alone even for an instant, he thought quickly. No one was going to take advantage of him while he slipped out to summon the doctor. He would open the door, stick out his head, and yell for Holmes. If the others wakened, the hell with them.

He grasped the knob, turned it noisily, and pulled the door open. He thrust out his head and opened his mouth.

.   .   .   .

To Ellery it seemed that he was struggling upward along the black glassy side of an animate abyss, striving to keep from slipping back to the cauldron of fire raging below. He battered his hands and bruised his fingers on the hard smooth jeering walls, and in his head was an inferno that matched the bl~ze in intensity. His head began to puff, to swell, to burst. He was sliding, sliding. . . . He awoke with a start, bathed in cold perspiration.

The room was dark and he fumbled on the night-table for his wrist-watch. By its luminous dial he saw that it was five minutes past two. He crept groaning out of bed, his body an aching mess of damp flesh and protesting muscles, and groped for his clothes.

The house was very still as he slipped out of his room and made his way up the corridor. The landing bulb was burning and to his blinking eyes everything seemed normal. All doors were shut.

He reached the end of the corridor and paused outside Xavier's room. He had made no noise walking, the door was shut, and there was no reason to suppose that any-one, including his father, had heard him. The thought filled him with a sudden surge of alarm. Lord, what applied to him might very well have applied to some-one else ! Suppose the old gentleman . . .

But the old gentleman, as he knew from varied and pleasant experience, was quite capable of taking care of himself. And then there was the revolver, which already had——

Shaking aside his fears as childish, he opened the door and said softly : " El, dad. Don't be alarmed." There was no response. He pushed the door farther and then froze to the spot, his heart stopping.

The Inspector lay on the floor near the door, face down, the revolver a few inches from his motionless hand.

Dazedly he shifted his gaze to the bed. The drawer of the night-table before it was open. Mark Xavier's right hand dangled to the floor, clutching something. His body lay half out of the bed, head hanging horribly. What Ellery could see of the face sickened him— twisted features contorted by impossible pain, the lips curled wolfishly back in a grin to expose the teeth and oddly bluish gums.

The man was dead.

But he had not died of the festering bullet in his lung. Ellery divined that even before he glimpsed the evidence. The tortured face, as if Xavier had died in exquisite agony ; significant. And significant, too, the empty vial that lay on the rug some feet from the bed, dropped there by a defiant hand.

Mark Xavier had been murdered.

PART IV

" I felt as if I was going crazy. Just plain crazy. I sat there and they stood over me and nobody said anything and all the while that damned bloody shirt lay there with the light on it and I could see his face even though he was a stiff in the Morgue. So I came through. I couldn't stand it. I felt as if I was going crazy. I confessed."—A. F.'s Statement to the Press While Awaiting Execution at Sing Sing Prison, November 21, 19—.

CHAPTER XV

THE RING

How long Ellery stood there he never knew. His brain was racing madly, but his muscles refused to respond and his heart had turned to granite in his breast.

It was so much like the nightmare, he thought, a continuation of the horrid dream he had been having. Perhaps he was still dreaming. . . . After the first lightning scrutiny of the man on the bed his head had wrenched about and he had fastened his gaze upon the supine figure of his father. Dead. . . . His father was dead. His brain reeled before the enormity of the fact. His father was dead. The shrewd grey eyes would never twinkle again. Those thin nostrils would never more flare in anger. That old throat would never mutter and growl at petty annoyances, nor chuckle with sly humour. Those tireless little legs . . . His father was dead.

Then he experienced a vast impersonal surprise. Something wet was trickling down his cheeks. He was crying ! Anger at himself made him shake his head violently, and suddenly he felt life and hope and strength flood warmly back into his blood. His muscles relaxed. But this time only to tense again for a spring forward.

He flung himself on his knees beside the Inspector and tore at the old man's collar. There was a waxy paleness on his father's face and he was breathing stertorously. Breathing ! Then he was alive !

He shook the thin small body with glad insistent hands, crying : " Dad, wake up ! Dad, it's El ! " and smiling and panting and weeping like a demented man.

But the Inspector's grey bird-like little head only wabbled a little and his eyes remained closed.

Panic-stricken again, Ellery slapped the old man's cheeks, pinched his arm, pounded and pummelled him. . . . And then he stopped, sniffing and raising his head. The shock had dulled his physical faculties. He realised acutely now what subconsciously he had known from his first step into the room. There was a cloying odour in the place. Yes, now that he bent closer to his father's lips, it was stronger. . . . The Inspector had been chloroformed.

Chloroformed ! Then he had been taken off his guard, a murderer had beaten down his defences and—committed murder again.

With the thought came calmness and a dogged resolve. He saw with bitter clarity where he had gone wrong, how essentially blind he had been. Led blandly along by his own self-assurance, he now realised that the trail, far from ending, had merely come to a bend, with a long misty prospect beyond. But this time, he told himself with gritted teeth, it would be different. The murderer's hand had been forced. This had been not a crime of will or whim but of necessity. It had drawn the criminal against his will into the open. The corpse on the bed, what he had quickly seen in that first second's flash . . .

He stooped, lifted the light figure of his father in his arms, and carried him to the armchair. Depositing him gently there, Ellery opened the old man's shirt and shifted his body into a comfortable position. He felt beneath the shirt and nodded at the steady pound of the old man's heart against his palm. The Inspector would be all right—just a matter of sleeping it off.

Ellery rose and went to the bed, eyes narrowed. What was to be seen he meant to see at once, before anyone else should come upon the scene.

The dead man was an unsavoury sight. His chin and breast were covered with a thick greenish-brown semi-liquid, evil-smelling and nauseating. Ellery's eyes strayed to the vial on the floor and he went over and picked it up carefully. A few drops of a whitish liquid remained at the bottom. He sniffed the mouth of the vial and then with desperate decision tipped it so that a drop fell on his finger. Instantly he wiped this off and touched his tongue to the spot where the drop had fallen. He was rewarded with a quick fire on his tongue and a disagreeable sour taste. His finger tingled. A little sick, he spat into his handkerchief. The stuff was poison, undoubtedly.

He placed the vial on the night-table and dropped to his knees beside the hanging head of the dead man. A swift glance into the open drawer of the table and the floor about the dead man's right hand had told him the incredible story. The drawer was cluttered with much the same assortment of games that occupied Ellery's own night-table drawer, but the customary deck of cards was gone. They now lay scattered on the floor beside the bed.

And the object that Mark Xavier's dead hand clutched so tightly was one of them.

Ellery removed it from the rigid fingers with difficulty. He shook his head at what he saw. He had been wrong. It was not a card ; it was *half* a card. His glance went to the floor and he soon picked out the other half lying on top of the rest of the strewn paste-boards.

That Mark Xavier should have torn a card in two was not remarkable, he reflected quickly, considering the fact that his dead brother had shortly before set the precedent. Nor was it remarkable that the card Xavier tore was not a six of spades ; for *that* bubble, he thought, had been for ever pricked.

What did pique him was that the card was a knave of diamonds.

.   .   .   .

Now why, he said fretfully, to himself, a knave of diamonds? Of all the fifty-two cards in the deck?

The fact that the torn half was in Xavier's right hand had no helpful significance. It was where it should have been. Left-handed, the poisoned lawyer in his last moments of consciousness had reached out to the table, pulled open the drawer, fumbled until he found the deck, opened it, picked out the knave of diamonds, dropped the rest of the deck on the floor, held the card in both hands, torn it with the left, thrown away one half with the left, and died with the other half clutched in his right hand.

Ellery rooted about among the fallen pasteboards. The six of spades was there, an innocent member of the ensemble.

He rose, frowning, and picked up the vial again. Holding it close to his mouth by the lip, he breathed hard upon the glass, turning the vial around as he did so to cover the surface with his condensed breath. No marks of fingerprints appeared. The murderer, as before, had been careful.

He set the vial down on the table and went out of the room.

.   .   .   .

The corridor was empty as before, and all the doors shut.

Ellery strode down the length of the hall to the last door on his right, listened for a moment with his ear close to the panels, heard nothing, and went in. The room was dark. He heard now a man's soft breathing across the room.

He groped for the bed, found it, felt about, and then

shook the sleeper's arm gently. The arm stiffened and he felt the man's body jerk with alarm.

"It's all right, Dr. Holmes," said Ellery softly. "It's Queen."

"Oh!" The young physician yawned with relief. "Gave me something of a turn." He switched on the lamp on the table beside his bed. Then, when he caught sight of Ellery's expression, his jaw dropped. "Wh-what's the matter?" he gasped. "What's happened? Has Xavier——?"

"Please come at once, Doctor. There's work for you."

"But—who——?" began the Englishman vaguely, his blue eyes liquid with alarm. Then he jumped out of bed, draped a dressing-gown about his shoulders, slipped his feet into carpet-slippers, and followed Ellery without another word.

Ellery reached the door of Xavier's bedroom and stood back. He motioned Holmes to precede him. Holmes stopped short on the threshold, staring.

"Oh, good God," he said.

"Not so very good to Xavier," murmured Ellery. "Our cunning little playfellow with the homicidal tendencies has been at work again, you see. I wonder how dad—— Let's get inside, Doctor, before anyone hears us. I most particularly want your opinion in private."

Dr. Holmes stumbled across the sill and Ellery followed, shutting the door quietly behind him.

"Tell me what he died of, and when."

For the first time Dr. Holmes saw the still figure of the Inspector outstretched on the chair. His eyes widened with horror. "But, great heavens, man, your father! Did he—was he——?"

"Chloroform," said Ellery briefly. "I want you to bring him round as soon as you can."

"Well, then, what are you standing there for?" shouted the young man, his eyes blazing. "Get busy, can't you ? To hell with Xavier ! Open those windows wide—wide as you can get them ! ''

Ellery blinked and then sprang to obey. Dr. Holmes bent over the Inspector, listened to his heart, pulled up his eyelids, nodded, and bounded off to the adjoining lavatory. He returned in a moment with several towels soaked in cold water.

'' Get him as close to the windows as you can,'' he said more calmly. '' Fresh air is imperative—fresh as you can get it in this ghoulish place,'' he muttered aside. '' Quickly, man ! '' They picked the chair up between them and carried it close to the open windows. The physician bared the Inspector's chest and slapped the sopping towels on the smooth flesh. Another he applied to the relaxed face, like a barber's hot towel—curled all about the face but leaving the nostrils exposed.

'' He seemed all right,'' said Ellery anxiously. '' Don't tell me——''

'' No, no, there's nothing wrong with him. How old is he ? ''

'' Not quite sixty.''

'' Good health ? ''

'' Hard as nails.''

'' Then this won't hurt him. If we're to get him out of it we've got to adopt heroic measures. Get a couple of those pillows from the bed.''

Ellery brought the pillows, filched from the dead man, and stood waiting rather helplessly. '' What now ? ''

Dr. Holmes glanced briefly at the bed. '' Can't put him there. . . . Get hold of his legs. We'll stretch him across the arms of the chair. Head lower than the rest of the body.''

They raised the old man's body easily and turned him around. Dr. Holmes stuffed the big pillows under the Inspector's back. The old man's head hung over one arm.

" Legs as high as you can get them."

Ellery circled the chair and obeyed.

" Firmly now." The physician bent over the hanging head and grasped the old man's jaws. He squeezed until the mouth opened, and then he reached in and pulled out the Inspector's tongue. " There ! That's better. I could shoot him full of adrenalin, or strychnine, or some of that new stuff, alpha-lobeline, but I don't think it will be necessary. I think he'll come round with just a little assistance ; he's been under the influence for some time. Steady ! I'm going to try artificial respiration. With an oxygen tank. . . . Well, I haven't any handy, so—— Steady."

He bent over the Inspector's torso and set to work. Ellery watched stormily.

" How long will it take ? "

" Depends upon how much he's inhaled. Ah, that's good ! It won't be long now, Queen."

In five minutes a strangled moan came from the old man's throat. Dr. Holmes worked steadily on. A moment later he stopped and pulled away the face towel. The Inspector's eyes were opening dazedly, and he was licking his lips as if his mouth were dry.

" All right now," said Dr. Holmes almost cheerfully, standing up. " He's out of it. Well, Inspector, how do you feel ? "

The first word the Inspector said was : " Lousy."

．　　．　　．　　．　　．　　．　　．　　．

Three minutes later he was sitting in the armchair, face buried in his hands. Aside from a mild nausea, he felt no ill effects.

" What gets me," he muttered brokenly, " is how I was tricked. That makes me responsible for that man's death on two counts. Lord. . . . Fell for the oldest gag. I stuck my head out, neglecting to douse the light.

Naturally I was a perfect target for anyone skulking out in the dark hall. Whoever it was—was waiting for me. Knew that when I came out it could only be because Xavier was conscious and I was going for you, Doctor. So he—or she—or it, or whoever it was pressed a wet cloth over my nose and mouth and held one arm over my throat. Soaked in chloroform. I was so taken off my guard I didn't even have a chance to make a fight of it. I didn't go off right away but I got weak—dizzy—felt the gun drop, and then . . . ''

" No sense in looking for the saturated cloth," said Ellery quietly. " Whoever used it has disposed of it down a drain by this time, I suppose. Is there chloroform in the laboratory, Doctor ? "

" Naturally. Lucky you've been eating so lightly to-day, Inspector. On a full stomach——" The young man shook his head and turned to the bed.

The Queens watched without speaking. In the old man's eyes there was a sick horror. Ellery gripped his shoulder comfortingly.

" Hmm," murmured Dr. Holmes, eyeing the mess on the dead man's chin and the contorted features. " Poison, eh ? " He leaned over and sniffed at the partly open mouth. " Yes, indeed." He looked around, spied the vial on the table, and picked it up.

" I tasted it," said Ellery wearily. " It's sour, and it burned my tongue."

" Good lord ! " cried Holmes. " I hope you didn't take much of it. Why, this is a deadly corrosive poison. Oxalic acid dissolved in water ! "

" I was careful. I suppose that comes from the laboratory, too ? "

Dr. Holmes grunted assent and turned back to the corpse again. When he straightened up his eyes were thoughtful. " He's been dead about an hour. Mouth forced open and the oxalic poured down his throat.

You can see the marks on his cheeks and jaw where the fingers gripped him. Poor chap ! He died in horrible pain."

" He could have removed that deck of cards from the drawer, I suppose, and torn one of them in two after he was poisoned and his poisoner left ? "

" Yes. As for the murderer's certainty that death would follow, I might point out that oxalic's always fatal in one hour, sometimes a good deal less. His generally debilitated condition didn't help." Dr. Holmes eyed the cards on the floor curiously. " Another——— ? "

" Another."

The Inspector rose and stumbled to the bed.

. . . .

Ellery let himself out of the room and stood still in the corridor outside, taking stock. Someone in this house was lying on a bed of thorns, writhing under the necessity for waiting, waiting. He wondered if he had the temerity to break into each room without noise and flash a strong light suddenly upon the face of each sleeper. But the women. . . . He pursed his lips thoughtfully.

The door opposite the spot where he stood led, he knew, to Ann Forrest's room. He marvelled silently at the apparent fact that the young woman had heard nothing of the attack upon the Inspector, the murderer's movements and departure, and all the swishing events that had ensued. He hesitated, then crossed quickly and pressed his right ear against the door. He could hear nothing. So he gripped the knob slowly and slowly turned it until it would turn no more. Then he pushed. To his astonishment, the door held. Miss Forrest had locked herself in !

" Now why the devil did she do that ? " he thought as he tiptoed down the corridor toward the next door.

" Obviously, for protection. From what ? The invisible hand of death ? " He chuckled to himself. " How dat ol' debil Night breeds drama ! Did she have a presentiment ? Did she lock the door from reasons of general caution ? *Tsk !* I haven't paid half enough attention to Miss Forrest."

The room next to the young woman's was occupied by the Carreau twins. They, at least, were coerced by no unhealthy fears. The door gave readily to his touch and he stole in and listened. Their rhythmic breathing was reassuring. He stole out again and crossed the hall.

Directly opposite the door to the twins' room was the door to the room to which Mrs. Wheary had assigned the gigantic fat gentleman named Smith. Ellery did not hesitate. He went in noiselessly, crept about until his fingers found the light-switch on the wall near the door, riveted his eyes upon the spot in the darkness from which came an elephantine snorting, and then snapped the switch. The room sprang into being, revealing the mountainous figure of Smith sprawled on the bed, pyjama-coat unbuttoned and rolls of pink unhealthy-looking flesh rising and falling with the tempestuous tide of his breathing.

The man's eyes opened instantly, frightened and yet wary. He flung up his arm more quickly than Ellery would have believed possible in a man of his ponderous size, as if he half expected a blow, a shot, something menacing and lethal.

" It's Queen," murmured Ellery, and the big fat arm dropped. Smith's froggy eyes blinked in the light. " Just an amiable visit, my friend. Been sleeping soundly ? "

" Huh ? " The man stared stupidly.

" Come, come, rub the sleep out of your eyes and rise from the—ah—groaning pallet of your dreams." Ellery

took in the details of the room ; he had never been inside
it before. No, there was only one other door, open, as
in Xavier's room ; and that led, as he could see, to the
usual lavatory.

" What's the big idea ? " croaked Smith, sitting up.
" What's happened ? "

" Another comrade has gone to join his Maker,"
replied Ellery gravely. " The slaughter, you see, has
become epidemic."

The huge jaw dropped. " S-somebody else been
m-m-mur——"

" Friend Xavier." Ellery put his hand on the door-
knob. " Get into a dressing-gown and go next door.
You'll find the Inspector and Dr. Holmes there. See
you later."

He ducked out quickly, leaving the fat man to gape
after him with tardily dawning horror.

Ellery recrossed the hall, ignoring the door next to
Smith's. That led, he knew, to an unoccupied room.
He tried the door of Mrs. Carreau's chamber. It gave
way and, after a moment of indecision, he shrugged
and stepped inside.

Immediately he knew he had made a mistake. No
rhythmic breathing here ; no breathing at all. Odd !
Was it possible the gentlewoman from Washington was
absent from her bed at three in the morning ? But the
realisation of error flashed over him even as his thoughts
eddied about the puzzle of her absence. She was not
absent. She was sitting there, sitting at the foot of a
chaise-longue, holding her breath, her eyes glowing in
the faintest of moonlight coming through the windows
off the balcony.

His foot kicked against a piece of furniture, and she
screamed . . . a shrill scream that raised the hair at the
base of his scalp and sent prickles of ice down his spine.

" Don't ! " he whispered, stepping forward. " Mrs.

Carreau ! It's Ellery Queen. For God's sake, stop that noise."

She had leaped from the *chaise-longue*. When he found the switch and turned it on, he saw her crouched with her back to the farthest wall, eyes lambent with terror, hands clutching the folds of her négligée to her.

Sanity returned to her eyes. She drew the négligée more closely about her slim figure. " What are you doing in my bedroom, Mr. Queen ? " she demanded.

Ellery blushed. " Ah—a very proper question. Can't say I blame you for screaming. . . . By the way, what are *you* doing up at this hour of the morning ? "

She compressed her lips. " I don't see, Mr. Queen . . . It was so stifling, and I couldn't sleep. But you still haven't——"

Ellery, feeling like a fool, frowned and turned to the door. " There ! I hear the others coming to your rescue. The point is, Mrs. Carreau, I came to tell you——"

" What's happened ? Who screamed ? " snapped the Inspector from the doorway. Then he stalked in, glaring from Ellery to Mrs. Carreau. The twins popped their heads in from the communicating door. Dr. Holmes and Miss Forrest, Smith, Mrs. Xavier, Bones, the house-keeper—all in various stages of undress—crowded in the corridor doorway, craning over the Inspector's shoulder.

Ellery dabbed his damp forehead and grinned weakly. " My fault entirely. I crept into Mrs. Carreau's room— with the most innocent intentions in the world, I assure you !—and very properly she took fright and let out that appalling feminine blast. I daresay she thought I was attempting to play lusty Tarquinius to her Lucretia."

The hostile glances directed at him made Ellery blush again, this time in anger.

" Mr. Queen," said Mrs. Xavier frigidly, " I must say this is the strangest conduct from a supposed gentle-man ! "

" Now, look here, all of you ! " cried Ellery, exasper-
ated. " You simply don't understand. Good lord ! I——"

Miss Forrest said quickly : " Of course. Let's not be
idiotic, Marie. . . . You're both dressed, both you and the
Inspector, Mr. Queen. What—what's the matter ? "

" Time," growled the Inspector. " As long as you're
all awake we might's well tell you. And let's not, as
Miss Forrest says, cover up all the important facts with
suspicions of my son's morals. He's foolish sometimes,
but not *that* foolish. Mr. Queen was coming to tell you,
Mrs. Carreau—when you screamed—that there's been
another attack."

" Attack ! "

" That's the ticket."

" A—a *murder* ? "

" Well, he's mighty dead."

Their heads moved slowly to changing inquisitorial
positions, searching one another's faces, tallying. . . .

" Mark," said Mrs. Xavier thickly.

" Yes, Mark." The Inspector stared grimly about.
" He was poisoned and put out of the way before he
could tell what he started out to tell earlier this evening.
I won't mention the little matter of my own part in the
affair, although you may be interested to learn that the
same scoundrel gave me a dose of chloroform. Yes,
Xavier's gone."

" Mark's dead," repeated Mrs. Xavier in the same
thick dull tones, and suddenly burying her face in her
hands she began to sob.

Mrs. Carreau, pale and stiff, stalked to the communicating door and put her arms about the shoulders
of her sons.

.   .   .   .

There was no sleep for any of them that night. They
all seemed reluctant to return to their bedrooms ; and

they remained huddled together with the gregarious instinct of frightened animals, starting at every night-sound.

With rather savage satisfaction Ellery insisted upon escorting them, one by one, into the dead man's bedroom for a view of the body. He watched them very closely. But if anyone was acting he could not detect the deception. They were merely a group of badly scared people. Mrs. Wheary fainted during her part of the performance and had to be revived with cold water and smelling salts. The twins, bewildered and very small boys now, were excused from participation in the test.

By the time it was over and the dead lawyer had been removed to share the refrigerator in the laboratory with his brother, an angry dawn was coming up.

The Queens stood in the death-room and looked gloomily at the tumbled empty bed.

" Well, son," said the Inspector with a sigh, " I guess we may as well give up. It's too much for me."

" It's because we're blind ! " cried Ellery, making a fist. " The evidence is all here. Xavier's clue. . . . Oh, hell, it just needs *thinking* over. And my head is spinning."

" One thing," said the old gentleman grumpily, " I s'pose we ought to be thankful for. He's the last. He wasn't mixed up in the direct motive behind his brother's kill, I'm sure. He was done in to keep him from spilling who the murderer is. Now how the deuce did he *know* ? "

Ellery started out of a brown study. " Yes, I suppose that's important. How he knew. . . . By the way, did you ever stop to speculate *why* Xavier framed his sister-in-law in the first place ? "

" So much has happened——"

" It's very simple. With John Xavier dead, Mrs. Xavier inherited. But Mrs. Xavier is the last of her line. No children. If anything happened to her, who'd get the estate ? "

" Xavier ! " exclaimed the Inspector, staring.

" Exactly. His frame-up was a clever means of getting her out of his way to a sizable fortune without soiling his own hands with blood."

" Well, I'll be damned." The Inspector shook his head. " And I thought——"

" What did you think ? "

" That there was something between those two." He frowned. " I couldn't see anyone but Mark Xavier as the reason why Mrs. Xavier should be willing to take the blame for a crime she knew she didn't commit. If she thought he did it, and she was desperately in love with him. . . . But that doesn't wash with his framing *her*."

" Such things have happened," said Ellery dryly. " I shouldn't discount it merely because it sounds wrong. Passionate women in love with their brothers-in-law can generally be counted upon to do unorthodox things. That female's half-cracked, anyway. But I'm not worried about that." He went to the night-table and picked up the torn half of the diamond knave which Xavier had held in his dead hand. " It's this little jigger that disturbs me. I can understand why Xavier should have thought of leaving a card-clue, even though there are pencil and paper in the same drawer from which he took the deck. . . ."

" There are ? "

" Certainly." Ellery waved a weary hand. " But he had a precedent. With his trained legal mind—he was sharp, don't doubt that—he saw his opportunity. You see, the name of the murderer was on his lips just before he lost consciousness. When he came to, it was still there, waiting. He remembered the cards. His mind was clear. Then the murderer came. Helpless, he was forced to swallow the oxalic acid from the vial. The cards were on his mind. . . . Oh, it's not the strangest thing that's happened."

" You don't like it," said the Inspector slowly.

" Eh ? Nonsense ! "

Ellery went to one of the windows and looked out upon the crimsoning world. The Inspector joined him in silence, putting his right hand on the window and resting his weight against it in a tired, dejected attitude.

" Fire's a damned sight worse," he muttered. " Cripes, my head's like a pumpkin ! It's always at the back of my mind. Feel that blast of heat ? . . . And then there's the crime—the crimes. What the devil *did* Xavier mean by that jack of diamonds ? "

Ellery half-turned away from the window, his shoulders sagging. Then he stiffened and his eyes went wide. He was glaring at the Inspector's hand on the window.

" What's the matter now ? " said the Inspector peevishly, glancing at his hand. Then he too stiffened, and for a moment both of them stared at his small delicate blue-veined hand with its loose and wrinkled skin quite as if a finger were missing.

" My ring ! " gasped the Inspector. " It's gone ! "

CHAPTER XVI

THE DIAMOND KNAVE

"Now that," said Ellery slowly, "*is* remarkable. When did you lose it?" Instinctively he glanced at his own hand, on which gleamed a very odd and beautiful ring, a mediæval trinket which he had picked up not long before in Firenze for a few *lire*.

"Lose it!" The Inspector threw up his hands. "I didn't lose it, El. I had it only last night, this morning. Why, I remember seeing it on my fourth finger about twelve-thirty, when I looked at my watch."

"Come to think of it," scowled Ellery, "I recall seeing it on your finger before I left you to take a nap last night, and I *didn't* see it when I found you on the floor at two." His lips tightened. "By thunder, it's been stolen!"

"Now there," said the Inspector sarcastically, "is a deduction. Sure it's been stolen. Stolen by that thieving scoundrel who put me to sleep and knocked Xavier off!"

"Undoubtedly. Hold those straining horses of yours." Ellery was pacing up and down now with furious strides. "I'm more fascinated by the theft of your ring than by anything that's happened so far. How risky! And all for what? For a ten-dollar plain gold wedding-band of the old-fashioned sinker variety that would fetch a dollar Mex at a pawnshop!"

"Well," said the Inspector shortly, "it's gone. And, by God, I'll have the eye teeth of the so-and-so who stole it. It belonged to your mother, my son, and I wouldn't have taken a thousand dollars for it." He started for the door.

" Here ! " cried Ellery, catching his arm. " Where are you going ? "

" To search every damn' one of 'em down to their skins ! "

" Nonsense, dad. Look here," said Ellery eagerly. " Don't spoil everything. I tell you that ring is a—is the *case* ! I don't know why, but when I recall the previous thefts of valueless rings . . ."

" Well ? " said the Inspector with drawn brows.

" It fits somehow. I know it does. But give me time. You won't accomplish anything by searching people and places. The thief certainly isn't stupid enough to have kept it on his person, and even if you turn it up in the house somewhere you won't know who hid it. Let it ride, please. For a while, anyway."

" Oh, very well. But I'm not forgetting it. And before we get out of this place—if we ever do—I'll have it or know the reason why." Had he been able to look into the near future he would not have spoken so confidently.

.   .   .   .

With the inexorable advance of the fire a deadly stillness settled down upon *Arrow Head* and its little band of helpless tenants. They were physically and mentally exhausted, and spiritually demoralised. Not even the menace of the bloodstained invisible creature in their midst could overshadow the greater menace that was creeping upon them from the air and the woods. There was no longer any attempt at dissimulation. The women were frankly hysterical and the men pale and worried. With the advance of day the heat became intolerable. The air was filled with drifting ashes which smudged their skins and clothes and made breathing a pain. There was no haven to which they could flee. The interior of the house was a shade less hot than the open summit, but here there was no breeze and the stillest of air. Yet few of them—the women especially—dared go alone to seek the temporary relief of the showers in their personal lavatories. They were afraid to be alone—afraid of one another, of the silence, of the fire.

Amiable conversation had died entirely. Driven to the group by their individual fears, nevertheless they sat and glared at one another with the most naked suspicion. Their nerves were stripped raw. The Inspector wrangled with Smith ; Miss Forrest snapped at Dr. Holmes, who lapsed into the most stubborn of silences ; Mrs. Xavier spoke sharply to the Carreau twins, who were haplessly wandering about ; Mrs. Carreau flew to their defence ; the two women had bitter words. . . . It was horrible and nightmarish. With the heavy smoke eddying about them ceaselessly now, they might have been creatures in torment consigned to an eternal hell by a particularly cynical Satan.

There was no longer any flour. They ate together, bitterly and without appetite, at the communal table in the dining-room, taking what nourishment they could from the eternal tinned fish. From time to time their eyes went to the Queens without hope. They all seemed to recognise, in their apathy, that if salvation was to come it would come at the hands of father and son. But the Queens ate stolidly, saying nothing for the excellent reason that there was nothing to say.

After luncheon they did not seem to know what to do. Magazines were picked up and riffled and glanced through with eyes that did not see ; people wandered about ; no one said anything at all. By reason of some curious development they seemed to be taking the murder of Mark Xavier more tragically than the murder of the master of the house. The tall lawyer had been a definite personality ; reticent, dour, frowning, his presence had always charged the atmosphere of a room with positive electricity ; and now that he was no longer among them they felt his absence so keenly that the silence was a pain.

And all the while they coughed, and their eyes smarted, and they sweltered in their clothes.

The Inspector could stand it no longer. " Now look here ! " he shouted suddenly, startling them into rigidity. " This can't keep on. We'll all go batty. Why don't you get along upstairs and duck under showers, or play tiddledywinks or something ? " He waved his arms, red of face. " Why don't you stop this milling about like a herd of cows with their tongues torn out ? Go on, all of you ! Git ! "

Dr. Holmes sucked a white knuckle. " The ladies are afraid, Inspector."

" Afraid ! Afraid of what ? "

" Well, of being alone."

" Hmm. There's somebody here who isn't afraid of the devil out of hell." Then the old gentleman softened. " Well, that's understandable, I suppose. If you want to," and his voice grew cynical again, " we'll escort you all to your rooms, one by one."

" Oh, don't jest, Inspector," said Mrs. Carreau wearily. " It—it's just that it gets on one's nerves."

" Well, I think the Inspector's perfectly right," exclaimed Miss Forrest, dropping a six-months' old copy of *Vanity Fair* on the floor with a thud. " *I'm* going upstairs and drown myself in mountain water and I defy any—any *two* murdering rascals to stop me ! "

" That's the spirit," said the Inspector with a shrewd glance at her. " And if you'll all get yourselves into the same frame of mind, we'll be a lot better off. This is the Twentieth Century, and it's daytime, and you've all got eyes and ears, so what the deuce are you afraid of ? Shoo, the lot of you ! "

And so, after a while, the Queens were left alone.

    .   .   .   .

They drifted out upon the terrace, shoulder to shoulder, a pair of sorely harrassed and miserable men. The sun was high and it broiled the almost volcanic rocks outside until they shimmered in the heat. The vista was comfortless and devastating.

" Might's well stew here as inside," grunted the Inspector, and he sank into a chair. His face was streaming grime.

Ellery dropped beside him, groaning.

They sat there for a long time. The house inside was oppressively quiet. Ellery's eyes had closed and his hands were loosely clasped on his chest as he lay slumped on his spine. They suffered the heat to fry their aching bones without vocal protest, sitting as still as they could.

The sun began to droop toward the west. It sank lower and lower and the two men sat still. The Inspector had drifted into a troubled doze : he sighed in his sleep convulsively from time to time.

Ellery's eyes were closed, too, but he was not asleep. His brain had never been more alert. The problem. . . . He had already gone over it in his mind a dozen times, probing for loopholes, striving to recall unimportant details, or details that might be important but did not seem to be. One never knew. There was something about the first murder, a matter of scientific fact, that kept bobbing to the surface of his thoughts. But each time he strove to catch and fix it, it slipped away only to submerge again. And then there was that knave of diamonds. . . .

He sat up as if he had been shot, tingling in every fibre. The Inspector's eyes flew open.

" What's the matter ? " he mumbled sleepily.

Ellery sprang from the chair and then stood still, listening. " I thought I heard . . ."

Alarmed, the old man rose. " Heard what ? "

" In the living-room." Ellery started across the terrace toward the French windows on the other side.

There was a scuffling sound from the direction of the living-room and the two men halted, tensed. Out of one of the French windows stepped Mrs. Wheary, red as a lobster, her hair wet and dishevelled, a dust-cloth in her hand. She was breathing heavily.

She halted on catching sight of the two men and beckoned mysteriously. " Inspector Queen, Mr. Queen, sir. Would you mind coming——? There's something very queer . . ."

They hurried to the nearest window and peered inside. But the room was empty.

" What's queer ? " said Ellery sharply.

The housekeeper pressed a grimy hand to her bosom. " I—I heard someone doing something, sir. . . ."

" Come, come " said the Inspector impatiently. " What's up, Mrs. Wheary ? "

" Well, sir," she whispered, " not having anything to do, I mean cooking and such, and feeling a—a little nervous, I decided to try and straighten things up a bit on the ground floor. We've been that upset, you know, sir, what with—with . . ."

" Yes, yes ? " .

" Anyway, everything being so cindery and all, I thought I'd run over the furniture with a cloth and try to get things a little clean again." She glanced nervously over her shoulder at the empty room. " I started in the dining-room and was just about half through when I heard a funny sound from—from the living-room here."

" Sound ? " Ellery frowned. " We didn't hear anything."

" It wasn't very loud, sir. Just a sort of pecking—I can't describe it. Anyway, I thought maybe someone might have come back to the living-room for a magazine or something, you see, and was going to keep on when I thought : ' Perhaps it's—something *else*.' So I tiptoed to the door and started to open it as softly as I could——"

" That was very brave, Mrs. Wheary."

She blushed. " I guess I must have made some noise with the door, sir, because when I'd opened it a bit and peeped in . . . there wasn't anything, you see. The noise must have scared—whoever—it was away, and he—she —oh, sir, I'm all mixed up ! "

" You mean whoever it was heard you coming and beat it back through the hall-door," snapped the Inspector. " Well, is that all ? "

" No, sir. I went in," faltered Mrs. Wheary, " and almost the first thing I saw . . . I'll show you."

She stepped heavily back into the living-room and the Queens followed with drawn brows.

She led them across the big room in the direction of the fireplace. Her fat forefingers shot up and pointed accusingly at the walnut-stained metal door of the wall-cabinet in which the Inspector had placed for safe-keeping the pack of playing-cards found on Dr. Xavier's desk the morning of the first murder.

There were scratches on the stout lock, and on the floor directly beneath lay a thin-edged fire-tool from the fireplace.

.   .   .   .

" Someone's been at the cabinet," muttered the Inspector. " Well, I'll be double-damned."

He strode forward and examined the marks on the door with a professional eye. Ellery picked up the fire-tool, regarded it thoughtfully for a moment, and then tossed it aside.

" Hunh," grunted the Inspector. " Just like trying to pick the lock of a bank-vault with a matchstick. But why the devil did he do it ? There's nothing in here but that pack of cards."

"Very curious," murmured Ellery. "*Very* curious. I suggest you open our little cache, dad, and see what's to be seen."

Mrs. Wheary stared at them with open mouth. "Do you think——" she began with an inquisitive gleam in her eyes.

"What we think, Mrs. Wheary, we think," said the Inspector severely. "You did a good job in keeping your eyes and ears open, but now you've got to do an even better job keeping your mouth shut. D'ye understand?"

"Oh, yes, sir!"

"That's all, then. Go back to your dusting."

"Yes, sir." Rather reluctantly she went away, closing the door of the dining-room behind her.

"Now let's see," growled the old gentleman, whipping out his key-wallet. He found the key to the cabinet and opened the door.

Ellery started. "I see you've still got that key."

"Sure I've still got the key." The Inspector stared at him.

"And that's another very curious item. By the way, I suppose this is the only key to the cabinet?"

"Don't worry, I checked up on that the other day."

"I'm *not* worrying. Well, let's see what's inside."

The Inspector pulled the door wide and they peered in. Except for the deck of cards the repository was empty, as before. And the cards lay quite where the Inspector had placed them. It was evident that the cabinet had not been opened since the old man had last turned the key in its lock.

He took out the deck and together they examined it. It was the same deck, beyond a doubt.

"Odd," muttered Ellery. "I really can't see why. . . . Lord, is it possible we missed something in looking over the cards originally?"

" There's one thing sure," said the Inspector thought-fully. " We were all together upstairs when I asked about a hiding-place for the cards and Mrs. Wheary told me about this cabinet and the key. She even said it was empty, I think ; and it was. So they all knew I was going to put the deck here. Since there's nothing else in the cabinet——"

" Of course. These cards are evidence. Evidence con-cerning Dr. Xavier's murder. It stands to reason that only the murderer would have motive to come after them. There are two things we can derive from this incident, dad, now that I analyse it : it was the murderer who sneaked in here and tried to break into the cabinet, and the reason he did it was that there's something about this deck which we've missed, apparently, and which he wanted to destroy because in some way it's damaging. Let's see those blasted things ! "

He snatched the deck from his father's hand and hurried to one of the small round tables. Spreading the cards out, face up, he examined each one with minute care. But there were no clear fingerprints on any of them ; what marks there were were unrecognisable smudges. Then he turned them over and scrutinised the backs with as little result.

" Appalling," he muttered. " There *must* be some-thing. . . . If it's not a question of a positive clue, logi-cally it must be a *negative*——"

" What are you talking about ? "

Ellery scowled. " I'm fishing. A clue isn't always the presence of something. Very often it's the absence of something. Let's see." He shoved the cards together, patted them neatly into a pile, and then to his father's astonishment began to count them.

" Why, that's—that's asinine ! " snorted the Inspector.

" No doubt," murmured Ellery, busy counting. "Forty-four, forty-five, forty-six, forty-seven, forty-eight——"

he stopped and his eyes blazed. " Do you see what I see ? " he shouted. " Forty-nine, fifty—and *that's all* ! "

" That's all ? " echoed the Inspector blankly. " There ought to be fifty-two in a full deck. No, this ought to have fifty-one ; the six of spades you took away, the torn one. . . ."

" Yes, yes, there's one card missing," said Ellery impatiently. " Well, we'll soon find out which one it is." Rapidly he began to separate the cards into suits. When he had four piles, each devoted to a single suit, he took up the pile of clubs. They were complete from deuce to ace, he found at once ; and, throwing them aside, examined the hearts. Complete. Spades—complete except for the six, and the two halves of the six reposed in the pocket of one of his suits upstairs. Diamonds. . . .

" Well, well, well," he said softly, staring down at the cards. " We might have known. Under our eyes all the time and we never thought of the elementary precaution of counting the cards. Provocative, eh ? "

The missing card was the knave of diamonds.

CHAPTER XVII

THE KNAVE'S TALE

Ellery dropped the cards, strode to the French windows, drew all the drapes, hurried across the room, closed the corridor-door, went to the dining-room door and made sure it was secure, switched on several lamps, and then dropped into a chair near the table.

"Squat and let's talk this over. I begin to see many things I was blind to." He stretched his legs and lit a cigarette, peering through the smoke at his father.

The Inspector sat down, crossed his knees, and snapped: "So do I. Thank God there's a little daylight! Look here. Mark Xavier left the torn half of a jack of diamonds as a clue to his murderer when he himself was attacked and forcibly poisoned. And now we find that a jack of diamonds has been missing since the murder of John Xavier—missing from the deck he was handling at the time he was shot. What's that tend to show?"

"Precisely the right tack," said Ellery approvingly. "I should say the inevitable question arises: Is it possible that the jack of diamonds in Dr. Xavier's deck was also a clue to *Dr. Xavier's* murderer?"

"That's putting it mildly," retorted the Inspector. "Possible? Why, it's the only logical answer to the whole business!"

"It would seem so; although," sighed Ellery, "I'm wary of everything in this grotesque mélange of wickedness. I confess that it accounts perfectly for the murderer's attempt to steal the deck from the cabinet and keep us from discovering that the knave is missing. If Murderer equals Diamond-Jack in our equation, there's no question about it."

"And maybe I've got an idea about *that*," growled the old gentleman. "It's just struck me. But let's mull this jack business through thoroughly first. The whole thing's shaping up beautifully. Mark Xavier left a jack of diamonds as a clue to his murderer. A jack of diamonds figures—somehow—in the previous murder of his brother because the deck coming from that previous murder has *its* jack of diamonds missing. Is it possible— I'll be as Sister-Maryish as you—that the clue of a jack of diamonds was suggested to Mark as he lay dying *by something he'd seen when he found his brother's body*? "

"I see," said Ellery slowly. "You mean that when he popped into the study that night and found Dr. Xavier shot to death, *he found a jack of diamonds in the doctor's hand*? "

"Right."

"Hmm. It does check, circumstantially. At the same time, the fact that he himself left a jack of diamonds in his own encounter with the murderer might merely mean that he saw the murderer's face and thought of the same card-significance as a clue to identity as his brother had." He shook his head. "No, that's impossibly coincidental, especially with such an obscurity. . . . You're right. He left the jack of diamonds because his brother had. It was the same murderer in both cases, of course, and with his knowledge of what his brother had done he merely duplicated the clue. Yes, I think we may say that when he found John Xavier dead he also found a jack of diamonds in John Xavier's hand. Then he switched the clue, took away the jack—substituted the six of spades from the solitaire-game on the desk as a deliberate frame-up of Mrs. Xavier."

"Now that you're through making a speech," grinned the Inspector, in sudden high spirits, " *I'll* go on. Why'd he take the jack out of his brother's hand and put the spade-six there ? Well, we know his motive for wanting to get his sister-in-law out of the way——"

" Hold on," murmured Ellery. " Not so fast. We've forgotten something. Two things. One is a confirmation explaining why he selected a six of spades at all in the frame-up ; obviously, if John's hand already held a card, a card-clue was immediately suggested to his mind. The other is this : in switching the clue from the diamond-knave to the spade-six, why didn't Xavier simply put the jack back where it had come from—the deck on the desk?"

" Well . . . It's true that he did take the damned card away—we didn't find it, so he must have. Why ? "

" The only logical reason must be that even taking it out of his brother's dead hand and tossing it among the scattered cards on the desk, or slipping it into the deck," replied Ellery calmly, " *would not conceal the fact that it had been used as a clue.*"

" Now you're talking in riddles again. That doesn't make sense. How on earth could that be ? "

Ellery puffed thoughtfully. " We've a perfect explanation. In his own case he left a jack of diamonds—*torn in half.*" The Inspector started. " But doesn't that fit ? He himself found only *half* a jack, I say, in his brother's hand ! If he'd found a torn jack, obviously he couldn't leave it on the scene of the crime ; its torn condition would immediately have called attention to it, especially since he was leaving a torn six in its place. I maintain that logically he *must* have found a torn jack in his brother's hand as the only plausible explanation under the circumstances for his having taken it away. He took it away, I suppose, and destroyed it, feeling fairly certain that no one would think of counting the cards . . . as no one," he added, frowning, " would have, had not the murderer tried to steal the deck from the cabinet in this room."

" Well, that's all very good," snapped the Inspector, " but let's get on. *I'm* not questioning the ways of Providence. That was a break, my son. . . . The point is that—the six of spades having been a frame-up on Mark Xavier's part on his own confession—the only important thing we have left is this : in both crimes we know that the victim left a half-jack of diamonds as a clue to the murderer. The same clue, of course, means the same murderer. There's only one queer thing in this business. By taking away the half-jack from the scene of his brother's murder he was covering up that murderer—shifting the blame from the real murderer to Mrs. Xavier. Then in his own murder he ups and accuses the very one he'd saved from suspicion in the first case ! It looks a little screwy somewhere."

" Not at all. Mark Xavier," said Ellery dryly, " was scarcely the self-sacrificing or Robin-Hood type of scoundrel. He framed Mrs. Xavier purely out of the trite but universal gain-motive. Obviously he couldn't leave the jack-clue around. He wanted that frame-up to take. In other words, he ' saved ' our knave of diamonds not out of loyalty or affection, but purely for financial reasons. On his own death-bed it was a different story. . . . There's something else, too. When you accused him of being his brother's killer, he lost his nerve and was only too willing to blurt out the name of the real murderer—indicating two things : that essentially he had no overweening desire to protect that individual, especially when his own neck was in danger ; and secondly that he himself had probably solved the problem of who was meant to be indicated by the jack ! And there, incidentally, is the answer to your question about how Xavier knew who his brother's murderer was. The half-jack of diamonds in his brother's hand had told him."

" That all washes," muttered the Inspector. " And to keep him from spilling the bad news, the murderer bumped him off." He rose and took a turn about the room. " Yes, it all gets down to that jack of diamonds. If we knew whom John and Mark had in mind when they left the half-jack, we'd have our man. *If* we knew. . . ."

" We do know."

" Hey ? "

" I've been working the old brain-cells overtime since last night and they've clicked on all twelve." Ellery sighed. " Yes, if that's all there is to it the case is solved. Sit down, dad, and let's go into executive conference. I warn you—it's the craziest thing you ever heard of. More fantastic than the six of spades. And it's a solution that still needs considerable scrubbing up. Sit down, sit down ! "

The Inspector sat down with celerity.

· · · · · · · · · ·

An hour later, with the black-red night glaring outside, a demoralised company were assembled in the game-room. The Inspector stood at the foyer-door and ushered them in, one by one, in a very forbidding silence. They came in wearily and yet cautiously, eyeing his grim face with the most helpless kind of apprehensive resignation. Finding no consolation there, they sought Ellery's face ; but he was standing by the window looking out at the darkness beyond the terrace.

" Now that we're all here," began the Inspector in a tone as grim as his expression, " sit down and take a load off your feet. This is going to be our last get-together about the murders. We've been led one hell of a merry chase, I'll tell you that, and we're just about fed up on it. The case is solved."

" Solved ! " they gasped.

" Solved ? " muttered Dr. Holmes. " You mean you know who——"

" Inspector," said Mrs. Xavier in a low voice. " You haven't found—the right one ? "

Mrs. Carreau sat very still, and the twins glanced in some excitement at each other. The others drew in their breaths.

" Can't you understand English ? " snapped the Inspector. " I said solved. Go on, El. This is your party."

Their eyes shifted to Ellery's back. He swung about slowly. " Mrs. Carreau," he said with abruptness, " you're French in origin, I believe ? "

" I ? French ? " she repeated, bewildered.

" Yes."

" Why—of course, Mr. Queen."

" You know the French language thoroughly ? "

She was trembling, but she made a weak attempt to laugh. " But—certainly. I was brought up on irregular verbs and Parisian slang."

" Hmm." Ellery came forward and stopped before one of the bridge-tables. " Let me point out at once," he said without inflection, " that what I am about to say constitutes probably the most fantastic reconstruction of a clue in the history of the so-called ' clever ' crime. It is incredibly subtle. It's so far removed from the ordinary realm of observation and simple deduction as to partake of something out of *Alice in Wonderland*. And yet—the facts are here, and we cannot ignore them. Please try to follow me closely."

This remarkable preamble was received in the deepest silence. There was blank confusion, or so it seemed, on every face.

" You all know," continued Ellery calmly, " that when we found Mark Xavier's dead body we also found clutched in his hand—the correct hand, incidentally— a torn playing-card. The exhibit was half a knave of diamonds ; unquestionably intended to convey to our intelligences the identity of Xavier's murderer. What you don't know—or at least what most of you don't know—is that when Mark Xavier entered his brother's study the other night, discovered the body, and decided to leave a six of spades in the dead man's fingers as a false clue to Mrs. Xavier, there was already in the dead man's fingers another card."

" Another card ? " gasped Miss Forrest.

" Another card. It's unnecessary to tell you how we know this, but the fact remains that beyond a doubt Mark Xavier was compelled to wrench out of Dr. Xavier's stiff hand . . . half a knave of diamonds ! "

" Another one," whispered Mrs. Carreau.

" Precisely. In other words, both dying men left half a knave of diamonds as a clue to the identity of their murderer—their common murderer, obviously, since the same clue was used. What did they mean by half a knave of diamonds ? "

He searched their faces deliberately. The Inspector leaned against the wall, watching with bright eyes.

" No suggestions ? It's quite *outré*, as I've said. Well, let's examine it point by point. The ' knave ' element first. A curious coincidence, but scarcely more than that. Certainly a murderer may be termed a knave, but that scarcely helps anyone but the panting collector of classic understatements. The fact that ' knave ' is commonly called ' jack ' ? There is no Jack in our little company ; the only one to whom it might have applied, John Xavier, having himself been the first victim. Well, then, how about the suit-symbol—the diamond ? There's no question of gems involved ; the only possible connection here would be "—he paused—" the rings that seem to have been stolen. But none of these was a diamond ring. On the surface, then, no indication of what the meaning might be." And then he whirled so unexpectedly upon Mrs. Carreau that she shrank back in her chair. " Mrs. Carreau, what does the word *carreau* mean in French ? "

" *Carreau ?* " Her eyes became enormous brown pools.

" Why "—her eyes flickered—" it means so many things, Mr. Queen. A hassock, and a tailor's goose, and a lozenge, and a pane of glass . . ."

" And a ground floor, and a certain kind of tile. Quite so." Ellery smiled coldly. " There's also a very significant idiom : *rester sur le carreau*, which may be translated to : *to be killed on the spot*, a singularly felicitous French version of our Chicagoese expression . . . all of which however we may discount as irrelevant." He continued to eye her steadily. " But what else does *carreau* mean ? "

Her eyes fell. " I'm afraid—I don't know, Mr. Queen."

" And the French so sportively inclined ! Have you forgotten that in French the word 'diamond' as applied to playing-cards is *carreau* ? "

She was silent. Each face mirrored amazement and horror.

" But, good lord," breathed Dr. Holmes. " That's insane, Mr. Queen ! "

Ellery shrugged without removing his fixed glance from the shrinking woman. " I'm recounting facts, not fancies, Doctor. Doesn't it strike you as enormously significant that the fatal card is a diamond, that 'diamond' is *carreau* in French, and that we have several Carreaus in this house ? "

Miss Forrest jumped from her chair and advanced with white lips upon Ellery. " I have never heard such unmitigated and cruel nonsense in my whole life, Mr. Queen ! Do you realise what you're insinuating on the basis of such—such flimsy evidence ? "

" Sit down, please," said Ellery wearily. " I realise a good deal more, I think, my loyal lady, than you do. Well, Mrs. Carreau ? "

Her hands were twisting like snakes. " What do you expect me to say ? All I can say is that—you're making a terrible mistake, Mr. Queen."

The twins leaped from the sofa. "You take that back!" cried Francis, doubling his fists. "You can't s-say things like that about our mother!"

Julian shouted: "You're crazy, that's what you are!"

"Sit down, boys," said the Inspector quietly from the wall.

They glared at Ellery, but obeyed.

"Let me continue, please," said Ellery again in a tired voice. "I don't relish this any more than the rest of you. The word 'diamond' in the card sense is, as I've pointed out, *carreau*. Is there anything in our facts which bolsters this admittedly fantastic theory that a Carreau, so to speak, was designated by John and Mark Xavier when they left the jack of diamonds as clues to their murderer? Unfortunately there is." He waved his hand and repeated: "Unfortunately—there is."

From the wall came the Inspector's voice, calm and impersonal. "*Which one of you boys,*" he said clearly to the Siamese twins, "*killed those two men?*"

. . . .

Mrs. Carreau sprang to her feet and bounded across the intervening space like a tigress. She stood before the speechless boys, her arms outspread, her whole body vibrating with passion. "This has gone far enough!" she cried. "I think even you stupid men must see the absurdity of accusing these—these children of murder. My sons murderers! You're mad, both of you!"

"Absurdity?" Ellery sighed. "Please, Mrs. Carreau. You've evidently failed to grasp the significance of the clue. That card was not only a diamond, but a jack of diamonds. What is the appearance of the knave-card? *It represents two joined young men.*" Her mouth came open. "Ah, I see you're not quite so certain of its absurdity. Two joined young men—not old men, mind you, for

a king would have sufficed for that—but young men.
Joined ! Incredible ? I told you it was. But we *have* two
joined young men in this house, and they *are* named
Carreau, you see. What is one to think ? "

She sank on to the sofa beside the boys, unable to
speak. Their young mouths were working soundlessly.

" Moreover, we ask the question : Why was the card
torn in half in both instances, leaving—so to speak—only
one of the two joined men as a clue ? " Ellery continued
with weary inexorability. " Obviously because the dead
men intended to show that one, not both, of the Carreau
twins was the murderer. How could this be ? Well, if one
was dominated by the other, was compelled to be
present against his will because of sheer physical ina-
bility to hang back, was a mere bystander while the
other committed the actual crimes . . . Which of you
shot Dr. Xavier and poisoned Mark Xavier, boys ? "

Their lips quivered ; the fight had quite gone out of
them. Francis whispered in a voice close to tears : " But
—but we *didn't*, Mr. Queen. We didn't. Why, we—we
couldn't do . . . *that*. We just couldn't. And why should
we ? Why ? It's so . . . Oh, don't you see ? "

Julian shuddered. His eyes were fixed on Ellery's face
with a sort of fascinated horror.

" I'll tell you why," said the Inspector slowly. " Dr.
Xavier was experimenting with Siamese-twin animals
in his laboratory. You people had some notion when you
came up here that the doctor could perform a miracle,
could separate the boys surgically——"

" That's nonsense," muttered Dr. Holmes. " I've
never believed——"

" Exactly. You've never believed it could be done,
Holmes. It's never been done successfully, has it, with
twins of this type ? So I say that it was you who threw
the monkey-wrench into the works ; you went on record
as not ' believing,' you made these people doubt the

ability of Dr. Xavier. You talked to the twins, to Mrs. Carreau, about it, didn't you ? "

" Well . . . " The Englishman was writhing. " Perhaps I did advise them that it was a very dangerous experiment——"

" I thought so. And then something happened." The Inspector's eyes were bright marbles. " I don't know what, exactly. Maybe Dr. Xavier was stubborn, or insisted on going ahead. The boys, Mrs. Carreau, got frightened. It was a murder in self-defence, in a way——"

" Oh, don't you see how ridiculous that is ? " cried Miss Forrest. " How childish ? There was nothing Machiavellian about Dr. Xavier. He wasn't the ' mad scientist ' of the thrillers and movies. He *wouldn't* have gone ahead with such an operation without the full consent of all parties concerned. Besides, what was to prevent us from just leaving ? Don't you see ? It simply won't stand examination, Inspector ! " Her voice rang with triumph.

" Besides," snapped Dr. Holmes, " there was no certainty at all about the surgery. Mrs. Carreau brought the boys up here for observation only. Even had everything been otherwise settled, an operation here would have been impossible. But then Xavier's experiments on animals were a matter of pure research, antedating Mrs. Carreau's arrival. I assure you that Dr. Xavier never had anything in mind concerning these lads, Inspector, other than mere theory. This is all very shockerish, Inspector."

" Yes," exclaimed Miss Forrest again, her eyes flashing, " and now that I come to think of it, Mr. Queen, there's something fallacious in your *reasoning*. You claim that tearing the double-jack in half to achieve just one jack means the—the dead men were indicating one of two joined men. Suppose I say to you that the reason they tore the cards in half was to *prevent* anyone from believing that Francis and Julian did it ? I mean that if they'd left just the jack, which shows two joined figures, somebody might think of the twins. By tearing the two figures apart they might have been saying : ' *Don't* think the twins did it. It's just one unjoined person. That's why I'm not leaving a whole card ! ' "

"Brava," murmured Ellery. "That's genius, Miss Forrest. But unfortunately you're forgetting that the cards *were* diamonds, and that the only male Carreaus here *are* the twins."

She subsided, biting her lip.

Mrs. Carreau said steadily : " The more I think of it the more convinced I am that somehow this is all a hideous mistake. Surely you ·don't mean to—to arrest . . . " She stopped.

The Inspector, who was feeling uneasy, scratched his chin. Ellery did not reply ; he had turned back to the window again. "Well," the old man said, hesitating, " can you suggest another meaning for the card ? "

"No. But——"

" *You're* the detective," said Miss Forrest with a rebirth of spirit. " I still maintain the whole argument is—is lunatic."

The Inspector went to one of the windows and stepped out upon the terrace. After a moment Ellery followed.

.   .   .   .

" Well ? " he said.

" I don't like it." The Inspector gnawed his moustache. " There's a lot in what they say—not about the card business, but about that operation and all." He groaned. " A hell of a' lot. Why should one of those kids have bumped the doctor off ? I tell you I don't like it."

" We discussed that, I believe, before we tackled them," Ellery pointed out with a shrug.

"Yes, I know," said the old man miserably, "but——
Cripes, I don't know what to think. The more I think
the dizzier I get. Even if it's true and one of the lads is
a murderer, how the devil can we ever establish which
one ? If they refuse to talk——"

A gleam came into Ellery's troubled eyes. "The
problem has its interesting points. Even if one of them
confesses—we'll suppose the most convenient theory—
have you stopped to consider what a beautiful headache
the case would give America's prize legal talent ? "

"What d'ye mean ? "

"Well," murmured Ellery, "let's say young Francis
is our man. He confesses on the stand, exonerating Julian
who, it devolves, was under Francis's thumb and was
forced to stand by while Francis did the dirty work.
Julian, we prove, was completely innocent in both
intent and activity. So Francis is tried, convicted, and
condemned to death."

"Cripes," groaned the Inspector.

"I see you envision the possibilities. Francis is tried,
convicted, and condemned to death ; and all the while
poor Julian is forced to undergo extreme mental suffer-
ing, physical imprisonment, and finally the degradation
of—what ? Death ? But he's an innocent victim of
circumstances. Surgery ? Modern science—minus at
least the voice of the late Dr. John S. Xavier—says that
Siamese twins with a common major organ cannot be
successfully disjoined ; result, death to the innocent boy
as well as to the guilty. So surgery is out. What then ?
The law says a person condemned to death shall be
executed. Shall we execute ? Clearly impossible without
also executing an innocent individual. Shall we not
execute ? Clearly in defiance of the *lex talionis*. Ah,
what a case ! The irresistible force meeting the immov-
able barrier." Ellery sighed. "I should really like to
confront a group of smug lawyers with this problem—

as neat a conflict of rights, I'll wager, as the whole history of criminal law has to offer. . . . Well, Inspector, what do you think *would* happen in your precious case ? "

" Let me alone, will you ? " mumbled his father. " You're always raising the most ridiculous questions. How do *I* know ? Am I God ? . . . Another week of this and we'll all be in a bughouse ! "

" Another week of this," said Ellery gloomily, looking at the frightful sky and trying to draw a breath without soiling his lungs, " and it begins to look as if we'll all be cold cinders."

" It does seem silly to break our heads about a matter of individual crime and guilt when we're one step from the last furnace ourselves," muttered the Inspector. " Let's go back inside. We'll have to take stock, organise, and do what we——"

" What's that ? " said Ellery sharply.

" What's what ? "

Ellery bounded off the terrace. He was down the steps in one leap and standing on the drive to stare up at the ruddy night-sky. " That noise," he said slowly. " Don't you hear it ? "

It was a faint rumbling roar and it seemed to emanate from a region of the heavens a great distance away.

" By George," cried the Inspector, scrambling to the ground, " I believe it's *thunder* ! "

" After all this horrible waiting, it doesn't seem . . . " Ellery's voice trailed off in a mutter. Their faces were raised to the skies nakedly, two white blurs of hope.

They did not turn at the pound and clatter of feet on the terrace.

" What is it ? " screamed Mrs. Xavier. " We heard . . . Is it thunder ? "

" Glo-o-ory ! " shrieked Miss Forrest. " If it's thunder it's rain ! "

The rumble was growing appreciably louder. It possessed a curiously living quality, and there was something metallic in its overtones. It rattled. . . .

" I've heard of such things before," cried Dr. Holmes. " It's an unusual meteorological phenomenon."

" What is ? " demanded Ellery, still craning at the sky.

" Under certain conditions of the atmosphere, clouds may very well form over the area of a widespread forest-fire. Condensation of moisture in the updraught of air. I read somewhere that fires of this sort have actually been extinguished by the clouds they themselves generated ! "

" Thank God," quavered Mrs. Wheary.

Ellery turned suddenly. They were lined up at the rail of the terrace—a row of pale straining faces raised to the sky. On every face but one there was livid hope. Only on Mrs. Carreau's delicate features sat horror, the horror of realisation. If it were rain, if the fire were blotted out, if communication were re-established . . . Her grip tightened on the shoulders of her sons.

" Don't thank Him yet, Mrs. Wheary," said Ellery in a savage tone. " We were mistaken ; it's not thunder. Don't you see that red light up there ? "

" Not thunder ? . . . "

" Red light ? "

They squinted in the direction of his pointing arm. And they all caught sight of the rapidly moving, unwinking little pinprick of bright red against the dark-wine of the heavens.

It was accompanied by the thunder, and it was headed for the summit of Arrow Mountain.

But the thunder was the sound of a motor, and the red pinprick was the night riding-light of an aeroplane.

CHAPTER XVIII

THE LAST REFUGE

THEY sighed *en masse*, a horrible sigh that held the death of hope. Mrs. Wheary uttered a heart-rending moan and Bones's voice startled them with a sudden vicious curse that hissed through the moist air like brimstone.

The Miss Forrest cried : " It's a 'plane ! They've—they've come for us ! They've news for us ! "

Her cries roused them. The Inspector yelled : " Mrs. Wheary ! Bones ! Somebody ! Put on every light in the house ! The rest of you get things that'll burn—anything —get busy ! We'll build a bonfire out here so he can see us ! "

They tumbled over one another in their haste. Bones began to hurl the terrace chairs over the rail. Mrs. Wheary vanished through one of the French windows. The women clattered down the steps and began to carry the chairs over, the gravel and rocks, away from the house. Ellery scrambled into the house and emerged a few moments later with two armfuls of old newspapers, magazines, and loose papers. The twins, their personal predicament forgotten in the excitement of the present, staggered off the porch under the weight of an over-stuffed chair from the now brilliantly illuminated living-room. They looked like scurrying ants in the darkness. . . .

The Inspector squatted on his thin hams and struck a match with a hand that trembled slightly. The tall pile of inflammable miscellany dwarfed his slender figure. He applied the flame to the bed of paper beneath the pile and rose hastily. They crowded around, jealous of the hot breeze that was tearing at the tiny flame. And all the while they kept their staring eyes upon the heavens.

The flame licked hungrily at the papers and with a crackle caught the makeshift kindling they had piled at the bottom of the pyre. In an instant the bed of the pyre was ablaze, and they shielded their faces and retreated from the blast of heat.

They held their breaths as they watched the red light. It was very near now, and at their altitude the roar of the aeroplane was deafening. Difficult as it was to estimate how far above their heads the aviator was winging, they realised that he could not be more than a few hundred feet above the summit of the mountain. And the invisible craft with its single red eye swooped nearer and nearer.

Then suddenly it was thundering overhead and—past.

In that single instant they had caught sight dimly in the upward illumination of their bonfire against the crimson sky of a small monoplane with an open cockpit.

" Oh, he's—he's gone past ! " moaned Miss Forrest.

But then the red light dipped and swerved to take a new direction, and it came swiftly back at them in a graceful arc.

" He's seen the fire ! " shrieked Mrs. Wheary. " Praise be, he's seen us by the fire ! "

The pilot's manœuvres were baffling. He kept circling the crest of the mountain as if he were uncertain of the terrain, as if he did not quite know what to do. And then, incredibly, the red light began to recede.

" Good God," said Dr. Holmes hoarsely, " isn't he going to land ? Is he leaving us ? "

" Land ? Nonsense ! " snapped Ellery, straining aloft.

" How could anything but a bird land on this tormented patch of rock ? He's levelling off for a straight swoop. What do you think he's been doing up there—playing tag ? He's been studying the ground. I think—something is primed to happen."

Before they could catch their breaths he was hurtling toward them with a scream of rushing wind and a thunder of propeller that made their eardrums ache. Down, down he came in a daring swoop that rooted them to the ground with horrified admiration. What was the madman attempting ? All their numbed brains could imagine was that he was bent on suicide.

He was only a hundred feet away now, and so low that they unconsciously ducked. His landing-gear barely cleared the tops of the trees at the margin of the summit. Then like lightning he was upon them—a rushing winged thing with belching vitals and hoarsely vibrating body—and past, away. Before they could recover he was past the summit, his wing tipped already as he climbed against the bloody moon in another spiral.

But now they understood that his madness had been cold sanity, and his foolhardiness courage.

A small white object had dropped like a plummet from the cockpit, hurled by a dark overhanging human arm, to fall with a crash not twenty feet from the fire.

The Inspector was over the treacherous ground like a monkey and clutching the fallen object in a twinkling. His fingers shook as he unwrapped several sheets of paper from the stone to which it had been bound.

They huddled about him, clawing at his coat.

" What is it, Inspector ? "

" What does he say ? "

" Is it—over ? "

" For God's sake, tell us ! "

The Inspector squinted at the typewritten lines in the leaping light of the bonfire, reading feverishly. And as he read, the lines of his grey face lengthened, and his shoulders sagged, and all the glitter of hope and life went out of his eyes.

They read their doom in his face. Their grimy wet cheeks became flaccid, with the flaccidity of the dead.

The Inspector said slowly : " Here it is." And he read in a low dull voice :

Temporary Headquarters
Osquewa

INSPECTOR RICHARD QUEEN :

I regret to have to inform you that the forest-fire in Tomahawk Valley and this section of the Tepee range, and most particularly on Arrow Mountain where you are bottled up, is absolutely out of control. There is no longer any hope that we will be able to get it under control. It is climbing the Arrow very fast and unless a miracle happens will soon sweep the summit.

We have hundreds of people fighting it and the casualties have mounted day by day. Scores have been overcome by smoke or badly burned, and the whole hospital corps of this and surrounding counties is taxed to the limit. The list of dead is now twenty-one. We have tried everything, including blasting and cross-fires. But now we have to admit we are licked.

There is no way out for you people at Dr. Xavier's place on the Arrow. I suppose you know that already.

This message is being dropped by Ralph Kirby, the speed flyer. When you have read this note signal him and he will know you have got the message all right and will drop a load of medicines and foodstuffs for you in case you have run out. We know you have plenty of water. If there were any way to take you people off by 'plane we would do it, but it is impossible. I know the nature of the ground at the top of the Arrow and it is far too broken up to permit a landing without fatal damage to the machine and almost certain death to the pilot. Not even a gyroplane could make it, even if we had one, which we have not.

I have asked the advice of the forest rangers on your predicament and they suggest one of two things, or both. If the wind is right build a fire in unburned woods to fight the fire coming up. This is no good because the winds around the top are too tricky, always shifting. The other thing is to dig a wide trench at the edge of the timber on the summit in the hope that the fire will not be able to jump over it. You might also remove all the dry brush and vegetation around the house as an additional safety measure. Keep the house damped down. There is only one thing to do with this fire and that is to let it burn itself out. It has already devastated the timberland for miles and miles around.

Keep a stiff upper lip and make a real fight of it. I have taken the liberty of notifying Police Headquarters in New York City about where you are and the pickle you are in. They are keeping the wires hot. I am damn sorry, Inspector, I cannot do more. Good luck to all of you. I won't say good-bye.

> (Signed) WINSLOWE REID,
> Sheriff, Osquewa.

"At least," said Ellery with a wild and bitter laugh in the ghastly silence that followed, "he's a newsy sort of chap, isn't he? Oh, God."

. . . .

The Inspector, in a daze, stepped as close to the fire as he dared and waved his arms slowly, without energy. Instantly the airman still circling above straightened out again and repeated his former manœuvres. This time when he roared by above their heads a large round bundle dropped from the cockpit. He circled twice again, as if reluctant to leave, came close once more, waggled his wings in a grim salute, and then darted off into the the night. None of them so much as stirred a finger until the red light vanished in the thickest darkness of the distance.

Then Mrs. Carreau sank to the ground, sobbing as if her heart would break. The twins cowered behind her, their teeth chattering.

"Well, what the hell are we waiting for?" bellowed Smith suddenly, waving his huge arms like a windmill. His eyes were staring madly from his head and rivulets of perspiration poured down his gross cheeks. " You read what that damn' Sheriff wrote ! Build a fire ! Dig a trench ! For the love of God, let's get busy ! "

" No fire," said Ellery quietly. " The wind's crazy up here. It might set the house ablaze."

" Smith's right about the trench, anyway," panted Dr. Holmes. " We can't just stand here like—like cattle waiting for slaughter. Bones—get those spades and picks out of the garage ! "

Bones cursed vilely and darted off into the darkness.

" I guess," said the Inspector in a stiff unnatural voice, " that it's the only thing to do. Dig. Dig until we smother." He drew a deep breath and something of the old martinet returned to his bearing. " All right ! " he snapped. " We dig. Everybody. Get as much of your clothing off as you decently can. Women—the boys—everybody help. We start right now and we don't finish till *we're* finished."

" How much time have we ? " whispered Mrs. Xavier.

Smith thrashed off into the darkness and disappeared in the smoky woods. Dr. Holmes stripped off his jacket and necktie and hurried after Bones. Mrs. Carreau rose, no longer sobbing. Mrs. Xavier did not stir ; she continued to stare after Smith.

They were whirling dervishes in a nightmare that grew steadily more fantastic.

Smith blundered back, materialising out of the smoke. " It's not far now ! " he snarled. " The fire ! Just a short way below ! Where the hell are those tools ? "

Then Bones and Dr. Holmes came staggering out of the darkness under a load of iron implements and the nightmare began in earnest.

To give them light Mrs. Wheary, physically the weakest, kept the fire burning with fresh fuel supplied by the twins, who dragged from the house all the portable furniture they could find. A high wind had risen and swept the sparks of the bonfire about with alarming abandon. Meanwhile the Inspector had marked off the three-quarter circle rimming the timberline which was to be dug. The women were set to uprooting the dry bushes from the crevices of the stony ground ; these they added to the fire from time to time as additional fuel. The smoke rose from the summit like the signal-fire of a race of gigantic Indians. They coughed and cried and toiled and sweated, and their arms became lead weights that were torture to lift. Miss Forrest, impatient in her frenzy, soon stopped tearing out brush and ran to help with the digging.

The men laboured silently, conserving their breath. Their arms rose and fell, rose and fell. . . .

When dawn broke—a turbulent smoky red dawn— they were still digging. Not fiercely now, but with the steadiness of inhuman desperation. Mrs. Wheary had collapsed by the dying fire ; she lay limply on the rocks, moaning and ignored. All the men were stripped to the waist now, their bodies glistening with body-oil where they were not coated with grime and soot.

No one had even cast a glance at the padded bag of food and medicines dropped by the aviator.

At two in the afternoon Mrs. Carreau collapsed. At three Mrs. Xavier. But Ann Forrest laboured on, although she staggered with each feeble thrust of the spade.

Then at four-thirty the spade dropped from her nerveless fingers and she sank to the ground. " I—can't —go on," she gasped. " I—can't."

At five Smith fell and could not rise. The others toiled on.

At twenty minutes past six, after twenty hours of incredible labour, the trench was finished.

.   .   .   .

They dropped where they were, their streaming clotted skins pressed to the scarred earth in the last oblivious spasm of exhaustion. The Inspector, stretched groaning on the ground, looked like a felled dwarf, one of the toilers of Vulcan's smithy. His eyes were sunken deep in his head and they were circled by purple rings. His mouth was open, gasping for air. His grey hair stuck wetly to his head. His fingers were bleeding.

The others were in scarcely better condition. Smith still lay where he had fallen, a mountain of quivering flesh. Ellery was a slim long sooty ghost. Bones was a dead man. The women were huddles of soiled ripped garments. The twins sat on a rock, heads hanging. Dr. Holmes lay still, eyes closed, nostrils twitching ; his white skin was a shambles.

They lay for more than an hour without moving.

Then the twins stirred, and croaked something to each other, and rose and tottered into the house. They returned after a long time lugging three pails of cold water, and doggedly set about reviving the victims of exhaustion.

Ellery came to with a gasp as icy water sloshed over his palpitating torso. He sat up, groaning, at first with bewilderment in his bloodshot eyes. Then memory returned, and he grinned feebly at the white faces of the twins. " To forgive—is divine, eh ? " he croaked, and struggled to his feet. " How long——? " He could not go on.

" It's half-past seven," mumbled Francis.

" Lord."

He stared about. Mrs. Carreau, revived, was stumbling up the steps of the porch. Bones had disappeared. The Inspector sat quietly on his haunches where he had fallen, glaring numbly at his blood-clotted hands. Mrs. Xavier was on her knees, rising. Ann Forrest and Dr. Holmes lay on their backs now, side by side, staring at the darkening sky. Smith was rumbling something evil and incoherent in the depths of his throat. Mrs. Wheary . . .

"Lord," he croaked again, blinking.

The wracked word was torn out of his mouth by a sudden overwhelming blast of boiling wind. His ears were filled with a stupendous roaring. Smoke belched out of the woods.

Then he saw the fire, the vanguard of the fire. It was sucking greedily away at the trees at the margin of the summit.

It had reached them at last.

. . . .

They began to run toward the house. Fear revived their glands and sent hot secretions into their blood which electrified their muscles and gave them new strength.

On the terrace they halted by silent consent and stared wildly back.

The whole cut circle of the timber's edge had burst into flame. The crackling roar, the searing heat, sent them reeling into the house after a moment, away from that terrifying arc of pure fire which the wind was bending slowly inward in a solid sheet fifty feet high. Through the French windows of the front rooms they stared in speechless panic at the hellish world outside. The wind was rising, still rising. The sheet of flame bent lower, tenaciously. Millions of riven sparks drove upon the house. The trench, their pitiful trench . . . would it hold?

Smith shouted : "All for nothing. All that work. Trench. . . . Hell, it's *funny* !" and he began to shriek with hysterical laughter. "Trench," he gasped, "trench," and the creases of his belly swelled over his belt as he bent double, tears streaming down his dirty cheeks.

" Stop it, you ass," said Ellery hoarsely. " Stop——"
and in the midst of the sentence he broke off with a cry
and darted out on to the terrace again.

The Inspector screamed : " *Ellery !* "

His lean figure scrambled over the rail and he began
to run. Above him, before him, loomed a wall of flame.
It seemed as if he meant to throw himself into the fire.
His half-naked body twisted and turned as he dodged
among the rocks. Then he stooped, wavered, picked
something up, and came stumbling back.

His torso was dull red with the heat and his face was
black. " Food," he panted. " Mustn't forget the sack
of food." His eyes blazed. " Well, what are you idiots
waiting for ? The trench is a fizzle ! And that damned
wind——"

They crouched before the wind, moaning with it.

" No time for anything but to get under cover,"
croaked Ellery. " The house is burning in a hundred
places already and we couldn't stop it now with a
brigade. A few pails of water over the gables . . . " He
laughed himself, a demon dancing against a backdrop
of fire. " The cellar—where's the cellar, for God's sake ?
Doesn't anyone know where the cellar is ? Lord, what
unmitigated idiots ! Talk, will you, somebody ? "

" The cellar," they chanted obediently, fixing glassy
eyes on his face. They were a company of half-naked
dead, dirty white Zombies in a purgatory of their own.
" The cellar."

" Behind the stairs," gurgled Mrs. Xavier ; her gown
was torn away from one shoulder and her hands were
bruised and blackened. " Oh, hurry, hurry."

And then they were tumbling down the hall. Mrs.
Xavier made for a thick solid door set beneath the rising
stairs which led to the upper floors. They jostled one
another in their frantic efforts to get through the doorway.

"Dad," said Ellery quietly. "Come on."

The Inspector started, wiped his white lips with a shaking hand, and followed. Ellery stumbled to the kitchen through a hall cloudy with bitter smoke ; he dug madly in the closets, tossing things about. He found pans, pots, kettles. "Fill 'em up from the tap," he directed, between hacking coughs. "Hurry. We'll need water. Lots of it. No telling how long we'll be. . . ."

They struggled down the hall with their slopping burdens. At the cellar-door Ellery shouted : "Holmes ! Smith ! Get this water down ! " and without waiting they staggered back to the kitchen for more.

They made six trips, filling all the large containers they could find—tin buckets, an empty butter-tub, wash basins, an old boiler and other objects as variegated and nondescript. And then, at last, Ellery stood at the top of the stairs as the Inspector tottered down into the cool cement chamber, as gloomy and dark and vast as a mountain cavern.

"Is the bag of food down there, somebody ? " he croaked before he closed the thick door.

"I've got it, Queen," called up Dr. Holmes.

Ellery slammed the door shut. "One of you women give me some cloth—anything."

Ann Forrest struggled to her feet. Beside Ellery in the darkness she ripped off her dress.

"I don't suppose I'll—need it much longer, Mr. Queen," she said, and her voice trembled even as she laughed.

"Ann ! " cried Dr. Holmes. "Don't ! There's the material of the bag——"

"Too late," she said, almost gaily ; but her lips quivered.

"Good girl," muttered Ellery. He grabbed the dress and began to tear it into strips. The scraps he stuffed at the bottom of the door. When he rose, he put his arm about the girl's white shoulders and together they descended to the cement floor below.

Dr. Holmes was waiting with a filthy old khaki coat which reeked of dampness. " Dug it up here. One of Bones's winter coats," he said hoarsely. " Ann—I'm sorry. . . . "

The tall girl shivered and draped the coat about her shoulders.

Ellery and Dr. Holmes bent over the sack which had been dropped by the airman and ripped it open. Protected by thick padding were bundles of medicine bottles—antiseptics, quinine, aspirin, salves, morphine ; and hypodermics, adhesive tape, absorbent cotton, bandage. There were other bundles, too—sandwiches, a whole ham, loaves of bread, jars of jam, bars of chocolate, thermos bottles of hot coffee. . . .

The two men doled out the food and for some time there was no sound but that of champing jaws and long gulps. The thermos bottles passed around from hand to hand. They ate slowly, savouring each mouthful. In each mind was the same thought : that this might be their last earthly dinner. . . . Finally they could eat no more, and Ellery gathered the remains of the meal carefully and stowed them in the sack again. Dr. Holmes, his naked torso crisscrossed by welts and scratches, went among them quietly with the antiseptics, cleansing their wounds, taping, bandaging. . . .

Then there was no more to be done, and he sank upon an old egg-crate and buried his face in his hands.

They sat about on old packing-cases, in the coal-bin, on the stone floor. A single bulb shed weak yellow light above them. Faintly they could hear the dull roar of the fire outside. It seemed nearer, much nearer.

Once they were startled by a series of booming explosions.

"The gasoline in the garage," muttered the Inspector. "There go the cars."

No one replied.

And once Bones rose and disappeared in the darkness. When he returned he rasped : "Cellar windows. I've stuffed 'em full of old metal things and flat stones."

No one replied.

And so they sat, drooping and hopeless, too exhausted too weep or sigh or stir, staring dully at the floor . . waiting for the end.

CHAPTER XIX

THE QUEEN'S TALE

Hours passed, how many they neither knew nor cared. In that vast dim cavern there was no night or day. The puny illumination of the feeble bulb was their sun and moon. They sat like stones and except for their uneven breathing they might have been already dead.

For Ellery it was a queer vertiginous experience. His thoughts veered from death to life, from barely glimpsed vistas of remembered fact to flitting phantoms of his aroused fancy. Pieces of the puzzle returned to annoy him. They persisted in invading his brain-cells and storming his consciousness. At the same time he chuckled mirthlessly to himself at the instability and inconsistency of the human mind, which stubbornly wrestled with problems of comparative unimportance while the big things were ignored or at best evaded. What did one murderer more or less matter to a man facing his own extinction? It was illogical, infantile. He should be occupied with making his private peace with his private gods; instead he worried about trivialities.

Finally, too weak to resist, he sighed and gave himself over wholly to thoughts of the case. The others about him receded; he closed his eyes and brooded with a weary return of his old concentrative energy.

.   .   .   .

When he opened them again after the passage of an eternity nothing had changed. The twins still crouched at the feet of their mother. Mrs. Xavier still sat upright on a packing-case, her head resting against the rough cement wall, eyes closed. Dr. Holmes and Miss Forrest still sat side by side, shoulder to shoulder, unmoving. Smith still squatted on an old box, head bowed and naked arms dangling between his Falstaffian thighs. Mrs. Wheary still lay in a heap on the coal pile, her arm flung over her eyes; and Bones still sat crosslegged beside her, as unblinking as a graven image.

Ellery shivered and stretched his arms. The Inspector, seated on a box beside him, stirred.

"Well?" mumbled the old man.

Ellery shook his head, struggled to his feet, and stumbled up the cellar stairs. They moved then and regarded him dully.

He sat down on the top step and pulled out a little of the stuffing in the crevice below the door. A puff of thick smoke made him blink and cough. He replaced the stuffing hastily and weaved his way downstairs again.

They were listening, listening to the hissing roar of the flames. It came from directly overhead now.

Mrs. Carreau was crying. The twins stirred uneasily and tightened their grip on her hands.

"Isn't the air—getting worse?" asked Mrs. Xavier thickly.

They sniffed. It was.

Ellery squared his shoulders. "Look here," he croaked. They looked. "We're on the verge of a particularly unpleasant death. I don't know what the human animal is supposed to do, how he's supposed to act in a crisis like this, when the last hope is gone, but I know this: I for one refuse to sit still like a gagged sacrifice and pass out in silence." He paused. "We haven't long, you know."

"Ah, shut up," snarled Smith. "We've had enough of your damn' gab."

" I'm afraid not. You're the type, old friend, who loses his head at the last moment and goes about bashing his brains out against the nearest wall. I'll thank you to remember that you've a certain amount of sheer pride to live up to." Smith blinked and lowered his eyes. " As a matter of fact," continued Ellery, coughing, " now that you've chosen to engage in conversation, there's a little mystery connected with your obese majesty I very earnestly desire to clear up."

" Me ? " mumbled Smith.

" Yes, yes. We're in the last confessional, you see, and I should think you wouldn't want to meet your slightly astigmatic Maker before making a clean breast of things."

" Confessing what ? " snapped the fat man, bridling.

Ellery eyed the other cautiously. They were sitting up now, listening and for the moment interested. " Confessing that you're a damned blackguard."

Smith struggled to his feet, clenching his fists. " Why, you——"

Ellery strode over to him and, placing his hand on the man's fleshy chest, pushed. Smith collapsed with a crash on his box. " Well ? " said Ellery, standing over him. " And are we to fight like wild beasts at the last, too, Smith, old chap ? "

The fat man licked his lips. Then he jerked his head up and cried defiantly : " Well, and why not ? We'll all be roast meat in a little while anyway. Sure I blackmailed her." His lips sneered. " Fat lot of good it'll do you now, you damn' meddling noseybody ! "

Mrs. Carreau had stopped crying. She sat up straighter and said quietly : " He's been blackmailing me for sixteen years."

" Marie—don't," begged Miss Forrest.

She waved her hand. " It doesn't matter now, Ann. I——"

" He knew the secret of your sons, didn't he ? " murmured Ellery.

She gasped. " How did you know ? "

" That doesn't matter now, either," he said a little bitterly.

" He was one of the physicians in attendance at their —their birth. . . . "

" You dirty fat hog," growled the Inspector with a flicker of anger in his eyes. " I'd like to smash your fat face in——"

Smith cursed weakly.

" Discredited, thrown out of his profession since," said Miss Forrest savagely. " Malpractice. Of course ! He came up here, trailed us to Dr. Xavier's, managed to see Mrs. Carreau alone——"

" Yes, yes," sighed Ellery. " We know all the rest." He looked up at the door above their heads. There was only one course, he knew ; he must keep them interested, boiling, frightened—anything so long as they did not think of that blazing horror roaring over their heads. " I'd like to tell you a—story," he said.

" Story ? " muttered Dr. Holmes.

" The story of the most remarkable case of stupid deception I have ever encountered." Ellery sat down on the first step ; he coughed a little and his bloodshot eyes flickered. " Before I tell my little tale, isn't there some-one here who, like Smith, has a confession to make ? "

There was silence. He searched their faces slowly, one by one.

" Stubborn to the last, I see. Well, then, I'll dedicate my last—the next few moments to the job." He massaged his bare neck and looked up at the little bulb. " I say stupid deception. The reason I say it is that the whole thing was as incredible and fantastic a plot as was ever conceived and perpetrated by an unbalanced mind. Under ordinary circumstances it shouldn't have fooled me for an instant. As it was, it took me some time to realise how utterly far-fetched it was."

" What was ? " said Mrs. Xavier harshly.

" The ' clues ' left in the dead hands of your husband and your brother-in-law, Mrs. Xavier," murmured Ellery. " After a while I came to see that they were impossible. They were much too subtle to have emanated from the thoughts of dying men. Too subtle and too complicated. Their very subtlety is what made their use by the murderer stupid. They flew in the face of the normal. As a matter of fact, if not for the fortuitous appearance of myself upon the scene, in all probability their intended meaning would never have been penetrated. I say this not in a spirit of egotism, but because in a way my own mind is as warped as the mind of the murderer. I have the tortuous mind. And so, fortunately, has the murderer." He paused and sighed. " As I say, then, after a while I suspected the validity of the clues, and after another while—here, thinking—I discarded them. And in a flash I saw the whole dismal thing, the whole dismal and clever and stupid and astounding thing."

He paused again, moving his tongue in his dry mouth. The Inspector was staring at him in bewilderment.

" What no earth *are* you talking about ? " croaked Dr. Holmes.

" This, Doctor. Where we first went off the track was in our blind assumption that this case presented only one instance of a frame-up—Mark Xavier's frame-up of Mrs. Xavier ; in our assumption that the knave-of-diamonds clue in Dr. Xavier's murder really had been left by Dr. Xavier."

" You mean, El," demanded the Inspector, " that the lawyer *didn't* find a half-jack in his brother's hand that night in the study ? "

" Oh, he found the half-jack all right," said Ellery

wearily, " and that's the crux of the matter. Mark also assumed that his brother John had left the half-jack as a clue to the murderer. It was, like ours, an utterly false assumption."

" But how could you know that ? "

" By a fact I've just recollected. Dr. Holmes after examining the body of his colleague stated that Dr. Xavier had been a diabetic, that because of this pathological condition *rigor mortis* had set in very early, in a matter of minutes rather than hours. We know that Dr. Xavier had died at about one o'clock in the morning. Mark Xavier had found the body at two-thirty. By that time *rigor* had long been complete, then. Now Dr. Xavier's right hand was clenched, holding the six of spades, when we found the body in the morning, and the left hand was spread out on the desk, flat, palm down, fingers stiff and straight. But if *rigor* had set in a few minutes after death, then those hands must have been in *that same condition* when Mark Xavier found the body an hour and a half after his brother died ! "

" Well ? "

" But don't you see ? " cried Ellery. " If Mark Xavier found his brother's right hand clenched and the left hand rigidly flat, then he could not *unclench* the right hand or *clench* the left without breaking the stiff dead fingers or leaving clear signs of the enormous pressure necessary to be exerted. If he had to manipulate the dead hands, he had also to leave them as they were. There's no question, then, but that Mark found John's right hand clenched and left hand unclenched, as *we* found them. Now we know that Mark substituted the six of spades for the jack of diamonds. In what hand therefore must the jack of diamonds have been when Mark made the substitution ? "

" Why, the right, the clenched hand, of course," muttered the Inspector.

"Exactly. The jack of diamonds was in Dr. Xavier's right hand; all Mark had to do was go through the same procedure you yourself went through, dad, when you took the six out of the dead man's hand; that is, merely separate the stiff clenched fingers sufficiently to make the card drop out. Then he inserted the six and forced the fingers back the infinitesimal fraction of an inch into the clutching position. He simply couldn't have found the jack in John's left hand, for that would mean that he would have had to unclench the left hand and leave it flat against the desk—impossible without, as I say, leaving brutal signs of the act, which did not exist upon examination of the body."

He stopped and for a moment there was only the terrifying crackle above their heads. Occasionally in the past few moments there had been a dull thud on the floor above. Now there was another. . . . But they scarcely heard. They were in the grip again of fascinated interest.

"But what——" began Miss Forrest, rocking to and fro.

"Don't you see it yet?" said Ellery almost cheerfully. "Dr. Xavier was right-handed. I've proved long ago that a right-handed man tearing a card in two would tear with his right, crumple with his right—or if he didn't crumple, at least throw the discarded half away with his right, since it made no difference which half he retained and which he threw away, both halves being exactly the same. This would leave the automatically retained half in his *left*. But I've demonstrated that the retained half must have been in Dr. Xavier's right when Mark found him. Therefore Dr. Xavier had never torn that card at all. Therefore some one else had torn that jack and left it in his right hand. *Therefore that half-jack*, meant to incriminate the twins, *was also a frame-up*, and the twins must be held entirely innocent of the murder of Dr. Xavier."

They were too stupefied to smile or show relief or do anything but gape at him. It did seem a small matter, Ellery thought, with death lurking for them all, innocent and guilty, beyond the closed door above.

" Since the first frame-up," he went on quickly, " was arranged before two-thirty, before Mark blundered upon the scene of the crime, I think we have a perfect right to assert that the first frame-up of the Carreau boys by means of the jack of diamonds had been arranged by the murderer. Unless we go into the far-fetched theory that *that* framer wasn't the murderer either, that that framer came before Mark but followed the murderer ; in other words, that there were *two* framers besides the murderer." He shook his head. " Much too fantastic. The framer of the twins was the murderer."

" This business about the *rigor* proving that it was the murderer and not Dr. Xavier who left the jack of diamonds accusing the twins," said the Inspector dubiously, interested despite himself, " sounds a—well, a little arbitrary to me. It doesn't sound very convincing."

" That ? " Ellery smiled in his desperate effort to take their minds off the flames. " Oh, I assure you it's fact, not theory. I can confirm it. But before I do that I want to point out that logically another question then arose : was the murderer of Mark Xavier the same as the murderer of his brother ? Despite the overwhelming probability that the same individual committed both crimes, we had no logical right to assume it. I didn't assume it. I proved it to my own satisfaction.

" For what was the state of affairs just before Mark's murder ? The man had lapsed into unconsciousness just before he could reveal what he claimed was the name of his brother's murderer. Dr. Holmes asserted that there was every chance the wounded man would recover consciousness in a few hours. Every one was present to hear that assertion. Who therefore was in the greatest danger should Mark recover consciousness ? Obviously, if we are to recognise the most elementary truth about cause and effect, the person who thought he was going to be unmasked by the dying man ; that is, the person with the guilty conscience, Dr. Xavier's murderer. Consequently I say that, under these special and weighty circumstances, it would be flying in the face of reason to doubt that it was John Xavier's murderer who crept into Mark's bedroom the other night and poisoned him to keep him for ever silent. And, mind you, this is true whether Mark *really* knew who the murderer was or not ! The mere threat was sufficient to force the murderer's hand."

" No quarrel with that," muttered the Inspector.

" Actually, we have confirmation of this. Let's suppose the alternative : that there were two murderers, that the killer of Mark was a different person from the killer of John. Would such a second killer have chosen the worst possible time to commit his crime ?—worst possible, I say, since he knew that Mark was under guard by a professional detective, and armed to boot ? No, the only person who would have risked this danger was someone who *had* to risk it ; who had to kill Mark not any time, but that very night, before Mark could come back to his senses and speak up. So I say, and I don't think there can be any logical or psychological weakness in the argument, that we are dealing with only one criminal."

" Nobody's questioned that. But how can you confirm your conclusion that it was the murderer, not Dr. Xavier, who left the jack of diamonds accusing the boys ? "

" I was coming to that. I don't have to confirm it, really. We've the murderer's own confession that he framed the twins after killing Dr. Xavier."

" Confession ? " They all gaped with the Inspector at that.

" Of action rather than speech. I daresay most of these good folk would be astonished to learn that after Mark Xavier's death some one tampered with the lock of the cabinet in which was secreted the deck of cards found on Dr. Xavier's desk."

" What ? " said Dr. Holmes, astonished. " I didn't know that."

" We didn't advertise it, Doctor. But after Xavier's murder someone monkeyed with the lock of the wall-cabinet in the living-room. What was in the wall-cabinet ? The deck of cards which had come from the scene of Dr. Xavier's murder. What was the only signi-ficant thing about that deck of cards which would, for any reason whatever, justify someone's tampering with the lock of the cabinet ? The fact that its jack of diamonds was missing. But *who knew* that the jack of diamonds was missing from that first deck ? Only two persons : Mark Xavier and the murderer of Dr. John Xavier. But Mark Xavier was dead. Therefore the tampering was done by the murderer.

" Now what could the murderer's motive in tampering with that cabinet have possibly been ? Did he want to steal or destroy the cards ? No."

" How the devil can you say that ? " growled the Inspector.

" Because every one in the house knew there was only one key to the cabinet, that the cabinet contained only the cards, and most important that the sole key was in your possession, dad." Ellery chuckled grimly. " How does that prove the murderer didn't want to steal or destroy the cards ? It leads to the proof. If the murderer wanted to get his claws on that deck, *why didn't he take the key from you* while he had you unconscious, helpless on the floor of Mark Xavier's bedroom ? The answer is that he *didn't* want the key, *didn't* want to get into the cabinet, *didn't* want to steal or destroy the cards ! "

" All right, even if that's so—for heaven's sake why did he tamper with the cabinet at all if he didn't want to get in ? "

" A very pertinent question. The only possible alternative is that he merely wanted to *call attention* to the deck of cards. There was even a confirmation of this : his whole effort to break into a metal cabinet with a puny little fire-tool showed that his intentions were directional rather than acquisitive."

" I'll be damned," said Smith huskily.

" No doubt. At any rate it was evident that the whole thing was a blind, a ruse, a device to call our attention to that first deck, to get us to re-examine it and discover that the jack was missing. But who could have had motive to call our attention to the missing jack ? The twins, whom the missing jack accused ? Had they tampered with the cabinet it could only have been with the determination to destroy the deck. I've just proved that the purpose of the tamperer was to call attention to the deck—the last thing in the world the twins, had they been guilty, would have wanted. Therefore the twins didn't tamper with the lock. But I've also shown that the one who tampered with the lock was the murderer. Therefore, again, the twins—one or both of them —were not the murderer. Therefore, finally, the twins were framed by the murderer . . . which is what I set out, eons ago, to demonstrate."

Mrs. Carreau sighed. The Carreau boys were staring at Ellery with naked worship in their eyes.

Ellery rose and began to stride about restlessly. " Who *was* the murderer—this framer-murderer ? " he demanded in a strident unnatural voice. " Was there any sign, any evidence, any clue that might point to the criminal's identity ? Well, there was ; and I've just figured it out—when," he added lightly, " it's too late to do anything about it but pat myself on the back."

" Then you know ! " cried Miss Forrest.

" Certainly I know, my dear girl."

" Who ? " croaked Bones. " Who was the damned——" He glared about, his bony fists quivering. His gaze lingered longest on Smith.

" The murderer, aside from the general insipidity of trying to create fantastic ' clues ' which in the normal course of events no one would have been able to interpret," continued Ellery hastily, " made one extremely bad mistake."

" Mistake ? " The Inspector blinked.

" Ah, but what a mistake ! Forced upon the murderer by outraged Nature—a most inevitable mistake, a mistake which resulted from an abnormality. In killing Mark and chloroforming the Inspector, this person "— he paused—" stole the Inspector's ring."

They stared at the old gentleman stupidly. Dr. Holmes said in a thick voice : " What—another ? "

" It was a most inoffensive little ring," said Ellery dreamily, " a plain gold wedding-band worth not more than a few dollars. Yes, Doctor, another of those piquant thefts of valueless rings the story of which both you and Miss Forrest related rather reluctantly on the night of our arrival. Queer, isn't it, that such a peculiar and seemingly irrelevant fact should have tripped the murderer up ? "

" But how ? " The Inspector coughed through a be-grimed handkerchief which he was holding to his mouth and nose. The others were all wrinkling their noses and stirring with a new uneasiness ; the air was foul.

" Well, why was the ring stolen ? " cried Ellery. " Why was Miss Forrest's, and Dr. Holmes's ? Any suggestions ? "

No one replied.

" Come, come," jeered Ellery, " lighten the last hour with a game of wits. I'm sure you can see some of the possible motives."

His cutting voice brought their heads about again. " Well," said Dr. Holmes in a mutter, " it couldn't be that they were stolen for their value, Queen. You've pointed that out yourself."

" Quite right." And blessings on your quick head, Ellery thought, for keeping the ball rolling. " Nevertheless, thank you. Any one else ? Miss Forrest ? "

" Why . . ." She licked her dry lips ; her eyes were extraordinarily bright. " It couldn't have been for—well, sentimental reasons, Mr. Queen. None of the rings had any but the most personal value, I'm sure. I mean—to the owner. Certainly none to the thief."

" A neat way of putting it," applauded Ellery. " You're quite right, Miss Forrest. Come, come, don't relax ! Make this interesting."

" Could it be," ventured Francis Carreau timidly, " that one of the rings in the house had a well, a hidden cavity or something that contained a secret or a poison of some kind ? "

" I was just thinking that," said Julian, coughing.

" Ingenious." Ellery grinned with difficulty. " Possible in the case of the thefts of the other rings, I suppose, but even that possibility is banished when you consider that the same person—obviously the same person—stole the Inspector's ring, Francis. By no stretch of the imagination could you say that the thief was looking for a hidden cavity in the *Inspector's* ring, Francis. Any more ? "

" By God," growled the Inspector suddenly. He rose and looked about him, a slender little Gandhi, with suspicious eyes.

" The old sleuth at last ! I wondered when you'd get it, dad. You see, the theft of the Inspector's ring shows clearly that all the thefts had no other purpose than . . . *mere possession.*"

Dr. Holmes started and began to say something. Then he shrank within himself, strangling the words and riveting his gaze on the stone floor.

" Smoke ! " shrieked Mrs. Xavier, rising and glaring at the stairs.

They jumped at the word, ghastly under the yellow light. Smoke was eddying from the stuffing Ellery had inserted beneath the cellar door.

He snatched up one of the tin pails and scrambled up the steps. He dashed the contents of the pail on the smouldering material, and with a hiss the smoke vanished.

" Dad ! Get that big tub of water up here. Here, I'll help you." Between them they got the butter-tub up-stairs. " Keep the door wet. We'll want to stave off the inevitable for as long . . ." His eyes were glittering as he bounded downstairs again. " Just a little more, friends, just a little more," he said like a barker striving to keep the attention of a restless crowd. His last words were drowned in the splash of water as the Inspector feverishly wet down the door. " I said mere possession. Do you know what that means ? "

" Oh, please," panted someone. They were staring, horrified, at the door, all standing now.

" You'll listen," said Ellery savagely, " if I have to shake every one of you. *Sit down.*" Dazed, they obeyed. " That's better. Now *listen.* The indiscriminate thefts of such concrete articles as valueless rings can mean only one thing—kleptomania. A kleptomania devoted exclu-sively to the stealing of rings, any kind of rings, but rings. I say that because nothing else has apparently been stolen." They were listening again, forcing themselves to

listen, forcing themselves to do anything but think of
the inferno blazing over their heads. The thuds of falling
débris came incessantly now, like the clump of clods on a
lowered coffin. " In other words, find a kleptomaniac
in this group and you'll have the murderer of Dr. Xavier
and Mark Xavier, and the framer of the boys."

The Inspector hurried down, panting, for more water.

" So," said Ellery with a ferocious scowl, " I propose
as the last act of my worthless life to do that very thing."
He raised his hand suddenly and began to tug at the
very odd and beautiful ring on his little finger. They
watched him, entranced.

He got it off after a struggle and placed it on one
of the old boxes. The box he pushed gently into the
centre of the group.

Then he straightened up and took a few backward
steps, and said no more.

Their eyes were fastened upon that small gleaming
trinket as if it were salvation, instead of the symbol of
a desperate trick. Even the coughing had ceased. The
Inspector came down and added his eyes to the fixed
battery. And no one spoke at all.

Poor fools, thought Ellery with an inward groan.
Don't you realise what's happening, what I'm doing?
And he kept his expression as savage as he could make it,
glaring coldly about him. He wished with fierce yearn-
ing that at this moment, when their attention was
wholly caught, when for the fluttering instant they
turned their faces away from death, that death would
come crashing and smoking upon them through a collapsed ceiling, so that their lives might be snuffed out
with no warning and no pain. And he continued to
glare.

They remained that way without moving during an
infinite interval. The only sounds were the thuds above
them, and the faint steady hissing of the flames. The

chill in the cellar had long since vanished, to be replaced by an insidious stuffy heat that choked their nostrils.

And then she screamed.

.   .   .   .

Oh, blessed Lord, thought Ellery, my trick has worked. As if it matters ! Why couldn't she stick it out until the end ? But then she was always a poor weak fool impressed with her own stupid cunning.

.   .   .   .

She screamed again. " Yes, I did it ! I did it, and I don't care ! I did it and I would do it over again—damn his soul, wherever he is ! "

She gulped for breath and a mad glint came into her eyes. " What's the difference ? ". she shrieked. " We're all dead, anyway ! Dead and in hell ! " She flung her arm at the petrified figure of Mrs. Carreau, crouched over the trembling twins. " I killed—him—and Mark because he knew ! *He* was in love with that—that . . ." Her voice gurgled off in an incoherent mutter. And it rose again. " She needn't deny it. That whispering, whispering, eternal whispering——"

" No," whispered Mrs. Carreau. " It was just about the children, I tell you. There was never anything between us——"

" It was my revenge ! " cried the woman. " I made it seem as if those—those sons of hers had killed him . . . to make her suffer, to make her suffer as she made me suffer. But Mark spoiled the first one. When he said he knew who did it, I had to kill him. . . ."

They let her rave. She was completely mad now ; there was froth at the corners of her mouth.

" Yes, and I stole them, too ! " she shouted. " You thought I couldn't stand it, putting that ring there——"

" Well, you couldn't," croaked Ellery.

She paid no attention. " That's why *he* retired, after
. . . He found out—about me. He tried to cure me,
take me away from the world, from temptation." Tears
were falling now. " Yes, and he was succeeding, too,"
she screamed, " when *they* came—that woman and her
devil's litter. And the rings, the rings . . . I don't care !
I'm glad to die—glad, do you hear ! *Glad !* "

It was Mrs. Xavier, the old Mrs. Xavier of the smoking black eyes and heaving breast, tall and swaying in
her tattered gown, her skin streaked with tears and
grime.

She drew a deep shuddering breath, looking quickly
about her, and then before any of them could move, to
their horror she sprang across the cleared space, bowled
the petrified Inspector to one side so that he staggered
to keep his balance, and scrambled up the cellar stairs
with the agility of insane desperation. Before Ellery
could follow her she had torn open the cellar door,
stopped short, screamed once more, and then plunged
through the burst of smoke directly into the flames in
the corridor outside.

   .   .   .   .

Ellery was after her in a flash. The smoke and fire
made him reel back, coughing and choking. He called
urgently, called and coughed and called again in the
inferno before him. There was no reply.

And so, after a while, he pushed the door shut and
crammed the fragments of Ann Forrest's dress back in
the crack at the bottom. The Inspector staggered up
with more water, a stumbling automaton.

" Why," whispered Miss Forrest with surprise, " she's
—she's . . ." She laughed hysterically and flung herself
into Dr. Holmes's arms, sobbing and laughing and choking in horrible sequence.

The Queens came slowly down the stairs.

" But, El," croaked the Inspector plaintively, like a child, " how—why—I don't understand." He passed his sooty hand over his forehead, wincing.

" It was there all the time," muttered Ellery ; his own eyes were dead. " John Xavier loved trinkets, had drawers full of them. But not a single ring. Why ? " He licked his lips. " It could only have been, when I thought of kleptomania, because the one nearest and dearest to him—who but his wife ?—was the klepto-maniac. He was keeping her particular temptation away from her."

" Mrs. Xavier ! " shrilled Mrs. Wheary suddenly, rigid on the coal heap. Her body was shaking spasmodically.

Ellery sank upon the bottom step and buried his face in his hands. " The futility of the whole damned thing," he said bitterly. " You were right from the beginning, dad—right for the wrong reasons. The extraordinary thing is that when she was accused of her husband's murder the other day *she confessed*. Good God, don't you understand ? She confessed ! Her confession was sincere. She wasn't shielding anybody. She caved in, poor weak creature that she—was." He shivered. " What an idiot I was. By demonstrating that the evidence upon which she was accused was false evidence I cleared her and gave her the opportunity of capitalising her exoneration, of feeding our suspicion that she was shielding somebody. How she must have laughed at me ! "

" She isn't laughing—now," said Mrs. Carreau hoarsely.

Ellery did not hear. " But I was right about the frame-up," he muttered. " She *was* framed—by Mark Xavier, as I explained. But the amazing thing about it—the most remarkable part of it all—was that Mark Xavier in framing Mrs. Xavier was unconsciously *framing the real murderer* ! By sheer accident. Don't you see the ghastly irony of that ? Putting the noose about the neck of the guilty person when he thought her innocent ! Oh, he really thought the twins guilty when he first framed her, I'm convinced of that. Maybe later on he came to suspect the truth ; I think he did. Remember that day we saw him trying to get into Mrs. Xavier's bedroom ? He had realised, from her manner when she had confessed to the crime, that by accident he *had* framed the right one, and wanted to implicate her even more by leaving some other damaging clue. We'll never know. It was she who left that jack of diamonds in Mark's hand after poisoning him ; he never had a chance. I never believed that—that a dying man would . . . could . . ." He stopped, his head hanging.

Then he looked up and stared at them. He tried to smile. Smith had sunk into a terrified stupor, and Mrs. Wheary was threshing about on the coal, moaning piteously.

" Well," he said, with an effort. " I've got *that* off my chest. I suppose now . . ."

He stopped again, and even as he stopped they all jumped to their feet, babbling : " What was that ? What was that ? "

It had been a reverberating clap, a sound that shook the house to its foundations and echoed faintly against the surrounding hills.

The Inspector was up the stairs in three bounds. He jerked open the door, shielding his eyes with his arm from the flames. He peered out and up.

He caught a glimpse of the sky—the upper floors had tumbled in long before, charred ruins. Before his feet there was the most peculiar phenomenon—a boiling of millions of little spears. From their sharp points came a steady hissing. Clouds of vapour, more evanescent than smoke, were rising all about.

He closed the door and came down the stairs with

infinite care, as if every step were a prayer and a bene-
diction. When he got to the bottom they saw that his
face was whiter than paper and that there were tears in
his eyes.

" What is it ? " croaked Ellery.

The Inspector said brokenly : " A miracle."

" A miracle ? " Ellery gaped with stupid open mouth.

" *It's raining.*"